UNDER THE BANYAN TREE & OTHER STORIES

By the same author

NOVELS OF MALGUDI

Swami and Friends
The Bachelor of Arts
The Dark Room
The English Teacher
Mr. Sampath – The Printer of Malgudi
The Financial Expert
Waiting for the Mahatma
The Guide
The Man-Eater of Malgudi
The Vendor of Sweets
The Painter of Signs
A Tiger for Malgudi
Talkative Man
The World of Nagaraj
Grandmother's Tale

RETOLD LEGENDS

Gods, Demons and Others
The Ramayana
The Mahabharata

STORIES

A Horse and Two Goats
An Astrologer's Day and Other Stories
Lawley Road
Malgudi Days

MEMOIRS

My Days

TRAVEL

My Dateless Diary
The Emerald Route

ESSAYS

Next Sunday
Reluctant Guru
A Writer's Nightmare
The World of the Story-Teller

UNDER THE BANYAN TREE & OTHER STORIES

R.K. NARAYAN

INDIAN THOUGHT PUBLICATIONS

INDIAN THOUGHT PUBLICATIONS
No. 38, Thanikachalam Road
T.Nagar, Madras 600 017

UNDER THE BANYAN TREE

81-85986-14-2

First published in Great Britain in 1985
by William Heinemann Ltd.,
and in the US by Viking Penguin Inc.

First Indian Edition 1992
Reprint 2003

Printed in India at
Sudarsan Graphics
27, Neelakanta Mehta Street, T.Nagar, Chennai-600 017

CONTENTS

INTRODUCTION vii
Nitya 1
House Opposite 10
A Horse and Two Goats 14
The Roman Image 31
The Watchman 39
A Career 43
Old Man of the Temple 50
A Hero 56
Dodu 61
Another Community 67
Like the Sun 73
Chippy 77
Uncle's Letters 82
All Avoidable Talk 87
A Snake in the Grass 93
The Evening Gift 96
A Breath of Lucifer 102
Annamalai 117
The Shelter 145
The Mute Companions 149

At the Portal 153
Four Rupees 157
Flavour of Coconut 161
Fruition at Forty 166
Crime and Punishment 170
Half a Rupee Worth 175
The Antidote 181
Under the Banyan Tree 187
GLOSSARY 193

INTRODUCTION

Out of the twenty-eight stories in the following pages, the first two were written this year, while the rest are—well, I won't call them old, as the date of a story is immaterial. A writer does not germinate, grow, and decay in the manner of a piece of vegetation. The conception seems to me irrelevant; a writer's output over the years cannot be studied as bio-historical material. A writer's early stories need not be worse than his later ones, and his so-called middle period may exhibit a dull competence rather than genius. I have faith in datelessness. A date-stamp may be necessary for a periodical, but not for a story. I came to this conclusion after trying to arrange the following stories in chronological order according to the year of publication. It didn't work, even in the few instances where I could guess the date. Then I tried to organize them according to the mood or theme of each, which again failed. Hence the only course left was to pick up a story at random, give it a number, and when all the stories were thus numbered and arranged, the collection displayed a strange but convincing pattern of affinities and contrasts.

I, for one, am prepared to assert that all theories of writing are bogus. Every writer develops his own method or lack of method and a story comes into being for some unknown reason and anyhow. The process involved cannot be stated theoretically. Once I was present at a lecture on creative writing. The lecturer began with: "All writing may be divided into two groups—good writing and bad writing. Good books come out of good writing while bad writing produces failures." When touching on the subject of the short story, the lecturer said: "A short story must be short and have a story." At this point I left unobtrusively, sympathizing with the man's predicament.

If asked, I cannot explain how a story comes to be written. All that I can say is that at one time I found material for my stories in the open air, market-place, and streets of Mysore. At an early stage of my life I enjoyed a lot of freedom, no one in our family minding my non-economic style of living. I read a little, also attempted to write, and went out on long walks along the tanks, parks, and avenues, or climbed the hill which looms over our city; and during some part of the day I watched also the crowds at the market—not deliberately or consciously to pick up a subject but for the sheer pleasure of watching people. The very first story I wrote was about a one-armed beggar who stood in the middle of a narrow street in front of a coffee-house and sailed forth with upheld palm when he spotted young men emerging from the restaurant in a merry, convivial mood. I wrote my first short story about him under the title "The One-Armed Giant." I remember clearly the first line—"One armed, he certainly was, but he was no more a giant than you or I"—which sounded excellent. I don't remember much of the story, which is lost in oblivion, originally published in *The Hindu* of Madras nearly four decades ago. The editor was generous enough to accept it although as I recollect it revolved round a flimsy theme—of the beggar's obsessive desire to acquire an old jacket. Following its publication I became a regular writer for *The Hindu.* The driving force was the need to write two stories a month to survive. Most of the stories in the present volume were born out of desperation to meet the deadline on alternate Thursdays for the Sunday column.

As I have mentioned, I realized that the short story is the best medium for utilizing the wealth of subjects available. A novel is a different proposition altogether, centralized as it is on a major theme, leaving out, necessarily, a great deal of the available material on the periphery. Short stories, on the other hand, can cover a wider field by presenting concentrated miniatures of human experience in all its opulence.

A story may have its origin in a personal experience or a bit of observation or a conversation overheard. "A Breath of Lucifer" was dictated by me into a cassette when I had to spend ten days in bed with eyes bandaged following a cataract operation, and was attended on by a crazy male nurse. "Annamalai" is almost a documentary of a strange personality who served as a watchman in my bungalow for fifteen years; "A Horse and Two Goats" was suggested by an American friend's visit to my house one evening in a station wagon, crammed with an enormous clay horse which he had picked up at a wayside village. "The Shelter" developed out of a whispered conversation between a couple, overheard during a bus journey.

About the arrangement, as I have already mentioned, it is not chronological. The only compulsion I admitted to myself was to place "Nitya," which is the story of a sparkling young mind, with rebellion at heart, at the head of the collection, and at the end the story of an old Story-Teller who concludes his career by taking a vow of silence for the rest of his life, realizing that a Story-Teller must have the sense to know when to stop, and not wait for others to tell him.

R. K. Narayan
February 21, 1984

Nitya

Nitya, at six on Friday morning," said his father determinedly, "we leave by bus." Nitya had noticed preparations at home for this trip, Mother planning a packed lunch for three and filling a basket with coconut, flowers, and incense for worship at the temple. Nitya very well knew how much he was involved in their plans. His mother had talked of nothing else whenever he stepped into the kitchen for coffee. "After all, a vow has to be fulfilled," she would keep repeating. Nitya would try to change the subject, banter, joke about it, and run away. They had made a vow to God in a distant hill that Nitya's head would be shaved clean and his hair offered with due rites if his life was spared. That was when he was two years old and stricken with whooping cough and convulsions. Now he was twenty, and although the time limit for fulfilment seemed to be past, yet, they felt, it would not be safe or proper to postpone further. When casually turning the leaves of an old diary, Father discovered the record of their promise to God. Mother, too, recollected having knotted a little coin in a piece of cloth as a reminder, although she could not trace it now. The promise and the diary were lost sight of during Nitya's growing years when the family suddenly found itself drawn into a legal battle over their property. The case was prolonged year after year through the labours of a specially gifted lawyer on the opposite side who could manoeuvre a postponement out of the toughest judge at a crucial point, with the idea of starting it all over again before a new judge in due course. Father was determined to fight it out as the will was unequivocally in his favour and made him sole heir to the property. By the time the final decision came his assets had dwindled, his lawyer himself had changed from a scintillating youth of promise to a toothless character in a frayed gown haunting the corridors of the civil court.

Today, when Father mentioned a firm date for the trip, Nitya protested, "It doesn't concern me, your twenty-year-old promise. You had no business to pawn my scalp without consulting me."

"You were only two years old then."

"You should have done it when you could handle my head as you pleased."

"But you were very sick and for a long time, too."

"I have survived, which proves that the disease died rather than me and so where is God's hand in this, if there is a God and if he is interested in my hair?"

His parents were aghast at his manner of talk. Mother pleaded, "Whatever you do, don't talk like that."

Father admonished, "Nitya, you must not be blasphemous. If God hadn't responded to our prayers and saved your life . . ." He could not complete the sentence.

"Was it a bargain?" Nitya asked leeringly.

"Yes," replied his father. "It was indeed a bargain and there can be no going back on it."

"Very well, but the head offered for a shave was not yours. You have been carrying on negotiations with a commodity that did not belong to you."

"It was for your welfare."

"Did I ask for it?" Nitya asked puckishly. His mother burst into tears. Father remarked with a scowl, "You talk like a sinner, cold and godless. Wonder where you inherited it from."

At this point their neighbour, an alcoholic who had stationed himself in front of the house listening to their debate, suddenly thundered from the street, "Silence! I am wifeless. Others have two or three—selfish bastards!" He had been a chief engineer in government service, but was dismissed for drunkenness, and later abandoned by his family, too. Nitya loved his antics as he strode up and down the street shouting obscenities after visits to the tavern at the market. Nitya had noted in his private journal: "The merry engineer mistook the kitchen for the toilet, and that proved too much for his better half." Now on the pretext of sending him away, Nitya went down the steps and escaped his parents. Later, however, his father kept a close watch on him and clung to him till they reached their seats in the yellow bus at the market gate on Friday.

Father looked triumphant with Nitya secure at his side in the bus, and engaged him in small talk. Mother sat away from them in a back row, enjoying the company of women returning to their villages. The bus passed through Ellaman and crossed Nallappa's Grove and climbed the other bank of the river, splashing up water. The driver displayed immense self-assurance and goaded his bus on with reckless gusto. Passengers were tossed sideways and jolted up and down, but no one minded except Nitya. "What sort of journey is this?"

"You must learn to be patient, my boy, ours is a poor country. We cannot afford the luxuries they have in Bombay or Madras." The passengers, mostly villagers, were happy chatting and laughing and also exchanging jokes with the conductor from time to time. Passengers got in and out all along the route whenever the bus stopped with its wheels screeching and churning up dust. At certain points the bus became almost empty, at others overcrowded, the conductor shouting, "Move up, move up." People got in somehow and stayed on somehow, packed to the windscreen. No one protested, but parted with their coins cheerfully. The conductor, hanging on the footboard precariously, pocketed all the cash, which inspired Nitya to note in his diary, "The bus rocks and sways, and sighs with its burden, but won't burst yet. Perhaps the last straw is yet to arrive. But the real question is, Who owns this? Definitely not this conductor, though he grows heavier every minute with the coins dropping like manna into his pocket."

"You should get down here and walk up to that hill, the bus can't take you there," said the conductor at a stop. They struggled their way out of the bus, Mother carrying her bundle of offerings and food delicately through the crush. As the bus started on its way again, Father asked the driver, "When are you returning?"

"At five, six, or seven; if you miss, tomorrow morning."

The temple perched on a hillock was visible across the field, but it was impossible to judge the distance. A track formed by the tread of feet meandered through the fields. They had to cross in single file with Nitya in the middle, Father ahead, and Mother bringing up the rear. Nitya reflected, Afraid I might run away, they are sandwiching me. But what chance have I, trapped by slush and vegetation on both sides of this narrow path.

An hour's walk brought them to a hamlet skirting the base of the hillock. Nitya was on the point of asking, Why come so far, if God is everywhere? I could as well have surrendered my head to our Vinayak Street barber, who shaves you at your doorstep. As if reading his mind, Father began to explain, "This temple was established by our ancestors five hundred years ago—earlier; it's on this hill that Kumara annihilated the demon whose name I can't recollect now."

"Demon is a demon, whatever the name," said the young man. Father ignored his quip and continued, "The temple was built by a Chola king who ruled these parts, and in course of time it was turned over to the care of our ancestors."

"How are you sure?" Nitya asked.

"You've got into the habit of questioning everything."

"I just want to know, that's all."

"Well, it is all recorded in copper plate, stone pillars, and palm leaves, from which deductions are made by scholars. Don't imagine you are the only wise man. There is a document in the temple in palm leaf mentioning my great-grandfather by name and committing our family to the expenses of the annual Chariot Festival. I pay them two hundred rupees a year and twenty measures of rice for a public feast on that day. They come to the town for collections in December, ten days before the festival. . . . Luckily, a copy of this document is in my possession with the receipts of annual payments which clinched the issue in our favour at the appellate stage." Nitya noted later in his diary, "Even at this distance and on a consecrated spot my father is unable to keep his mind off the civil court, verily like the engineer of his wifelessness." When they came to the border of the village, Father slowed his steps and, with a slight frown, threw a general question in the air: "Where is everybody?" as if the reception committee had failed him.

He halted at a corner and shouted, "Hey, Rama," and a group of women and boys emerged from some corner and came running on seeing him. They invited him into their homes. Father said impatiently, "Yes, later. First the temple. Call the headman."

"They are all away weeding," said a woman, and turning to a young man jabbed his cheek with her forefinger and said, "Run up and tell Rama that the Trustee is come." The boy shot off like an arrow. They dragged out of their homes an assortment of furniture and put it up in the shade of a tree, and then bustled about and conjured up a bunch of bananas and a jug of milk for the visitors and laid the fare on a wooden stool. Nitya cried, "Oh, just what I need," and tried to reach out for a fruit, but Father said, "Not now, after the vow." (Nitya noted in his diary, "Not now, but after the vow, says God through my father in a perfect rhyme, while the banana wilts in the tray and the milk curdles irreparably.") The headman arrived. After the initial courtesies, much business talk ensued, with a crowd standing around and listening intently. Father inquired authoritatively, "Where is the priest? The temple must be opened. We have to leave by the evening bus."

The headman said out of courtesy, "Must you? You may spend the night at the rest house, sir. You have come after a long time."

Immediately, Nitya protested, "You may both stay back if you choose, but I want to catch the bus," feeling nostalgic for his evening group at the College Union. Mother said, "Be patient." But Nitya replied, "I've much to do this evening." Father said, "What could be more important than your duty to God? Be patient, having come so far."

The temple priest, his forehead ablaze with sacred ash and vermilion, shoulder wrapped in a red shawl, a lanky person with a booming voice, arrived, dangling a large key in an iron hoop. After greeting the Trustee in the correct manner, he plunged straight into business, cataloguing his demands.

"The well at the temple needs to be deepened. The temple lock must be replaced. It is worn out, sir. These are very bad days. We are finding it difficult to get flowers for the worship. We were getting supplies from the other village. But they raise their rates each time and are very irregular too. They have to come up from the other side of the hill and don't like it, and so have started a rumour that they see a wolf or panther prowling around, and have stopped coming altogether."

"Nonsense, only an excuse," cried Father. "No panther or tiger in these parts, never heard such rubbish in my life."

"He mentioned wolf, not tiger," corrected Nitya.

"What if? It is just gossip and nonsense—the rumour-mongers!" Father cried with passion, looking outraged at the notion of any wild life in the vicinity of his ancestral temple. He dismissed the subject peremptorily and commanded, "Get the barber down. My son's tonsure today whatever happens," and the assembly looked with fresh interest at Nitya's head, at which he simpered, squirmed, and ran his fingers through his crop. The priest turned to a little fellow in the crowd and said, "Don't bite your nail, you fool! Go to the tank bund and tell Raghavan to come up with his tin box immediately, this very second. Run, run." The little messenger was off like a shot again.

They started up the hill, led by the priest, a crowd following. It was a short climb, but Nitya's mother panted and rested in three places, while Father hovered around her and fidgeted impatiently. The climb ended at the door of the temple, which was unlocked, and two large doors were pushed open. It was a little shrine with a granite-pillared hall and paved corridor around the sanctum, which housed an image on a pedestal. Father became grim and devout. Mother shut her eyes and recited a prayer. The priest lit the wicks in the sanctum and the image began to glow with the oil anointed on it and gradually took shape. The priest was grumbling, "Even this oil is adulterated nowadays." He had managed to secure a handful of marigolds and nerium and stuck them on the image. While they were all in this state of elation, the young messenger returned from his mission and bellowed from the door, "The barber's house is locked, not a soul there."

"Did you ask the neighbours?"

"They don't know. They only saw the family go out for the bus with their baggage."

Nitya cried aloud, "God is great, really."

Father commented, "This is the worst of it, having one barber for the whole place. He thinks he can do what he pleases. One and only Padmavathi for a whole city, as the saying goes," he said, unable to contain himself. His wife said with a frown, "Hush! What awful words to utter in this place" (Padmavathi was a reference to a whore). Father glowered at her for checking him, but they were all assembled in the presence of God and could not engage in acrimony. Nitya giggled but suppressed himself when his father glanced in his direction. The headman said in a respectful whisper, "Raghavan cannot make both ends meet unless he ekes out with the fee for playing the pipe at weddings. It is their family tradition." Father leaned over to Mother and whispered, "For thousands of years somehow barbers have also been outstanding pipers and custodians of pure classical music." While this was going on, the priest sounded a bell and circled a camphor flame around the image and they stopped talking and were lost in meditation.

When the priest came out of the sanctum, bearing a tray with camphor flame, a discussion began as to what course of action the scriptures prescribed when an essential barber was absent.

"We are at the mercy of a single man," Father kept repeating monotonously, firmly suppressing the name "Padmavathi," which kept bobbing up again and again on his tongue. The priest put the tray back in the sanctum, came out, and joined the discussion. He finally said, gaping at Nitya's crop, which was the main topic of discussion and purpose of the trip, "Sometimes, the vow is taken to be fulfilled through a token performance with penalty added. These days young men will not allow barbers to come near them."

"They won't allow their terrifying whiskers to be touched either!" added Father.

"No tonsure is possible unless done in babyhood," said the priest.

"Too true, well spoken," said Nitya, pleased with the tenor of talks, and offered, "Get me a pair of scissors, and I will give you four inches of my front lock, the best available—that's all, and God will be satisfied. After all, with so many offerings, where can he keep his collection?"

The priest said, "The fruits and coconuts you have brought are adequate, leave them behind, and add whatever cash you can spare."

Father and Mother looked disappointed and kept throwing covetous glances at Nitya's head. Nitya felt relieved, but the relief threatened to be short-lived. Soon there was a commotion. Someone at the doorway announced excitedly, "Raghavan is coming up," followed by the appearance of a fat barber holding in his hand a tiny tin box. He was panting and perspiring; he stared at the gathering from the doorway, and without a word went straight to the well at the backyard, peeled off his vest, drew a pot of water and emptied it over his head, and reappeared, dripping and ready. "He never opens his razor box without a bath at first when he has to perform a tonsure ceremony," explained the priest admiringly. The barber explained, "I had only gone to a nearby farm for a baby's first shave, that was all."

"Not to play the pipe at a wedding?" someone asked.

"Oh, no. I have jealous neighbours who create false rumours to spoil my business. If I had known the Trustee was coming I would not have accepted even a thousand pieces of gold anywhere outside. When the boy came on a bicycle and told me, I snatched it from his hand and rode down immediately. Now I am ready, my master." Father and Mother looked pleased at this turn of events. Nitya giggled at the thought of the fat barber on the boy's bicycle. Father took Nitya by hand. "Let us sit on that stone platform in the corridor, that's where he shaves—"

Nitya shook himself free and said, "I agreed to give four inches of hair, it was up to you to have taken it. Now you have lost the opportunity, which must be seized by the forelock."

"Now, with this man here, we must fulfil the vow as originally promised," said Mother.

"Let Father use the barber if he likes. I'm not interested."

The barber started pleading and arguing. The priest edged up to Nitya with his pleas and said ingratiatingly, "You must not hurt your parents' feelings. Please move on to that platform, the barber is ready."

"But my head is not ready. You promised to accept four inches of my hair. Now you are demanding my head itself. Have you no logic or reason? No contentment or consistency? How can God tolerate fickle-minded people like you! Now I have changed my mind—I won't give even an inch . . ."

Both Father and Mother cried simultaneously, "Don't talk to the priest like that in his own temple." Nitya was angry, also hungry. They would not let him touch even one plantain out of the dozens offered by the villagers under the tree. While his parents stood staring at him helplessly, Nitya suddenly turned on his heel, dashed out, and sped downhill saying, "I will wait for you both at the bus stop, but only till the bus arrives. . . ."

House Opposite

The hermit invariably shuddered when he looked out of his window. The house across the street was occupied by a shameless woman. Late in the evening, men kept coming and knocking on her door—afternoons, too, if there was a festival or holiday. Sometimes they lounged on the pyol of her house, smoking, chewing tobacco, and spitting into the gutter—committing all the sins of the world, according to the hermit who was striving to pursue a life of austerity, forswearing family, possessions, and all the comforts of life. He found this single-room tenement with a couple of coconut trees and a well at the backyard adequate, and the narrow street swarmed with children: sometimes he called in the children, seated them around, and taught them simple moral lessons and sacred verse. On the walls he had nailed a few pictures of gods cut out of old calendars, and made the children prostrate themselves in front of them before sending them away with a piece of sugar candy each.

His daily life followed an unvarying pattern. Bird-like, he retired at dusk, lying on the bare floor with a wooden block under his head for a pillow. He woke up at four ahead of the rooster at the street corner, bathed at the well, and sat down on a piece of deerskin to meditate. Later he lit the charcoal stove and baked a few chapattis for breakfast and lunch and cooked certain restricted vegetables and greens, avoiding potato, onion, okra, and such as might stimulate the baser impulses.

Even in the deepest state of meditation, he could not help hearing the creaking of the door across the street when a client left after a night of debauchery. He rigorously suppressed all cravings of the palate, and punished his body in a dozen ways. If you asked him why, he would have been at a loss to explain. He was the antithesis of the athlete who flexed his muscles and watched his expanding chest before a mirror. Our hermit, on the contrary, kept a minute check of his emaciation and felt a peculiar thrill out of such an achievement. He was only following without questioning his ancient guru's instructions, and hoped thus to attain spiritual liberation.

One afternoon, opening the window to sweep the dust on the sill, he noticed her standing on her doorstep, watching the street. His temples throbbed with the rush of blood. He studied her person—chiselled features, but sunk in fatty folds. She possessed, however, a seductive outline; her forearms were cushion-like and perhaps the feel of those encircling arms attracted men. His gaze, once it had begun to hover about her body, would not return to its anchor—which should normally be the tip of one's nose, as enjoined by his guru and the yoga shastras.

Her hips were large, thighs stout like banana stalks, on the whole a mattress-like creature on which a patron could loll all night without a scrap of covering—"Awful monster! Personification of evil." He felt suddenly angry. Why on earth should that creature stand there and ruin his tapas: all the merit he had so laboriously acquired was draining away like water through a sieve. Difficult to say whether it was those monstrous arms and breasts or thighs which tempted and ruined men. . . . He hissed under his breath, "Get in, you devil, don't stand there!" She abruptly turned round and went in, shutting the door behind her. He felt triumphant, although his command and her compliance were coincidental. He bolted the window tight and retreated to the farthest corner of the room, settled down on the deerskin, and kept repeating, "Om, Om, Rama, Jayarama": the sound "Rama" had a potency all its own—and was reputed to check wandering thoughts and distractions. He had a profound knowledge of mantras and their efficacy. "Sri Rama . . . ," he repeated, but it was like a dilute and weak medicine for high fever. It didn't work. "Sri Rama, Jayarama . . . ," he repeated with a desperate fervour, but the effect lasted not even a second. Unnoticed, his thoughts strayed, questioning: Who was that fellow in a check shirt and silk upper cloth over his shoulder descending the steps last evening when I went out to the market? Seen him somewhere . . . where? when? . . . ah, he was the big tailor on Market Road . . . with fashionable men and women clustering round him! Master-cutter who was a member of two or three clubs. . . . Hobnobbed with officers and businessmen—and this was how he spent his evening, lounging on the human mattress! And yet fashionable persons allowed him to touch them with his measuring tape! Contamination, nothing but contamination; sinful life. He cried out in the lonely room, "Rama! Rama!" as if hailing someone hard of hearing. Presently he realized it was a futile exercise. Rama was a perfect incarnation, of course, but he was mild and gentle until provoked beyond limit, when he would storm and annihilate the evildoer without a trace, even if he was a monster like Ravana. Normally, however, he had forbearance, hence the repetition of his name only resulted in calmness and peace, but the present occasion demanded stern measures. God Siva's mantra should help. Did he not open his Third Eye and reduce the God of Love to ashes, when the latter slyly aimed his arrow at him while he was meditating? Our hermit pictured the god of matted locks and fiery eyes and recited aloud: "Om Namasivaya," that lonely hall resounding with his hoarse voice. His rambling, unwholesome thoughts were halted for a while, but presently regained their vigour and raced after the woman. She opened her door at least six times on an evening. Did she sleep with them all together at the same time? He paused to laugh at this notion, and also realized that his meditation on the austere god was gone. He banged his fist on his temples, which pained but improved his concentration. "Om Namasivaya . . ." Part of his mind noted the creaking of the door of the opposite house. She was a serpent in whose coils everyone was caught and destroyed—old and young and the middle-aged, tailors and students (he had noticed a couple of days ago a young B.Sc. student from Albert Mission Hostel at her door), lawyers and magistrates (Why not?) . . . No wonder the world was getting overpopulated—with such pressure of the elemental urge within every individual! O God Siva, this woman must be eliminated. He would confront her some day and tell her to get out. He would tell her, "Oh, sinful wretch, who is spreading disease and filth like an open sewer: think of the contamination you have spread around—from middle-aged tailor to B.Sc. student. You are out to destroy mankind. Repent your sins, shave your head, cover your ample loins with sackcloth, sit at the temple gate and beg or drown yourself in sarayu after praying for a cleaner life at least in the next birth . . ."

Thus went his dialogue, the thought of the woman never leaving his mind, during all the wretched, ill-spent night; he lay tossing on the bare floor. He rose before dawn, his mind made up. He would clear out immediately, cross Nallappa's Grove, and reach the other side of the river. He did not need a permanent roof; he would drift and rest in any temple or mantap or in the shade of a banyan tree: he recollected an ancient tale he had heard from his guru long ago. . . . A harlot was sent to heaven when she died, while her detractor, a self-righteous reformer, found himself in hell. It was explained that while the harlot sinned only with her body, her detractor was corrupt mentally, as he was obsessed with the harlot and her activities, and could meditate on nothing else.

Our hermit packed his wicker box with his sparse possessions—a god's image in copper, a rosary, the deerskin, and a little brass bowl. Carrying his box in one hand, he stepped out of the house, closing the door gently behind him. In the dim hour of the dusk, shadowy figures were moving—a milkman driving his cow ahead, labourers bearing crowbars and spades, women with baskets on their way to the market. While he paused to take a final look at the shelter he was abandoning, he heard a plaintive cry, "Swamiji," from the opposite house, and saw the woman approach him with a tray, heaped with fruits and flowers. She placed it at his feet and said in a low reverential whisper: "Please accept my offering. This is a day of remembrance of my mother. On this day I pray and seek a saint's blessing. Forgive me. . . ." All the lines he had rehearsed for a confrontation deserted him at this moment; looking at her flabby figure, the dark rings under her eyes, he felt pity. As she bent down to prostrate, he noticed that her hair was indifferently dyed and that the parting in the middle widened into a bald patch over which a string of jasmine dangled loosely. He touched her tray with the tip of his finger as a token of acceptance, and went down the street without a word.

A Horse and Two Goats

Of the seven hundred thousand villages dotting the map of India, in which the majority of India's five hundred million live, flourish, and die, Kritam was probably the tiniest, indicated on the district survey map by a microscopic dot, the map being meant more for the revenue official out to collect tax than for the guidance of the motorist, who in any case could not hope to reach it since it sprawled far from the highway at the end of a rough track furrowed up by the iron-hooped wheels of bullock carts. But its size did not prevent its giving itself the grandiose name Kritam, which meant in Tamil "coronet" or "crown" on the brow of this subcontinent. The village consisted of fewer than thirty houses, only one of them built with brick and cement. Painted a brilliant yellow and blue all over with gorgeous carvings of gods and gargoyles on its balustrade, it was known as the Big House. The other houses, distributed in four streets, were generally of bamboo thatch, straw, mud, and other unspecified material. Muni's was the last house in the fourth street, beyond which stretched the fields. In his prosperous days Muni had owned a flock of forty sheep and goats and sallied forth every morning driving the flock to the highway a couple of miles away. There he would sit on the pedestal of a clay statue of a horse while his cattle grazed around. He carried a crook at the end of a bamboo pole and snapped foliage from the avenue trees to feed his flock; he also gathered faggots and dry sticks, bundled them, and carried them home for fuel at sunset.

His wife lit the domestic fire at dawn, boiled water in a mud pot, threw into it a handful of millet flour, added salt, and gave him his first nourishment for the day. When he started out, she would put in his hand a packed lunch, once again the same millet cooked into a little ball, which he could swallow with a raw onion at midday. She was old, but he was older and needed all the attention she could give him in order to be kept alive.

His fortunes had declined gradually, unnoticed. From a flock of forty which he drove into a pen at night, his stock had now come down to two goats, which were not worth the rent of a half rupee a month the Big House charged for the use of the pen in their backyard. And so the two goats were tethered to the trunk of a drumstick tree which grew in front of his hut and from which occasionally Muni could shake down drumsticks. This morning he got six. He carried them in with a sense of triumph. Although no one could say precisely who owned the tree, it was his because he lived in its shadow.

She said, "If you were content with the drumstick leaves alone, I could boil and salt some for you."

"Oh, I am tired of eating those leaves. I have a craving to chew the drumstick out of sauce, I tell you."

"You have only four teeth in your jaw, but your craving is for big things. All right, get the stuff for the sauce, and I will prepare it for you. After all, next year you may not be alive to ask for anything. But first get me all the stuff, including a measure of rice or millet, and I will satisfy your unholy craving. Our store is empty today. Dhall, chili, curry leaves, mustard, coriander, gingelley oil, and one large potato. Go out and get all this." He repeated the list after her in order not to miss any item and walked off to the shop in the third street.

He sat on an upturned packing case below the platform of the shop. The shopman paid no attention to him. Muni kept clearing his throat, coughing, and sneezing until the shopman could not stand it any more and demanded, "What ails you? You will fly off that seat into the gutter if you sneeze so hard, young man." Muni laughed inordinately, in order to please the shopman, at being called "young man." The shopman softened and said, "You have enough of the imp inside to keep a second wife busy, but for the fact the old lady is still alive." Muni laughed appropriately again at this joke. It completely won the shopman over; he liked his sense of humour to be appreciated. Muni engaged his attention in local gossip for a few minutes, which always ended with a reference to the postman's wife, who had eloped to the city some months before.

The shopman felt most pleased to hear the worst of the postman, who had cheated him. Being an itinerant postman, he returned home to Kritam only once in ten days and every time managed to slip away again without passing the shop in the third street. By thus humouring the shopman, Muni could always ask for one or two items of food, promising repayment later. Some days the shopman was in a good mood and gave in, and sometimes he would lose his temper suddenly and bark at Muni for daring to ask for credit. This was such a day, and Muni could not progress beyond two items listed as essential components. The shopman was also displaying a remarkable memory for old facts and figures and took out an oblong ledger to support his observations. Muni felt impelled to rise and flee. But his self-respect kept him in his seat and made him listen to the worst things about himself. The shopman concluded, "If you could find five rupees and a quarter, you will have paid off an ancient debt and then could apply for admission to swarga. How much have you got now?"

"I will pay you everything on the first of the next month."

"As always, and whom do you expect to rob by then?"

Muni felt caught and mumbled, "My daughter has sent word that she will be sending me money."

"Have you a daughter?" sneered the shopman. "And she is sending you money! For what purpose, may I know?"

"Birthday, fiftieth birthday," said Muni quietly.

"Birthday! How old are you?"

Muni repeated weakly, not being sure of it himself, "Fifty." He always calculated his age from the time of the great famine when he stood as high as the parapet around the village well, but who could calculate such things accurately nowadays with so many famines occurring? The shopman felt encouraged when other customers stood around to watch and comment. Muni thought helplessly, My poverty is exposed to everybody. But what can I do?

"More likely you are seventy," said the shopman. "You also

forget that you mentioned a birthday five weeks ago when you wanted castor oil for your holy bath."

"Bath! Who can dream of a bath when you have to scratch the tank-bed for a bowl of water? We would all be parched and dead but for the Big House, where they let us take a pot of water from their well." After saying this Muni unobtrusively rose and moved off.

He told his wife, "That scoundrel would not give me anything. So go out and sell the drumsticks for what they are worth."

He flung himself down in a corner to recoup from the fatigue of his visit to the shop. His wife said, "You are getting no sauce today, nor anything else. I can't find anything to give you to eat. Fast till the evening, it'll do you good. Take the goats and be gone now," she cried and added, "Don't come back before the sun is down." He knew that if he obeyed her she would somehow conjure up some food for him in the evening. Only he must be careful not to argue and irritate her. Her temper was undependable in the morning but improved by evening time. She was sure to go out and work—grind corn in the Big House, sweep or scrub somewhere, and earn enough to buy foodstuff and keep a dinner ready for him in the evening.

Unleashing the goats from the drumstick tree, Muni started out, driving them ahead and uttering weird cries from time to time in order to urge them on. He passed through the village with his head bowed in thought. He did not want to look at anyone or be accosted. A couple of cronies lounging in the temple corridor hailed him, but he ignored their call. They had known him in the days of affluence when he lorded over a flock of fleecy sheep, not the miserable gawky goats that he had today. Of course he also used to have a few goats for those who fancied them, but real wealth lay in sheep; they bred fast and people came and bought the fleece in the shearing season; and then that famous butcher from the town came over on the weekly market days bringing him betel leaves, tobacco, and often enough some bhang, which they smoked in a hut in the coconut grove, undisturbed by wives and well-wishers. After a smoke one felt light and elated and inclined to forgive everyone including that brother-in-law of his who had once tried to set fire to his home. But all this seemed like the memories of a previous birth. Some pestilence afflicted his cattle (he could of course guess who had laid his animals under a curse), and even the friendly butcher would not touch one at half the price . . . and now here he was left with the two scraggy creatures. He wished someone would rid him of their company, too. The shopman had said that he was seventy. At seventy, one only waited to be summoned by God. When he was dead what would his wife do? They had lived in each other's company since they were children. He was told on their day of wedding that he was ten years old and she was eight. During the wedding ceremony they had had to recite their respective ages and names. He had thrashed her only a few times in their career, and later she had the upper hand. Progeny, none. Perhaps a large progeny would have brought him the blessing of the gods. Fertility brought merit. People with fourteen sons were always so prosperous and at peace with the world and themselves. He recollected the thrill he had felt when he mentioned a daughter to that shopman; although it was not believed, what if he did not have a daughter?—his cousin in the next village had many daughters, and any one of them was as good as his; he was fond of them all and would buy them sweets if he could afford it. Still, everyone in the village whispered behind their backs that Muni and his wife were a barren couple. He avoided looking at anyone; they all professed to be so high up, and everyone else in the village had more money than he. "I am the poorest fellow in our caste and no wonder that they spurn me, but I won't look at them either," and so he passed on with his eyes downcast along the edge of the street, and people left him also very much alone, commenting only to the extent, "Ah, there he goes with his two goats; if he slits their throats, he may have more peace of mind." "What has he to worry about anyway? They live on nothing and have none to worry about." Thus people commented when he passed through the village. Only on the outskirts did he lift his head and look up. He urged and bullied the goats until they meandered along to the foot of the horse statue on the edge of the village. He sat on its pedestal for the rest of the day. The advantage of this was that he could watch the highway and see the lorries and buses pass through to the hills, and it gave him a sense of belonging to a larger world. The pedestal of the statue was broad enough for him to move around as the sun travelled up and westward; or he could also crouch under the belly of the horse, for shade.

The horse was nearly life-size, moulded out of clay, baked, burnt, and brightly coloured, and reared its head proudly, prancing its forelegs in the air and flourishing its tail in a loop; beside the horse stood a warrior with scythe-like mustachios, bulging eyes, and aquiline nose. The old image-makers believed in indicating a man of strength by bulging out his eyes and sharpening his moustache tips, and also decorated the man's chest with beads which looked today like blobs of mud through the ravages of sun and wind and rain (when it came), but Muni would insist that he had known the beads to sparkle like the nine gems at one time in his life. The horse itself was said to have been as white as a dhobi-washed sheet, and had had on its back a cover of pure brocade of red and black lace, matching the multicoloured sash around the waist of the warrior. But none in the village remembered the splendour as no one noticed its existence. Even Muni, who spent all his waking hours at its foot, never bothered to look up. It was untouched even by the young vandals of the village who gashed tree trunks with knives and tried to topple off milestones and inscribed lewd designs on all walls. This statue had been closer to the population of the village at one time, when this spot bordered the village; but when the highway was laid through (or perhaps when the tank and wells dried up completely here) the village moved a couple of miles inland.

Muni sat at the foot of the statue, watching his two goats graze in the arid soil among the cactus and lantana bushes. He looked at the sun; it was tilted westward no doubt, but it was not the time yet to go back home; if he went too early his wife would have no food for him. Also he must give her time to cool off her temper and feel sympathetic, and then she would scrounge and manage to get some food. He watched the mountain road for a time signal. When the green bus appeared around the bend he could leave, and his wife would feel pleased that he had let the goats feed long enough.

He noticed now a new sort of vehicle coming down at full

speed. It looked like both a motor car and a bus. He used to be intrigued by the novelty of such spectacles, but of late work was going on at the source of the river on the mountain and an assortment of people and traffic went past him, and he took it all casually and described to his wife, later in the day, everything he saw. Today, while he observed the yellow vehicle coming down, he was wondering how to describe it later to his wife, when it sputtered and stopped in front of him. A red-faced foreigner, who had been driving it, got down and went round it, stooping, looking, and poking under the vehicle; then he straightened himself up, looked at the dashboard, stared in Muni's direction, and approached him. "Excuse me, is there a gas station nearby, or do I have to wait until another car comes—" He suddenly looked up at the clay horse and cried, "Marvellous," without completing his sentence. Muni felt he should get up and run away, and cursed his age. He could not readily put his limbs into action; some years ago he could outrun a cheetah, as happened once when he went to the forest to cut fuel and it was then that two of his sheep were mauled—a sign that bad times were coming. Though he tried, he could not easily extricate himself from his seat, and then there was also the problem of the goats. He could not leave them behind.

The red-faced man wore khaki clothes—evidently a policeman or a soldier. Muni said to himself, He will chase or shoot if I start running. Some dogs chase only those who run—O Siva, protect me. I don't know why this man should be after me. Meanwhile the foreigner cried, "Marvellous!" again, nodding his head. He paced around the statue with his eyes fixed on it. Muni sat frozen for a while, and then fidgeted and tried to edge away. Now the other man suddenly pressed his palms together in a salute, smiled, and said, "Namaste! How do you do?"

At which Muni spoke the only English expressions he had learnt, "Yes, no." Having exhausted his English vocabulary, he started in Tamil: "My name is Muni. These two goats are mine, and no one can gainsay it—though our village is full of slanderers these days who will not hesitate to say that what belongs to a man doesn't belong to him." He rolled his eyes and shuddered at the thought of evil-minded men and women peopling his village.

The foreigner faithfully looked in the direction indicated by Muni's fingers, gazed for a while at the two goats and the rocks, and with a puzzled expression took out his silver cigarette case and lit a cigarette. Suddenly remembering the courtesies of the season, he asked, "Do you smoke?" Muni answered "Yes, no." Whereupon the red-faced man took a cigarette and gave it to Muni, who received it with surprise, having had no offer of a smoke from anyone for years now. Those days when he smoked bhang were gone with his sheep and the large-hearted butcher. Nowadays he was not able to find even matches, let alone bhang. (His wife went across and borrowed a fire at dawn from a neighbour.) He had always wanted to smoke a cigarette; only once did the shopman give him one on credit, and he remembered how good it had tasted. The other flicked the lighter open and offered a light to Muni. Muni felt so confused about how to act that he blew on it and put it out. The other, puzzled but undaunted, flourished his lighter, presented it again, and lit Muni's cigarette. Muni drew a deep puff and started coughing; it was racking, no doubt, but extremely pleasant. When his cough subsided he wiped his eyes and took stock of the situation, understanding that the other man was not an Inquisitor of any kind. Yet, in order to make sure, he remained wary. No need to run away from a man who gave him such a potent smoke. His head was reeling from the effect of one of those strong American cigarettes made with roasted tobacco. The man said, "I come from New York," took out a wallet from his hip pocket, and presented his card.

Muni shrank away from the card. Perhaps he was trying to present a warrant and arrest him. Beware of khaki, one part of his mind warned. Take all the cigarettes or bhang or whatever is offered, but don't get caught. Beware of khaki. He wished he weren't seventy as the shopman had said. At seventy one didn't run, but surrendered to whatever came. He could only ward off trouble by talk. So he went on, all in the chaste Tamil for which Kritam was famous. (Even the worst detractors could not deny that the famous poetess Avaiyar was born in this area, although no one could say whether it was in Kritam or Kuppam, the adjoining village.) Out of this heritage the Tamil language gushed through Muni in an unimpeded flow. He said, "Before God, sir, Bhagwan, who sees everything, I tell you, sir, that we know nothing of the case. If the murder was committed, whoever did it will not escape. Bhagwan is all-seeing. Don't ask me about it. I know nothing." A body had been found mutilated and thrown under a tamarind tree at the border between Kritam and Kuppam a few weeks before, giving rise to much gossip and speculation. Muni added an explanation. "Anything is possible there. People over there will stop at nothing." The foreigner nodded his head and listened courteously though he understood nothing.

"I am sure you know when this horse was made," said the red man and smiled ingratiatingly.

Muni reacted to the relaxed atmosphere by smiling himself, and pleaded, "Please go away, sir, I know nothing. I promise we will hold him for you if we see any bad character around, and we will bury him up to his neck in a coconut pit if he tries to escape; but our village has always had a clean record. Must definitely be the other village."

Now the red man implored, "Please, please, I will speak slowly, please try to understand me. Can't you understand even a simple word of English? Everyone in this country seems to know English. I have gotten along with English everywhere in this country, but you don't speak it. Have you any religious or spiritual scruples against English speech?"

Muni made some indistinct sounds in his throat and shook his head. Encouraged, the other went on to explain at length, uttering each syllable with care and deliberation. Presently he sidled over and took a seat beside the old man, explaining, "You see, last August, we probably had the hottest summer in history, and I was working in shirt-sleeves in my office on the fortieth floor of the Empire State Building. We had a power failure one day, you know, and there I was stuck for four hours, no elevator, no air conditioning. All the way in the train I kept thinking, and the minute I reached home in Connecticut, I told my wife, Ruth, 'We will visit India this winter, it's time to look at other civilizations.' Next day she called the travel agent first thing and told him to fix it, and so here I am. Ruth came with me but is staying back at Srinagar, and I am the one doing the rounds and joining her later."

Muni looked reflective at the end of this long oration and said, rather feebly, "Yes, no," as a concession to the other's language, and went on in Tamil, "When I was this high"—he indicated a foot high—"I had heard my uncle say . . ."

No one can tell what he was planning to say, as the other interrupted him at this stage to ask, "Boy, what is the secret of your teeth? How old are you?"

The old man forgot what he had started to say and remarked, "Sometimes we too lose our cattle. Jackals or cheetahs may sometimes carry them off, but sometimes it is just theft from over in the next village, and then we will know who has done it. Our priest at the temple can see in the camphor flame the face of the thief, and when he is caught . . ." He gestured with his hands a perfect mincing of meat.

The American watched his hands intently and said, "I know what you mean. Chop something? Maybe I am holding you up and you want to chop wood? Where is your axe? Hand it to me and show me what to chop. I do enjoy it, you know, just a hobby. We get a lot of driftwood along the backwater near my house, and on Sundays I do nothing but chop wood for the fireplace. I really feel different when I watch the fire in the fireplace, although it may take all the sections of the Sunday *New York Times* to get a fire started." And he smiled at this reference.

Muni felt totally confused but decided the best thing would be to make an attempt to get away from this place. He tried to edge out, saying, "Must go home," and turned to go. The other seized his shoulder and said desperately, "Is there no one, absolutely no one here, to translate for me?" He looked up and down the road, which was deserted in this hot afternoon; a sudden gust of wind churned up the dust and dead leaves on the roadside into a ghostly column and propelled it towards the mountain road. The stranger almost pinioned Muni's back to the statue and asked, "Isn't this statue yours? Why don't you sell it to me?"

The old man now understood the reference to the horse, thought for a second, and said in his own language, "I was an urchin this high when I heard my grandfather explain this horse and warrior, and my grandfather himself was this high when he heard his grandfather, whose grandfather . . ."

The other man interrupted him. "I don't want to seem to have stopped here for nothing. I will offer you a good price for this," he said, indicating the horse. He had concluded without the least doubt that Muni owned this mud horse. Perhaps he guessed by the way he sat on its pedestal, like other souvenir sellers in this country presiding over their wares.

Muni followed the man's eyes and pointing fingers and dimly understood the subject matter and, feeling relieved that the theme of the mutilated body had been abandoned at least for the time being, said again, enthusiastically, "I was this high when my grandfather told me about this horse and the warrior, and my grandfather was this high when he himself . . ." and he was getting into a deeper bog of reminiscence each time he tried to indicate the antiquity of the statue.

The Tamil that Muni spoke was stimulating even as pure sound, and the foreigner listened with fascination. "I wish I had my tape-recorder here," he said, assuming the pleasantest expression. "Your language sounds wonderful. I get a kick out of every word you utter, here"—he indicated his ears—"but you don't have to waste your breath in sales talk. I appreciate the article. You don't have to explain its points."

"I never went to a school, in those days only Brahmin went to schools, but we had to go out and work in the fields morning till night, from sowing to harvest time . . . and when Pongal came and we had cut the harvest, my father allowed me to go out and play with others at the tank, and so I don't know the Parangi language you speak, even little fellows in your country probably speak the Parangi language, but here only learned men and officers know it. We had a postman in our village who could speak to you boldly in your language, but his wife ran away with someone and he does not speak to anyone at all nowadays. Who would if a wife did what she did? Women must be watched; otherwise they will sell themselves and the home." And he laughed at his own quip.

The foreigner laughed heartily, took out another cigarette, and offered it to Muni, who now smoked with ease, deciding to stay on if the fellow was going to be so good as to keep up his cigarette supply. The American now stood up on the pedestal in the attitude of a demonstrative lecturer and said, running his finger along some of the carved decorations around the horse's neck, speaking slowly and uttering his words syllable by syllable, "I could give a sales talk for this better than anyone else. . . . This is a marvelous combination of yellow and indigo, though faded now. . . . How do you people of this country achieve these flaming colours?"

Muni, now assured that the subject was still the horse and not the dead body, said, "This is our guardian, it means death to our adversaries. At the end of Kali Yuga, this world and all other worlds will be destroyed, and the Redeemer will come in the shape of a horse called Kalki; this horse will come to life and gallop and trample down all bad men." As he spoke of bad men the figures of his shopman and his brother-in-law assumed concrete forms in his mind, and he revelled for a moment in the predicament of the fellow under the horse's hoof: served him right for trying to set fire to his home. . . .

While he was brooding on this pleasant vision, the foreigner utilized the pause to say, "I assure you that this will have the best home in the U.S.A. I'll push away the bookcase, you know I love books and am a member of five book clubs, and the choice and bonus volumes mount up to a pile really in our living room, as high as this horse itself. But they'll have to go. Ruth may disapprove, but I will convince her. The TV may have to be shifted, too. We can't have everything in the living room. Ruth will probably say what about when we have a party? I'm going to keep him right in the middle of the room. I don't see how that can interfere with the party—we'll stand around him and have our drinks."

Muni continued his description of the end of the world. "Our pundit discoursed at the temple once how the oceans are going to close over the earth in a huge wave and swallow us—this horse will grow bigger than the biggest wave and carry on its back only the good people and kick into the floods the evil ones—plenty of them about—" he said reflectively. "Do you know when it is going to happen?" he asked.

The foreigner now understood by the tone of the other that a question was being asked and said, "How am I transporting it? I can push the seat back and make room in the rear. That van can take in an elephant"—waving precisely at the back of the seat.

Muni was still hovering on visions of avatars and said again, "I never missed our pundit's discourses at the temple in those days during every bright half of the month, although he'd go on all night, and he told us that Vishnu is the highest god. Whenever evil men trouble us, he comes down to save us. He has come many times. The first time he incarnated as a great fish, and lifted the scriptures on his back when the flood and sea waves . . ."

"I am not a millionaire, but a modest businessman. My trade is coffee."

Amidst all this wilderness of obscure sound Muni caught the word "coffee" and said, "If you want to drink 'kapi,' drive further up, in the next town, they have Friday market and there they open 'kapi-otels'—so I learn from passers-by. Don't think I wander about. I go nowhere and look for nothing." His thoughts went back to the avatars. "The first avatar was in the shape of a little fish in a bowl of water, but every hour it grew bigger and bigger and became in the end a huge whale which the seas could not contain, and on the back of the whale the holy books were supported, saved, and carried." Once he had launched on the first avatar, it was inevitable that he should go on to the next, a wild boar on whose tusk the earth was lifted when a vicious conqueror of the earth carried it off and hid it at the bottom of the sea. After describing this avatar Muni concluded, "God will always save us whenever we are troubled by evil beings. When we were young we staged at full moon the story of the avatars. That's how I know the stories; we played them all night until the sun rose, and sometimes the European collector would come to watch, bringing his own chair. I had a good voice and so they always taught me songs and gave me the women's roles. I was always Goddess Lakshmi, and they dressed me in a brocade sari, loaned from the Big House . . ."

The foreigner said, "I repeat I am not a millionaire. Ours is a modest business; after all, we can't afford to buy more than sixty minutes of TV time in a month, which works out to two minutes a day, that's all, although in the course of time we'll maybe sponsor a one-hour show regularly if our sales graph continues to go up . . ."

Muni was intoxicated by the memory of his theatrical days and was about to explain how he had painted his face and worn a wig and diamond earrings when the visitor, feeling that he had spent too much time already, said, "Tell me, will you accept a hundred rupees or not for the horse? I'd love to take the whiskered soldier also but no space for him this year. I'll have to cancel my air ticket and take a boat home, I suppose. Ruth can go by air if she likes, but I will go with the horse and keep him in my cabin all the way if necessary." And he smiled at the picture of himself voyaging across the seas hugging this horse. He added, "I will have to pad it with straw so that it doesn't break . . ."

"When we played *Ramayana,* they dressed me as Sita," added Muni. "A teacher came and taught us the songs for the drama and we gave him fifty rupees. He incarnated himself as Rama, and he alone could destroy Ravana, the demon with ten heads who shook all the worlds; do you know the story of *Ramayana*?"

"I have my station wagon as you see. I can push the seat back and take the horse in if you will just lend me a hand with it."

"Do you know *Mahabharata*? Krishna was the eighth avatar of Vishnu, incarnated to help the Five Brothers regain their kingdom. When Krishna was a baby he danced on the thousand-hooded giant serpent and trampled it to death; and then he suckled the breasts of the demoness and left them flat as a disc, though when she came to him her bosoms were large, like mounds of earth on the banks of a dug-up canal." He indicated two mounds with his hands.

The stranger was completely mystified by the gesture. For the first time he said, "I really wonder what you are saying because your answer is crucial. We have come to the point when we should be ready to talk business."

"When the tenth avatar comes, do you know where you and I will be?" asked the old man.

"Lend me a hand and I can lift off the horse from its pedestal after picking out the cement at the joints. We can do anything if we have a basis of understanding."

At this stage the mutual mystification was complete, and there was no need even to carry on a guessing game at the meaning of words. The old man chattered away in a spirit of balancing off the credits and debits of conversational exchange, and said in order to be on the credit sale, "Oh, honourable one, I hope God has blessed you with numerous progeny. I say this because you seem to be a good man, willing to stay beside an old man and talk to him, while all day I have none to talk to except when somebody stops by to ask for a piece of tobacco. But I seldom have it, tobacco is not what it used to be at one time, and I have given up chewing. I cannot afford it nowadays." Noting the other's interest in his speech, Muni felt encouraged to ask, "How many children have you?" with appropriate gestures with his hands.

Realizing that a question was being asked, the red man replied, "I said a hundred," which encouraged Muni to go into details. "How many of your children are boys and how many girls? Where are they? Is your daughter married? Is it difficult to find a son-in-law in your country also?"

In answer to these questions the red man dashed his hand into his pocket and brought forth his wallet in order to take immediate advantage of the bearish trend in the market. He flourished a hundred-rupee currency note and said, "Well, this is what I meant."

The old man now realized that some financial element was entering their talk. He peered closely at the currency note, the like of which he had never seen in his life; he knew the five and ten by their colours although always in other people's hands, while his own earning at any time was in coppers and nickels. What was this man flourishing the note for? Perhaps asking for change. He laughed to himself at the notion of anyone coming to him for changing a thousand- or ten-thousand-rupee note. He said with a grin, "Ask our village headman, who is also a moneylender; he can change even a lakh of rupees in gold sovereigns if you prefer it that way; he thinks nobody knows, but dig the floor of his puja room and your head will reel at the sight of the hoard. The man disguises himself in rags just to mislead the public. Talk to the headman yourself because he goes mad at the sight of me. Someone took away his pumpkins with the creeper and he, for some reason, thinks it was me and my goats . . . that's why I never let my goats be seen anywhere near the farms." His eyes travelled to his goats nosing about, attempting to wrest nutrition from minute greenery peeping out of rock and dry earth.

The foreigner followed his look and decided that it would be a sound policy to show an interest in the old man's pets. He went up casually to them and stroked their backs with every show of courteous attention. Now the truth dawned on the old man. His dream of a lifetime was about to be realized. He understood that the red man was actually making an offer for the goats. He had reared them up in the hope of selling them some day and, with the capital, opening a small shop on this very spot. Sitting here, watching towards the hills, he had often dreamt how he would put up a thatched roof here, spread a gunny sack out on the ground, and display on it fried nuts, coloured sweets, and green coconut for the thirsty and famished wayfarers on the highway, which was sometimes very busy. The animals were not prize ones for a cattle show, but he had spent his occasional savings to provide them some fancy diet now and then, and they did not look too bad. While he was reflecting thus, the red man shook his hand and left on his palm one hundred rupees in tens now, suddenly realizing that this was what the old man was asking. "It is all for you or you may share it if you have a partner."

The old man pointed at the station wagon and asked, "Are you carrying them off in that?"

"Yes, of course," said the other, understanding the transportation part of it.

The old man said, "This will be their first ride in a motor car. Carry them off after I get out of sight, otherwise they will never follow you, but only me even if I am travelling on the path to Yama Loka." He laughed at his own joke, brought his palms together in a salute, turned around and went off, and was soon out of sight beyond a clump of thicket.

The red man looked at the goats grazing peacefully. Perched on the pedestal of the horse, as the westerly sun touched off the ancient faded colours of the statue with a fresh splendour, he ruminated, "He must be gone to fetch some help, I suppose!" and settled down to wait. When a truck came downhill, he stopped it and got the help of a couple of men to detach the horse from its pedestal and place it in his station wagon. He gave them five rupees each, and for a further payment they siphoned off gas from the truck, and helped him to start his engine.

Muni hurried homeward with the cash securely tucked away at his waist in his dhoti. He shut the street door and stole up softly to his wife as she squatted before the lit oven wondering if by a miracle food would drop from the sky. Muni displayed his fortune for the day. She snatched the notes from him, counted them by the glow of the fire, and cried, "One hundred rupees! How did you come by it? Have you been stealing?"

"I have sold our goats to a red-faced man. He was absolutely crazy to have them, gave me all this money and carried them off in his motor car!"

Hardly had these words left his lips when they heard bleating outside. She opened the door and saw the two goats at her door. "Here they are!" she said. "What's the meaning of all this?"

He muttered a great curse and seized one of the goats by its ears and shouted, "Where is that man? Don't you know you are his? Why did you come back?" The goat only wriggled in his grip. He asked the same question of the other, too. The goat shook itself off. His wife glared at him and declared, "If you have thieved, the police will come tonight and break your bones. Don't involve me. I will go away to my parents. . . ."

The Roman Image

The Talkative Man said:

Once I was an archaeologist's assistant. I wandered up and down the country probing, exploring, and digging, in search of antiquities, a most interesting occupation, although cynics sometimes called us "grave-diggers." I enjoyed the work immensely. I had a master who was a famous archaeologist called Doctor something or other. He was a superb, timeless being, who lived a thousand years behind the times, and who wanted neither food nor roof nor riches if only he was allowed to gaze on undisturbed at an old coin or chip of a burial urn. He had torn up the earth in almost all parts of India and had brought to light very valuable information concerning the history and outlook of people of remote centuries. His monographs on each of his excavations filled several shelves in all the important libraries. And then, as our good fortune would have it, he received an inspiration that Malgudi district was eminently diggable. I am not competent to explain how he got this idea, but there it was. Word was brought to me that the great man was staying in the dak bungalow and was in need of an assistant. Within an hour of hearing it I stood before the great man. He was sitting on the floor with the most crazy collection of articles in front of him—pots and beads and useless coins and palm leaves, all of them rusty and decaying. He had a lens by his side, through which he looked at these articles and made notes. He asked me: "What do you know of the archaeological factors of your district?" I blinked. Honestly I didn't know there was any archaeology in our place. He looked at me through his old spectacles, and I realized that my living depended upon my answer. I mustered up all the knowledge of elementary history I had acquired in my boyhood, and replied: "Well, nothing has so far been done in any methodical manner, although now and then we come across some ignorant villagers ploughing up old unusual bits of pottery and metal."

"Really," he asked, pricking up his ears. "And what do they do with them?"

"They simply throw them away or give them to children to play with," I replied.

"Oh, too bad," he muttered. "Why couldn't you have collected these things in one place?"

"I will take care to do that hereafter, sir," I said; and that settled it. He engaged me on the spot at fifty rupees a month, and my main business was to follow him about and help him.

I had my wits alive, and within a month I was in a position to lead him by the hand. Not the slightest object escaped my notice. I picked up everything I saw, cleaned and polished it, and held it up for his opinion. Most times, I am sorry to confess, they were useless bits of stuff of known origin—namely, our own times. But I am glad to say that once I scored a hit.

We camped one week-end at Siral—a village sixty miles from the town. It is a lovely ancient place, consisting of a hundred houses. Sarayu River winds its way along the northern boundary of the village. The river here is broader than it is anywhere else in the district. On the other bank of the river we have the beginnings of a magnificent jungle of bamboo and teak. The most modern structure in the place was a small two-roomed inspection lodge. The doctor occupied one room and I the other. We were scouting the surroundings for a mound under which was supposed to be a buried city. This discovery was going to push the earliest known civilization three centuries farther back and rival Mohenjadaro in antiquity. We might be pardoned if we set about our business with some intensity. Our doctor somehow seemed to possess an inexplicable feeling of rivalry with the discoverers of Mohenjadaro and such other places. His greatest desire was to have a monopoly of the earliest known civilization and place it where he chose. This seemed to me a slight weakness in his nature, but pardonable in a great man, who had done so much else in life. This is all beside the point. Let me get on with the story. One day I had gone to the river for a bathe. It was an exhilarating evening; I had done a good day's work, assisting the doctor to clean up and study a piece of stained glass picked up in a field outside the village. The doctor kept gazing at this glass all day. He constantly shook his head and said: "This is easily the most important piece of work which has come under my notice. This bit of glass you see is not ordinary archaeological stuff, but a very important link. This piece of glass is really Florentian, which went out of vogue in A.D. 5. How did this come here? It is not found anywhere else in the world. If the identity of this is established properly we may ultimately have a great deal to say about the early Roman Empire and this part of India. This will revolutionize our whole knowledge of history." He talked of nothing but that the whole day. He trembled with excitement and lost all taste for food. He kept on muttering: "We must tread warily and not overlook the slightest evidence. Keep your eyes open. We are on the eve of great discoveries. . . ." And I caught this excitement and acquired a permanently searching look. I was in this state when I plunged into the waters of Sarayu that evening. I am a good diver. As I went down my hand struck against a hard object in the sandy bed. Feeling with my fingers, I found it to be a stone image. When I came to the surface again I came up bearing that image with me. Dripping with water, I sat on the river step, without even drying myself, and examined the image.

"This takes us on to an entirely new set of possibilities!" exclaimed the doctor in great joy. He keenly examined it by our tin lantern. It was a stone image a foot high, which had acquired a glass-like smoothness, having been under water for years. It had an arm, an eye, the nose, and the mouth missing. There were a few details of ornament and drapery, which the doctor examined with special care. It was 3 A.M. when he went to bed. An hour later the doctor peeped in at my doorway and announced: "This is a Roman statue. How it came to be found in these parts is a historical fact we have to wrest from evidence. It is going to give an entirely new turn to Indian history."

Within the next two months all the important papers and periodicals in the world published details of this discovery. Papers were read before historical associations and conferences. I came to be looked upon as a sort of saviour of Indian history, for the doctor insisted upon giving me my due share of fame. University honours came my way. I was offered lucrative positions here and there. It was finally decided that the image was that of a Roman Emperor called Tiberius II. It would be out of place to go into the details that led to this conclusion: but you need have no doubt that the doctor had excellent reasons for it. Besides the study of the image itself he went through some Roman texts which mentioned South India.

For the next few months we toured about a great deal lecturing on this subject and demonstrating. I went with my doctor to Madras and started work on a monograph on the subject. It was to be a monumental work covering over a thousand pages of demy size, full of photographs and sketches. You can understand why it should be so big when I tell you that it was going to be a combined work on early Roman history, Indian history, archaeology, and epigraphy. My name was going to appear as the joint author of the work. I realized that here was my future—fame, position, and perhaps some money, too. The doctor left me in entire charge of this work and went away to Upper India to continue a piece of work which he had already been doing. I sat in a large library the whole day, examining, investigating, studying, and writing. I became a fairly important person in learned societies. I worked from seven in the morning to eleven in the evening almost without a break, and throughout the day I had visits from people interested in the discovery. Papers and journals contained paragraphs now and then—"Archaeologist assistant working on monograph . . ."—and its progress was duly reported to the public. And then there came a time when the press could announce: "Monograph on which —— has been working for months now will be ready for publication in ten days. It is expected that this is going to make the richest contribution to Indian history. . . ." My fingers were worn out with writing. My eyes were nearly gone. I looked forward to the end of the work, when, as my doctor wrote: "You can have a holiday for three months in any hill station you like and forget the whole business. . . ." The manuscripts piled a yard high on my table.

It was at this stage that I had to visit Siral once again. I had to obtain measurements of the spot where the image was found. I left my work at that and hurried to the village. I plunged into the river and came up. I sat on the river step, still dripping with water, noting down figures, when a stranger came and sat near me. We fell to talking, and I told him about my work, in the hope of drawing out further facts. He was a rustic, and he listened to me without emotion. At the end of my narration he remained peculiarly moody and asked me to repeat facts about the image. He compressed his lips and asked: "Where do you say it came from?"

"Rome—"

"Where is that?"

"In Europe," I said. He stood still, puzzled, and I amplified: "Where the European people live—"

"I don't know about that—but if it is the image which you found in these parts I can tell you something about it. It is without nose and arm, isn't it?" I assented, not knowing what was coming. He said: "Follow me, if you want to know anything more about this image." He led me up the bank, along a foot track which wound through the jungle. We reached a hamlet a mile off. He stopped in front of a little shrine and said: "That image belonged to this temple." He led me into the shrine. We had to go stooping into it because of its narrow doorway and low roof. At the inner sanctum there was an image of Mari with a garland of yellow chrysanthemums around her neck, lit by a faint wick lamp. On one side of the sanctum doorway stood a dwarapalaka—a winged creature a foot high. My friend pointed at the image and said: "This formed a pair with the one you picked up, and it used to adorn that side of the doorway." I looked up where he pointed. I noticed a pedestal without anything on it. A doubt seized me. "I want to examine the figure," I said. He brought down the wick lamp; I examined by its flickering light the dwarapalaka. "Is this exactly like the one which was on that side?" It was a superfluous question. This image was exactly like the image I had found, but without its injuries.

"Where was this made?"

"I had it done by a stone-image maker, a fellow in another village. You see that hillock? Its stone is made into images all over the world, and at its foot is a village where they make images."

"Are you sure when it was made?"

"Yes, I gave an advance of twenty rupees for it, and how that fellow delayed! I went over to the village and sat up night and day for two months and got the pair done. I watched them take shape before my eyes. And then we collected about fifty rupees and gave it to him. We wanted to improve this temple." I put back the lamp and walked out. I sat down on the temple step. "Why do you look so sad? I thought you'd be pleased to know these things," he said, watching me.

"I am, I am—only I've been rather unwell," I assured him. "Can't you tell me something more about it: how it came to be found in the river?"

"Yes, yes," said my friend. "It was carried and thrown into the river; it didn't walk down there."

"Oh!" I exclaimed.

"That is a story. For this we went to the court and had the priest dismissed and fined. He cannot come near the temple now. We spent one thousand rupees in lawyer fees alone; we were prepared to spend all our fortune if only to see that priest removed. It went up to Malgudi court—we got a vakil from Madras."

"What was wrong with your priest?"

"No doubt he had a hereditary claim and took up the work when his father died, but the fellow was a devil for drink if ever there was one. Morning till night he was drinking, and he performed all the puja in that condition. We did not know what to do with him. We just tolerated him, hoping that some day the goddess would teach him a lesson. We did not like to be too harsh, since he was a poor fellow, and he went about his duties quietly. But when we added these two dwarapalakas at the doorway he got a queer notion in his head. He used to say that the two doorkeepers constantly harried him by staring at him wherever he went. He said that their look pricked him in the neck. Sometimes he would peep in from within to see if the images were looking away, and he'd scream, 'Ah, still they are watching me,' and shout at them. This went on for months. In course of time he began to shudder whenever he had to pass these doorkeepers. It was an acute moment of suspense for him when he had to cross that pair and get into the sanctum. Gradually he complained that if he ever took his eyes off these figures they butted him from behind, kicked him, and pulled his hair, and so forth. He was afraid to look anywhere else and walked on cautiously with his eyes on the images. But if he had his eyes on one, the other knocked him from behind. He showed us bruises and scratches sometimes. We declared we might treat his complaints seriously if he ever went into the shrine without a drop of drink in him. In course of time he started to seek his own remedy. He carried a small mallet with him, and whenever he got a knock he returned the blow; it fell on a nose today, on an arm tomorrow, and on an ear another day. We didn't notice his handiwork for months. Judging from the mallet blows, the image on the left side seems to have been the greater offender.

"The culmination came when he knocked it off its pedestal and carried it to the river. Next morning he declared he saw it walk off and plunge into the river. He must have felt that this would serve as a lesson to the other image if it should be thinking of any trick. But the other image never got its chance: for we dragged the priest before a law court and had him sent away."

Thus ended the villager's tale. It took time for me to recover. I asked: "Didn't you have to pick up the image from the water and show it to the judge?"

"No, because the fellow would not tell us where he had flung it. I did not know till this moment where exactly it could be found."

When I went back to Madras I was a different man. The doctor had just returned for a short stay. I told him everything. He was furious. "We have made ourselves mighty fools before the whole world," he cried.

I didn't know what to say. I mumbled: "I am so sorry, sir." He pointed at the pile of manuscripts on the table and cried: "Throw all that rubbish into the fire, before we are declared mad. . . ." I pushed the whole pile off the table and applied a matchstick. We stood frowning at the roaring fire for a moment, and then he asked, pointing at the image: "And what will you do with it?"

"I don't know," I said.

"Drown it. After all, you picked it up from the water—that piece of nonsense!" he cried.

I had never seen him in such a rage before. I wrapped the image in a piece of brown paper, carried it to the seashore, and flung it far into the sea. I hope it is still rolling about at the bottom of the Bay of Bengal. I only hope it won't get into some large fish and come back to the study table! Later a brief message appeared in all the important papers: "The manuscript on which Doctor —— and assistant were engaged has been destroyed, and the work will be suspended."

The doctor gave me two months' salary and bade me goodbye.

The Watchman

There was still a faint splash of red on the western horizon. The watchman stood on the tank bund and took a final survey. All the people who had come for evening walks had returned to their homes. Not a soul anywhere—except that obstinate angler, at the northern end, who sat with his feet in water, sadly gazing on his rod. It was no use bothering about him: he would sit there till midnight, hoping for a catch.

The Taluk office gong struck nine. The watchman was satisfied that no trespassing cattle had sneaked in through the wire fencing. As he turned to go, he saw, about a hundred yards away, a shadowy figure moving down the narrow stone steps that led to the water's edge. He thought for a second that it might be a ghost. He dismissed the idea, and went up to investigate. If it was anyone come to bathe at this hour . . . From the top step he observed that it was a woman's form. She stooped over the last step and placed something on it—possibly a letter. She then stepped into knee-deep water, and stood there, her hands pressed together in prayer. Unmistakable signs—always to be followed by the police and gruesome details, bringing the very worst possible reputation to a tank.

He shouted, "Come out, there, come out of it." The form looked up from the water. "Don't stand there and gaze. You'll catch a cold, come up whoever you are. . . ." He raced down the steps and picked up the letter. He hurriedly lit his lamp, and turned its wick till it burnt brightly, and held it up, murmuring: "I don't like this. Why is everyone coming to the same tank? If you want to be dead, throw yourself under an engine," he said.

The light fell upon the other's face. It was a young girl's, wet with tears. He felt a sudden pity. He said, "Sit down, sit down and rest . . . no, no . . . go up two more steps and sit down. Don't sit so near the water. . . ." She obeyed. He sat down on the last step between her and the water, placed the lantern on the step, took out a piece of tobacco, and put it in his mouth. She buried her face in her hands, and began to sob. He felt troubled and asked: "Why don't you rise and go home, lady?"

She sputtered through her sob: "I have no home in this world!"

"Don't tell me! Surely, you didn't grow up without a home all these years!" said the watchman.

"I lost my mother when I was five years old—" she said.

"I thought so . . ." replied the watchman, and added, "and your father married again and you grew up under the care of your stepmother?"

"Yes, yes, how do you know?" she asked.

"I am sixty-five years old," he said and asked, "Did your stepmother trouble you?"

"No, there you are wrong," the girl said. "She is very kind to me. She has been looking after me ever since my father died a few years ago. She has just a little money on hand left by my father, and she spends it on us."

The watchman looked at the stars, sighed for the dinner that he was missing. "It's very late, madam, go home."

"I tell you I've no home—" she retorted angrily.

"Your stepmother's house is all right from what you say. She is good to you."

"But why should I be a burden to her? Who am I?"

"You are her husband's daughter," the watchman said, and added, "That is enough claim."

"No no. I won't live on anybody's charity."

"Then you will have to wait till they find you a husband—"

She glared at him in the dark. "That's what I do not want to do. I want to study and become a doctor and earn my livelihood. I don't want to marry. I often catch my mother talking far into the night to her eldest son, worrying about my future, about my marriage. I know they cannot afford to keep me in college very long now; it costs about twenty rupees a month."

"Twenty rupees!" the watchman exclaimed. It was his month's salary. "How can anybody spend so much for books!"

"Till today," she said, "I was hoping that I would get a scholarship. That would have saved me. But this evening they announced; others have got it, not I. My name is not there—" and she broke down again. The watchman looked at her in surprise. He comprehended very little of all this situation. She added: "And when they come to know of this, they will try to arrange my marriage. Someone is coming to have a look at me tomorrow."

"Marry him and may God bless you with ten children."

"No, no," she cried hysterically. "I don't want to marry. I want to study."

The silent night was stabbed by her sobbing and some night bird rustled the water, and wavelets beat upon the shore. Seeing her suffer, he found his own sorrows in life came to his mind; how in those far-off times, in his little village home an epidemic of cholera laid out his father and mother and brothers on the same day, and he was the sole survivor; how he was turned out of his ancestral home through the trickery of his father's kinsmen, and he wandered as an orphan, suffering indescribable hunger and privation.

"Everyone has his own miseries," he said. "If people tried to kill themselves for each one of them, I don't know how often they would have to drown." He remembered further incidents and his voice shook with sorrow. "You are young and you don't know what sorrow is. . . ." He remained silent and a sob broke out of him as he said: "I prayed to all the gods in the world for a son. My wife bore me eight children. Only one daughter lives now, and none of the others saw the eleventh year. . . ." The girl looked at him in bewilderment.

The Taluk office gong struck again. "It is late, you had better get up and go home," he said.

She replied: "I have no home."

He felt irritated. "You are making too much of nothing. You should not be obstinate—"

"You don't know my trouble," she said.

He picked up his lantern and staff and got up. He put her letter down where he found it.

"If you are going to be so obstinate, I'll leave you alone. No one can blame me." He paused for a moment, looked at her, and went up the steps; not a word passed between them again.

The moment he came back to duty next morning, he hurried down the stone steps. The letter lay where he had dropped it on the previous night. He picked it up and gazed on it, helplessly, wishing that it could tell him about the fate of the girl after he had left her. He tore it up and flung it on the water. As he watched the bits float off on ripples, he blamed himself for leaving her and going away on the previous night. "I am responsible for at least one suicide in this tank," he often remarked to himself. He could never look at the blue expanse of water again with an easy mind. Even many months later he could not be certain that the remains of a body would not come up all of a sudden. "Who knows, it sometimes happens that the body gets stuck deep down," he reflected.

Years later, one evening as he stood on the bund and took a final survey before going home, he saw a car draw up on the road below. A man, a woman, and three children emerged from the car and climbed the bund. When they approached, the watchman felt a start at his heart; the figure and face of the woman seemed familiar to him. Though the woman was altered by years, and ornaments, and dress, he thought that he had now recognized the face he had once seen by the lantern light. He felt excited at this discovery. He had numerous questions to ask. He brought together his palms and saluted her respectfully. He expected she would stop and speak to him. But she merely threw at him an indifferent glance and passed on. He stood staring after her for a moment, baffled. "Probably this is someone else," he muttered and turned to go home, resolving to dismiss the whole episode from his mind.

A Career

The Talkative Man said:

Years and years ago I had a shop. It was in those days when Lawley Extension was not what it is now. It consisted of fewer than a hundred houses. Market Road being at least a mile off, the people living in the Extension looked on me as a saviour when I took up a little building, and on an auspicious day hung up a large board with the inscription: THE NATIONAL PROVISION STORES. I went from house to house and secured orders. I literally examined every pantry in the Extension and filled up the gaps. When the bell rang for the midday interval at the Extension Elementary School, children swarmed into my shop and carried off whatever sweets, ribbons, and fancy stationery I happened to keep. I did about twenty-five rupees credit and ten rupees cash sales every day. This gave us at least fifty rupees a month to live on. We paid a rent of five rupees and took a small house in Kabir Street, which was over a mile from my shop. I left at seven in the morning and returned home only at nine in the evening, after clearing the daily accounts.

A year and a half passed thus. One day a young fellow presented himself at my shop. He looked about twenty, very fair and bright. He wore a spotless dhoti and shirt.

"What can I do for you?" I asked, taking him to be a young customer.

In answer he brought his palms together in salute and said, "I need your help, sir. I will do whatever work you may give me in return for a little food and shelter and kindness."

There was something in the young fellow's personality which

appealed to me. Moreover, he had on his forehead three-finger width of sacred ash and a dot of vermilion between his eyebrows. He looked as if he had just come from a temple.

"I am very God-fearing, sir, and susceptible to religious influences."

I spoke to him for about an hour.

He said he belonged to a family of wealthy landholders in a village near Trichinopoly. His mother had died some years before. His father took a mistress who ill-treated the boy and consequently he ran away from home.

A touching story, I felt.

I directed him to my house. When I went home in the evening I found that he had already made himself a great favourite there. His life story had deeply moved my wife.

"So young!" she whispered to me, "and to think that he should be left at this age without a father or a mother!" she sighed. He had made himself lovable in a dozen ways already. He had taken my little son out for a walk. The youngster cried as soon as he came home, "Let Ramu stay in our house. He is great. He knows magic and can tame tigers and elephants." Ramu walked into the kitchen and offered assistance. At first my wife protested.

"Why won't you allow me to go near the oven, Mother?" he asked. "Is it because you think I can't cook? Give me a chance and see."

He made a dash for the bathroom, turned the tap on himself, and came out dripping. He took a handful of sacred ash and smeared it on his forehead. My wife was tremendously impressed. She let him do the cooking.

He prepared delicious food for us. We were all very pleased. After that he helped my wife with all the cleaning and scrubbing. He slept at night on the bare floor, refusing the mat and the pillow we offered.

He was the first to be up next morning. He lit the stove and woke up my wife. At midday he brought me my food. While I ate he attended to the school children who came into the shop. He handed them their knick-knacks with an expert hand. He charmed and amused them. He made them laugh. He beguiled them with an alternative when he had not on hand what they wanted.

It was inevitable that in a month he should be sharing with me the shop work. He had attractive ways about him. Customers liked to talk to him. Within a short time there was not a single home in the Extension where he was not treated as a member of the family. He knew the inside story of every family. He served everyone to the best of his capacity. Here he helped a man with his garden, and there he pleaded with a house-building contractor and had an estimate revised. He patched up quarrels. He tamed truants and sent them to school. He took part in all the extracurricular activities of the Extension Elementary School. He took an interest in the Club Movement. He dressed himself up for the occasion when the inspector visited the school, and arranged for the supply of garlands and flowers. And all this in addition to assisting me in the shop. He went every day to the market and purchased provisions from the wholesale merchants, sat down for hours on end in the shop and handed out things to customers, pored over the accounts till late at night, and collected all the bills.

As a result of Ramu's presence my business increased nearly tenfold. I had abundant rest now. I left the shop entirely in his hands. I went home for food at midday. After that I slept till three in the afternoon. And then I went to the shop, but stayed there only till five o'clock, when I went to an open space nearby and played badminton with some friends. I came to the shop again only at seven in the evening.

Once or twice my wife and I talked over the matter and tried to fix up a monthly pay for Ramu. We felt we ought not to be exploiting Ramu's friendliness. But when the subject was mentioned Ramu grew red in the face and said, "If you don't want me to stay with you any more, you may talk of salary again. . . ."

Five years passed thus. He aged with us. He lived with us through all our joys and sorrows. I had four children now. My business had prospered enormously. We were living in a bigger house in the same street. I took the shop building on a long lease. I had an immense stock of all kinds of provisions and goods.

I extended my business. I purchased large quantities of butter in all the nearby villages and sold them to butter and ghee merchants in Madras. This business gave me large profits. It kept me running between the villages and Madras. The shop was entirely in Ramu's hands.

At Madras I used to stop with a merchant in George Town. Once work kept me on there a little longer than I had anticipated. One evening just as I was starting out to post a letter for Ramu, a telegraph messenger stepped off his cycle and gave me an envelope. I tore open the cover and read: "Father dying of cholera. Must go at once. Return immediately. Ramu."

The next morning at five o'clock I got down at Malgudi. Ramu was at the station. He was going to Trichinopoly by the same train. The train halted only for a few minutes. Red-eyed and sobbing, Ramu said, "My father, father, cholera. Never thought he would get it. . . ." I consoled him. I had never seen him so broken. I said feebly, "He will be all right, don't worry. . . ." I had hardly the heart to ask him about the shop. He himself said, "I have handed the keys to Mother, and all the accounts and cash also. . . ."

"All right, all right, I will look to all that. Don't worry," I said.

The guard blew his whistle. Ramu jumped into a third-class compartment. The train jerked forward. He put his head out the window and said, "I will be back tomorrow by the night train, if my father gets better. . . . Whatever happens, I won't be away for more than fifteen days. Kittu has asked me to bring him"—his voice and face receded—"a wooden elephant on wheels. Please tell him that I will surely bring it. My namaskarams to Mother. . . ." Tears rolled down his cheeks. Even long after the train had left the platform he was still looking out of the window and gesticulating to indicate "I will surely be back soon. . . ."

Having some unfinished Madras business on hand, I could hardly go near the shop for a week. When I reopened, the first thing that I noticed was that the shop was empty. Except for a bag of coarse rice and a few bars of cheap soap, all the racks and containers were empty. I picked up the books and examined them. The entries were all in a mess. I put them away. Replenishing the stock was more urgent. I made out a list and went to the market.

Sadik Sait, my wholesale supplier, squatted amidst his cushions and welcomed me warmly. I owed my start in life to the unlimited credit he allowed me. After some preliminary, inconsequential talk, I put before him the list. He scrutinized it gloomily and shook his head. He said, "You want goods for about three hundred rupees. I wouldn't advise you to put up your dues. Why don't you take fifty rupees worth now? I am suggesting this only for your own convenience . . ." This was the first time in my life that he had spoken to me in this manner. And he explained, "Don't mistake me, friend. You are a business man, so am I. No use talking indirectly and vaguely. I will tell you what the matter is. Your account with us stands at Rs. 3,500—and if you had paid at least a single instalment for these three months, we should have felt happier. . . ."

"But, Sait, last month I sent four hundred to be given to you, and the month before three hundred and fifty, and the month before— There must be only a balance of—" He took out his ledger. There was only one payment made for four months when the bill stood at about a thousand. After that there had been purchases almost every day for about forty rupees.

"The young fellow said that business was very brisk and that you would clear the accounts when you returned from Madras."

My head swam. "I will see you again," I said, and went back to the shop.

I once again examined the books. The pages showed a lot of arrears to be collected. Next day I went round to collect all my bills. People looked surprised. "There must be some mistake. We paid our bills completely a fortnight ago. Otherwise Ramu wouldn't leave us in peace."

My wife said, "In your absence he was coming home nearly at twelve every night. He used to tell me that the accounts kept him late. 'How was business today?' I unfailingly asked every day. He replied, 'Business is good, bad, good and bad. Don't worry. Leave it all to me. I will manage.' "

An old man of Lawley Extension asked me, "Where is that boy you had?"

I told him.

"Look here," the old man said. "Keep this to yourself. You remember there lived next door to us those people from Hyderabad?"

"Yes, yes . . ."

"Your boy was gadding about with them a little too much. You know there was a tall, pretty girl with them. Your fellow was taking her out every evening in a taxi. He closed the shop promptly at six in the evening. Those people went back to Hyderabad a few days ago."

Later on I made inquiries in Market Road and learnt that Ramu had had stitched four tweed suits, eighteen silk shirts and other clothes worth about a hundred rupees, purchased leather suitcases, four pairs of pump shoes, two pairs of velvet slippers, a wrist watch, two rings, a brooch, silk saris, blouse pieces, and so on. I got in touch with a near relative of Ramu's employed in a bank in Madras. I learnt that his old father was hale and hearty, and there was no mention of cholera. Above all, Ramu was never known to have visited Trichinopoly. His whereabouts were unknown. The letter concluded: "Someone recently returned from a tour mentioned that he thought he caught a glimpse of Ramu in a large gathering during some music festival in Hyderabad. He was, however, not very certain about it. . . ."

I sold my shop and everything, paid off my creditors, and left Malgudi. I was a bankrupt, with a wife and four children to support. We moved from place to place, living on the charity of friends, relatives, and unknown people. Sometimes nobody would feed us and we threw ourselves down in a dark corner of some rest-house, and my ragged children cried till sleep overcame them. I needn't weary you with an account of my struggles. It is another story. I must tell you about Ramu. I have to add only this about my own career. Four years later I came across a coffee-estate owner in Mempi Hills, and he gave me a fresh start; and I must say, thanks to him, I have done very well indeed in the coffee trade.

Now about Ramu. A year ago I was panting up the steps of Thirupathi Hills. I had a vow to fulfil at the temple. I had passed two thousand steps when a familiar voice assailed my ears from among the group of mendicants lining the steps. I stopped and turned. And there he was, I could hardly recognize him now. I had seen him off at Malgudi station ten years before. His face was now dark, scarred, and pitted. His eyes were fixed in a gaze. I should have passed him without noticing if he hadn't called out for alms. His voice was still unchanged. I stopped and said, "Look here.'"

"I can't see, I am blind."

"Who are you? Where do you come from?" I asked in a voice which I tried to disguise with a little gruffness.

"Go, go your way. Why do you want to know all that?" he said.

I had often boasted that if I met him I would break his bones first; but this was not at all how I had hoped to see him again. I felt very confused and unhappy. I dropped a coin on his upraised palm and passed on. But after moving up a few steps I stopped and beckoned to another beggar sitting by his side. He came up. I held up an anna coin before him and said, "You may have this if you will tell me something about that blind man. . . ."

"I know him," said this beggar, who had no arms. "We keep together. He has arms, but no eyes; I have eyes, but no arms, and so we find each other helpful. We move about together. He is not a beggar like me, but a sanyasi. He came here two years ago. He had once much money in Hyderabad, Delhi, Benares, or somewhere. Smallpox took away his sight. His wife, a bad sort, deserted him. He is vexed with the world. Some pilgrims coming from the North brought him here. . . . But, surely you won't tell him I have spoken all this? He becomes wild if those days are mentioned. . . ."

I went back to Ramu, stood before him and watched him for a moment. I felt like shouting, "Ramu, God has punished you enough. Now come with me. Where is your sweetheart? Where is my money? What devil seized you?" But I checked myself. I felt that the greatest kindness I could do him was to leave him alone. I silently placed a rupee on his outstretched palm, and raced up the steps. At the bend I turned my head and had another look at him. And that was the last I saw of him. For when I returned that way four days later, he was not to be seen. Perhaps he had moved on to another place with his armless companion.

Old Man of the Temple

The Talkative Man said:

It was some years ago that this happened. I don't know if you can make anything of it. If you do, I shall be glad to hear what you have to say; but personally I don't understand it at all. It has always mystified me. Perhaps the driver was drunk; perhaps he wasn't.

I had engaged a taxi for going to Kumbum, which, as you may already know, is fifty miles from Malgudi. I went there one morning and it was past nine in the evening when I finished my business and started back for the town. Doss, the driver, was a young fellow of about twenty-five. He had often brought his car for me and I liked him. He was a well-behaved, obedient fellow, with a capacity to sit and wait at the wheel, which is really a rare quality in a taxi driver. He drove the car smoothly, seldom swore at passers-by, and exhibited perfect judgment, good sense, and sobriety; and so I preferred him to any other driver whenever I had to go out on business.

It was about eleven when we passed the village Koopal, which is on the way down. It was the dark half of the month and the surrounding country was swallowed up in the night. The village street was deserted. Everyone had gone to sleep; hardly any light was to be seen. The stars overhead sparkled brightly. Sitting in the back seat and listening to the continuous noise of the running wheels, I was half lulled into a drowse.

All of a sudden Doss swerved the car and shouted: "You old fool! Do you want to kill yourself?"

I was shaken out of my drowse and asked: "What is the matter?"

Doss stopped the car and said, "You see that old fellow, sir. He is trying to kill himself. I can't understand what he is up to."

I looked in the direction he pointed and asked, "Which old man?"

"There, there. He is coming towards us again. As soon as I saw him open that temple door and come out I had a feeling, somehow, that I must keep an eye on him."

I took out my torch, got down, and walked about, but could see no one. There was an old temple on the roadside. It was utterly in ruins; most portions of it were mere mounds of old brick; the walls were awry; the doors were shut to the main doorway, and brambles and thickets grew over and covered them. It was difficult to guess with the aid of the torch alone what temple it was and to what period it belonged.

"The doors are shut and sealed and don't look as if they had been opened for centuries now," I cried.

"No, sir," Doss said coming nearer. "I saw the old man open the doors and come out. He is standing there; shall we ask him to open them again if you want to go in and see?"

I said to Doss, "Let us be going. We are wasting our time here."

We went back to the car. Doss sat in his seat, pressed the self-starter, and asked without turning his head, "Are you permitting this fellow to come with us, sir? He says he will get down at the next milestone."

"Which fellow?" I asked.

Doss indicated the space next to him.

"What is the matter with you, Doss? Have you had a drop of drink or something?"

"I have never tasted any drink in my life, sir," he said, and added, "Get down, old boy. Master says he can't take you."

"Are you talking to yourself?"

"After all, I think we needn't care for these unknown fellows on the road," he said.

"Doss," I pleaded. "Do you feel confident you can drive? If you feel dizzy don't drive."

"Thank you, sir," said Doss. "I would rather not start the car now. I am feeling a little out of sorts." I looked at him anxiously. He closed his eyes, his breathing became heavy and noisy, and gradually his head sank.

"Doss, Doss," I cried desperately. I got down, walked to the front seat, opened the door, and shook him vigorously. He opened his eyes, assumed a hunched-up position, and rubbed his eyes with his hands, which trembled like an old man's.

"Do you feel better?" I asked.

"Better! Better! Hi! Hi!" he said in a thin, piping voice.

"What has happened to your voice? You sound like someone else," I said.

"Nothing. My voice is as good as it was. When a man is eighty he is bound to feel a few changes coming on."

"You aren't eighty, surely," I said.

"Not a day less," he said. "Is nobody going to move this vehicle? If not, there is no sense in sitting here all day. I will get down and go back to my temple."

"I don't know how to drive," I said. "And unless you do it, I don't see how it can move."

"Me!" exclaimed Doss. "These new chariots! God knows what they are drawn by, I never understand, though I could handle a pair of bullocks in my time. May I ask a question?"

"Go on," I said.

"Where is everybody?"

"Who?"

"Lots of people I knew are not to be seen at all. All sorts of new fellows everywhere, and nobody seems to care. Not a soul comes near the temple. All sorts of people go about but not one who cares to stop and talk. Why doesn't the king ever come this way? He used to go this way at least once a year before."

"Which king?" I asked.

"Let me go, you idiot," said Doss, edging towards the door on which I was leaning. "You don't seem to know anything." He pushed me aside, and got down from the car. He stooped as if he had a big hump on his back, and hobbled along towards the temple. I followed him, hardly knowing what to do. He turned and snarled at me: "Go away, leave me alone. I have had enough of you."

"What has come over you, Doss?" I asked.

"Who is Doss, anyway? Doss, Doss, Doss. What an absurd name! Call me by my name or leave me alone. Don't follow me calling 'Doss, Doss.'"

"What is your name?" I asked.

"Krishna Battar, and if you mention my name people will know for a hundred miles around. I built a temple where there was only a cactus field before. I dug the earth, burnt every brick, and put them one upon another, all single-handed. And on the day the temple held up its tower over the surrounding country, what a crowd gathered! The king sent his chief minister . . ."

"Who was the king?"

"Where do you come from?" he asked.

"I belong to these parts certainly, but as far as I know there has been only a collector at the head of the district. I have never heard of any king."

"Hi! Hi! Hi!" he cackled, and his voice rang through the gloomy silent village. "Fancy never knowing the king! He will behead you if he hears it."

"What is his name?" I asked.

This tickled him so much that he sat down on the ground, literally unable to stand the joke any more. He laughed and coughed uncontrollably.

"I am sorry to admit," I said, "that my parents have brought me up in such utter ignorance of worldly affairs that I don't know even my king. But won't you enlighten me? What is his name?"

"Vishnu Varma, the emperor of emperors . . ."

I cast my mind up and down the range of my historical knowledge but there was no one by that name. Perhaps a local chief of pre-British days, I thought.

"What a king! He often visited my temple or sent his minister for the Annual Festival of the temple. But now nobody cares."

"People are becoming less godly nowadays," I said. There was silence for a moment. An idea occurred to me, I can't say why. "Listen to me," I said. "You ought not to be here any more."

"What do you mean?" he asked, drawing himself up, proudly.

"Don't feel hurt; I say you shouldn't be here any more because you are dead."

"Dead! Dead!" he said. "Don't talk nonsense. How can I be dead when you see me before you now? If I am dead how can I be saying this and that?"

"I don't know all that," I said. I argued and pointed out that according to his own story he was more than five hundred years old, and didn't he know that man's longevity was only a hundred? He constantly interrupted me, but considered deeply what I said.

He said: "It is like this . . . I was coming through the jungle one night after visiting my sister in the next village. I had on me some money and gold ornaments. A gang of robbers set upon me. I gave them as good a fight as any man could, but they were too many for me. They beat me down and knifed me; they took away all that I had on me and left thinking they had killed me. But soon I got up and tried to follow them. They were gone. And I returned to the temple and have been here since . . ."

I told him, "Krishna Battar, you are dead, absolutely dead. You must try and go away from here."

"What is to happen to the temple?" he asked.

"Others will look after it."

"Where am I to go? Where am I to go?"

"Have you no one who cares for you?" I asked.

"None except my wife. I loved her very much."

"You can go to her."

"Oh, no. She died four years ago . . ."

Four years! It was very puzzling. "Do you say four years back from now?" I asked.

"Yes, four years ago from now." He was clearly without any sense of time.

So I asked, "Was she alive when you were attacked by thieves?"

"Certainly not. If she had been alive she would never have allowed me to go through the jungle after nightfall. She took very good care of me."

"See here," I said. "It is imperative you should go away from here. If she comes and calls you, will you go?"

"How can she when I tell you that she is dead?"

I thought for a moment. Presently I found myself saying, "Think of her, and only of her, for a while and see what happens. What was her name?"

"Seetha, a wonderful girl . . ."

"Come on, think of her." He remained in deep thought for a while. He suddenly screamed, "Seetha is coming! Am I dreaming or what? I will go with her . . ." He stood up, very erect; he appeared to have lost all the humps and twists he had on his body. He drew himself up, made a dash forward, and fell down in a heap.

Doss lay on the rough ground. The only sign of life in him was his faint breathing. I shook him and called him. He would not open his eyes. I walked across and knocked on the door of the first cottage. I banged on the door violently.

Someone moaned inside, "Ah, it is come!"

Someone else whispered, "You just cover your ears and sleep. It will knock for a while and go away." I banged on the door and shouted who I was and where I came from.

I walked back to the car and sounded the horn. Then the door opened, and a whole family crowded out with lamps. "We thought it was the usual knocking and we wouldn't have opened if you hadn't spoken."

"When was this knocking first heard?" I asked.

"We can't say," said one. "The first time I heard it was when my grandfather was living; he used to say he had even seen it once or twice. It doesn't harm anyone, as far as I know. The only thing it does is bother the bullock carts passing the temple and knock on the doors at night . . ."

I said as a venture, "It is unlikely you will be troubled any more."

It proved correct. When I passed that way again months later I was told that the bullocks passing the temple after dusk never shied now and no knocking on the doors was heard at nights. So I felt that the old fellow had really gone away with his good wife.

A Hero

For Swami events took an unexpected turn. Father looked over the newspaper he was reading under the hall lamp and said, "Swami, listen to this: 'News is to hand of the bravery of a village lad who, while returning home by the jungle path, came face to face with a tiger . . .'" The paragraph described the fight the boy had with the tiger and his flight up a tree, where he stayed for half a day till some people came that way and killed the tiger.

After reading it through, Father looked at Swami fixedly and asked, "What do you say to that?"

Swami said, "I think he must have been a very strong and grown-up person, not at all a boy. How could a boy fight a tiger?"

"You think you are wiser than the newspaper?" Father sneered. "A man may have the strength of an elephant and yet be a coward: whereas another may have the strength of a straw, but if he has courage he can do anything. Courage is everything, strength and age are not important."

Swami disputed the theory. "How can it be, Father? Suppose I have all the courage, what can I do if a tiger should attack me?"

"Leave alone strength, can you prove you have courage? Let me see if you can sleep alone tonight in my office room."

A frightful proposition, Swami thought. He had always slept beside his granny in the passage, and any change in this arrangement kept him trembling and awake all night. He hoped at first that his father was only joking. He mumbled weakly, "Yes," and tried to change the subject; he said very loudly and with a great deal of enthusiasm, "We are going to admit even elders in our cricket club hereafter. We are buying brand-new bats and balls. Our captain has asked me to tell you . . ."

"We'll see about it later," Father cut in. "You must sleep alone hereafter." Swami realized that the matter had gone beyond his control: from a challenge it had become a plain command; he knew his father's tenacity at such moments.

"From the first of next month I'll sleep alone, Father."

"No, you must do it now. It is disgraceful sleeping beside granny or mother like a baby. You are in the second form and I don't at all like the way you are being brought up," he said, and looked at his wife, who was rocking the cradle. "Why do you look at me while you say it?" she asked. "I hardly know anything about the boy."

"No, no, I don't mean you," father said.

"If you mean that your mother is spoiling him, tell her so; and don't look at me," she said, and turned away.

Swami's father sat gloomily gazing at the newspaper on his lap. Swami rose silently and tiptoed away to his bed in the passage. Granny was sitting up in her bed, and remarked, "Boy, are you already feeling sleepy? Don't you want a story?" Swami made wild gesticulations to silence his granny, but that good lady saw nothing. So Swami threw himself on his bed and pulled the blanket over his face.

Granny said, "Don't cover your face. Are you really very sleepy?" Swami leant over and whispered, "Please, please, shut up, granny. Don't talk to me, and don't let anyone call me even if the house is on fire. If I don't sleep at once I shall perhaps die—" He turned over, curled, and snored under the blanket till he found his blanket pulled away.

Presently Father came and stood over him. "Swami, get up," he said. He looked like an apparition in the semi-darkness of the passage, which was lit by a cone of light from the hall. Swami stirred and groaned as if in sleep. Father said, "Get up, Swami." Granny pleaded, "Why do you disturb him?"

"Get up, Swami," he said for the fourth time, and Swami got up. Father rolled up his bed, took it under his arm, and said, "Come with me." Swami looked at his granny, hesitated for a moment, and followed his father into the office room. On the way he threw a look of appeal at his mother and she said, "Why do you take him to the office room? He can sleep in the hall, I think."

"I don't think so," Father said, and Swami slunk behind him with bowed head.

"Let me sleep in the hall, Father," Swami pleaded. "Your office room is very dusty and there may be scorpions behind your law books."

"There are no scorpions, little fellow. Sleep on the bench if you like."

"Can I have a lamp burning in the room?"

"No. You must learn not to be afraid of darkness. It is only a question of habit. You must cultivate good habits."

"Will you at least leave the door open?"

"All right. But promise you will not roll up your bed and go to your granny's side at night. If you do it, mind you, I will make you the laughing-stock of your school."

Swami felt cut off from humanity. He was pained and angry. He didn't like the strain of cruelty he saw in his father's nature. He hated the newspaper for printing the tiger's story. He wished that the tiger hadn't spared the boy, who didn't appear to be a boy after all, but a monster. . . .

As the night advanced and the silence in the house deepened, his heart beat faster. He remembered all the stories of devils and ghosts he had heard in his life. How often had his chum Mani seen the devil in the banyan tree at his street-end. And what about poor Munisami's father, who spat out blood because the devil near the river's edge slapped his cheek when he was returning home late one night. And so on and on his thoughts continued. He was faint with fear. A ray of light from the street lamp strayed in and cast shadows on the wall. Through the stillness all kinds of noises reached his ears—the ticking of the clock, rustle of trees, snoring sounds, and some vague night insects humming. He covered himself so completely that he could hardly breathe. Every moment he expected the devils to come up to carry him away; there was the instance of his old friend in the fourth class who suddenly disappered and was said to have been carried off by a ghost to Siam or Nepal . . .

Swami hurriedly got up and spread his bed under the bench

and crouched there. It seemed to be a much safer place, more compact and reassuring. He shut his eyes tight and encased himself in his blanket once again and unknown to himself fell asleep, and in sleep was racked with nightmares. A tiger was chasing him. His feet stuck to the ground. He desperately tried to escape but his feet would not move; the tiger was at his back, and he could hear its claws scratch the ground . . . scratch, scratch, and then a light thud. . . . Swami tried to open his eyes, but his eyelids would not open and the nightmare continued. It threatened to continue forever. Swami groaned in despair.

With a desperate effort he opened his eyes. He put his hand out to feel his granny's presence at his side, as was his habit, but he only touched the wooden leg of the bench. And his lonely state came back to him. He sweated with fright. And now what was this rustling? He moved to the edge of the bench and stared into the darkness. Something was moving down. He lay gazing at it in horror. His end had come. He realized that the devil would presently pull him out and tear him, and so why should he wait? As it came nearer he crawled out from under the bench, hugged it with all his might, and used his teeth on it like a mortal weapon . . .

"Aiyo! Something has bitten me," went forth an agonized, thundering cry and was followed by a heavy tumbling and falling amidst furniture. In a moment Father, cook, and a servant came in, carrying light.

And all three of them fell on the burglar who lay amidst the furniture with a bleeding ankle. . . .

Congratulations were showered on Swami next day. His classmates looked at him with respect, and his teacher patted his back. The headmaster said that he was a true scout. Swami had bitten into the flesh of one of the most notorious house-breakers of the district and the police were grateful to him for it.

The Inspector said, "Why don't you join the police when you are grown up?"

Swami said for the sake of politeness, "Certainly, yes," though he had quite made up his mind to be an engine driver, a railway guard, or a bus conductor later in life.

When he returned home from the club that night, Father asked, "Where is the boy?"

"He is asleep."

"Already!"

"He didn't have a wink of sleep the whole of last night," said his mother.

"Where is he sleeping?"

"In his usual place," Mother said casually. "He went to bed at seven-thirty."

"Sleeping beside his granny again!" Father said. "No wonder he wanted to be asleep before I could return home—clever boy!"

Mother lost her temper. "You let him sleep where he likes. You needn't risk his life again. . . ." Father mumbled as he went in to change: "All right, molly-coddle and spoil him as much as you like. Only don't blame me afterwards. . . ."

Swami, following the whole conversation from under the blanket, felt tremendously relieved to hear that his father was giving him up.

Dodu

Dodu was eight years old and wanted money badly. Since he was only eight, nobody took his financial worries seriously. (He wanted money for many things—from getting a good stock of Chinese crackers for the coming Deepavali to buying a fancy pen-holder which his master at school was forcing on everybody at the point of the cane.) Dodu had no illusions about the generosity of his elders. They were notoriously deaf to requests. They jingled with coins when they moved about. And yet they were astonishingly niggardly. No elder would part with a single coin if he could help it.

Dodu's office was his dealwood box with the lid open. He had his office hours between any hour and any other hour of the day, just as it suited his fancy. When he wanted to do a bit of serious thinking, he would open the lid and squat in his box amidst its contents. And certainly the contents were not so fragile as to be crushed by the weight of their owner. All the discarded things of the household found their way into this box. Every evening Dodu would make a circuit round the house to gather "things," as he vaguely called them. The waste-paper basket in his father's room gave him a steady supply of attractive book jackets, brown wrapping paper, large envelopes, charming catalogues, and pieces of brown thread. From under the window of his big brother, he picked up yellow packets of Gold Flake cigarettes, shining cigarette-foils, razor blades, cardboard boxes. When his sister was not at home, he opened her box and appropriated bits of coloured thread.

Thus day by day the contents of his box increased. At the end of every week it overflowed, though it was the biggest box in the house. When it overflowed so much as to choke the space between its back and the wall and laid a trail across to the coat stand nearby, his father took notice. Dodu dreaded these periodic notice-takings of his father, which would always end in his emptying the box into the adjoining conservancy lane. The moment his father's back was turned, Dodu would run round to the conservancy lane and pick out the things that he couldn't really afford to throw away. For a whole hour he would remain broken-hearted. But mails were arriving every day for his father, and his sister was always buying coloured thread, and his brother was a confirmed smoker.

Dodu sat in his box and wondered what he could do for money. He wondered if he could try again a piece of business he had undertaken once before. His uncle from Madras had given him a rupee. Dodu had gone straight to the post office and bought twelve brown stamps, four green stamps, and four postcards. He then wrote in his scraggy hand a placard in Kannada, STAMPS FOR SALE, and hung it outside the window of his room, which opened on a side street. His chief customers were his elders at home (except his father), and they helped him to dispose of his postal commodities with a rapidity that astonished Dodu himself. He sold his goods with a profit of three pies over each item. People bought readily. Only one card was left in the end, and a neighbour came to buy it, and when Dodu quoted his price, he seemed outraged. He behaved like a madman and swore that he would report the matter to the police. Dodu was frightened. But all the same, he had enough courage left to ask what interest he should have in selling stamps and cards if it were not for the slight profit he got. And finally he parted with the last card for nothing in order to earn the goodwill of this noisy customer. The end was that Dodu's dream of investing over and over again his rupee and spending the profit just as he pleased was shattered. He not only did not realize any profit but lost his capital as well. He could not point to any particular hole through which his capital had leaked out. It had just diffused and faded away. The elders bought on credit and put off paying him. They seemed to be suffering from a chronic lack of "change." Dodu soon forgot all about the business and remained so until one afternoon someone walked into the house and demanded ten half-anna stamps and sixteen postcards. Father ordered the customer to go his way and he answered back that he certainly would have but for the announcement outside the window. Father tore the placard down, stamped on it, and shouted at Dodu. Dodu had forgotten to remove the STAMPS FOR SALE placard even after he had definitely closed down his business. That was the end of his business venture.

Now, sitting in his box, he was unconsciously summing up the lessons of his past experience. Lesson number one was that he could not expect help or sympathy from his elders. Lesson number two: if his uncle should give him a rupee again, it was not to be wasted on foolish schemes. Buying and selling stamps was a silly idea. The buying side of it was probably all right. As for selling, it did not come within the definition of the term. It was more giving away for nothing.

Looking out the window, he saw a man getting up a coconut tree. It was the Pests-Man.

Dodu jumped out of his box and walked up to the coconut tree. "Hi!" he cried, looking up. "How much do you earn every day?"

"About two rupees," replied the man from the treetop.

"Two rupees! Then you must be making a good lot of money! Don't you ever feel that you have too much of it?" asked Dodu.

The Pests-Man laughed and said something about wife and children at home. To Dodu this sum appeared immense: What could he not buy with all that money? Chinese crackers piled up and up to the very sky, and whole boxes full of sweets and pencils.

"Can I also earn?" Dodu asked.

"Certainly, why not?" replied the Pests-Man.

But what a huge thing a coconut tree was! One found the two rupees on its top. How did one climb it?

"Here, coconut-man," he cried. "Can that pest be found anywhere nearer?"

"No," replied the coconut-man, "it hides only on the top of the tree, and eats into the sap. I pluck it out and throw it down thus. And they pay me three annas per tree." He pulled out a few tender leaves and threw them down. Dodu picked up one. It was so attractive, long, tender, and pale. He casually scratched the pale surface with his thumb-nail. It made a mark, a clear mark, which turned red. He picked up another and wrote his name on it. It was equally wonderful. An idea struck him. He remembered an incident his brother had related to his mother. One of his brother's friends took a palmyra leaf with writings on it to some library and was paid for it. There was obviously money in it.

The next morning he dropped a casual inquiry and made his brother repeat the whole incident. His brother said that the Director of Archaeology, Dr. Iyengar, bought from someone a historical document written on palmyra leaf, for the Mysore Oriental Library. Dodu was very attentive when the library's name, whereabouts, and the Director's name were mentioned.

That afternoon he found his way to the library. His mind was already feasting on visions of a bumper Deepavali with no end of crackers.

The yellow building with its big dome awed him. He doubted if he would be allowed to enter it. Outside a door a peon, with his right knee drawn up, was dozing. Dodu informed him in a respectful tone: "I have come to see the master of this office on a very important business." The peon did not care. He was far too sleepy.

Dodu entered the building and felt terribly small. Everything looked powerful and big. All around there were stone images and stone slabs with a lot of writings on them. Many pundits wrapped in gaudy shawls were poring over long palm-scrips. Things were so imposing that Dodu almost decided to run out. He could hear the beats of his own heart reverberating through the long silent hall.

However, he took courage in both hands and stood at an immense table, on the other side of which a mighty man wearing a turban and spectacles was sitting.

"Sir," Dodu called in a respectful whisper, lowering his voice to the point of silence. The mighty man did not hear.

"Sir," Dodu repeated. This time, as if to compensate, his voice was indecently loud. And Dodu felt awkward.

The mighty man started at the noise, and looked about for the source of that "Sir," but could not locate it.

"Are you a doctor?" the voice asked. The mighty man was puzzled by the disembodied voice. He searched with his eyes and found a clump of black hair level with the top of his table. He pushed back his chair and rose. He was surprised to see an urchin, wearing dirty coat and shorts, standing at the other end of the table. He was accustomed to receiving only dignified scholars and students as visitors.

"What are you doing here?" he asked.

"I have come to see a doctor," replied Dodu. "Are you a doctor?"

"Yes. Who are you?"

Dodu climbed a chair and stood on it.

"If you are a doctor," Dodu said, "I have something interesting for you. I hear that you give a lot of money for palm leaves with writings on them. I hear that you pay a hundred rupees for such things." He pulled out of his pocket a few leaves crumpled into a ball and gave them to the doctor.

This was a refreshing change for the doctor from his serious work. He examined with keen delight the scrips. On one he found the figures of a jug, a nose, a horse, and the name "Dodu" in Kannada. On another leaf he found these interesting statements in Kannada: "The cow is a very tame animal. This is Rama's book." All these were copied from an old Kannada primer. The third bore on it in English: "Cot. Ox. Fig. Pear. Baby. AAAABCFG."

The doctor found no difficulty in deciphering the inscriptions. He had succeeded with far more difficult ones carved on stones and copper-plates by kings who lived hundreds of years ago. Dodu's handwriting—big, gawky, and irregular as it was—was, comparatively, a specimen of fine, recent calligraphy.

When he had finished, he paused and then burst into a hearty laugh.

Dodu was offended. He said (to himself) that the doctor had no business to laugh at him. If he did not want the palm leaves he might quietly give them back. Dodu would go and try to sell them to some other doctor. But he did not express anything aloud.

"Who told you that I give money for these things?" the doctor asked.

Dodu repeated what he had heard from his brother. The doctor's face was bright with amusement. "You are a very nice boy," he said; "you have brought just the thing I wanted. I will buy it."

He took the palm leaves and gave Dodu all the copper coins he had in his pocket. He had about four annas. Four annas in copper look immense. Dodu received the money with delight.

"Whose son are you?" asked the doctor.

Dodu preferred not to answer. This transaction was a secret.

"I don't know," he replied innocently. "My father goes to some office."

"What is your name?" asked the doctor.

Dodu paused and answered, "Ramaswami." That was also a lie. His real name was "Dodu" at home and "Lakshmana" at school.

"Well, Ramaswami," said the doctor, "can you go home safely? Always walk on the footpath. There are too many motor cars on the roads."

Dodu sat before an old woman who was selling edibles, and filled his pockets with fried groundnuts for three pies. He looked idly at the cows grazing in the green fields opposite, under the bright sun, and felt very happy and contented.

Another Community

I am not going to mention caste or community in this story. The newspapers of recent months have given us a tip which is handy—namely the designation: "One Community" and "Another Community." In keeping with this practice I am giving the hero of this story no name. I want you to find out, if you like, to what community or section he belonged; I'm sure you will not be able to guess it any more than you will be able to say what make of vest he wore under his shirt; and it will be just as immaterial to our purpose. He worked in an office which was concerned with insurance business. He sat at a table, checked papers and figures between noon and five p.m. every day, and at the end of a month his pay envelope came to his hands containing one hundred rupees. He was middle-aged now, but his passage from youth to middle age was, more or less, at the same seat in his office. He lived in a little house in a lane: it had two rooms and a hall and sufficed for his wife and four children, although he felt embarrassed when a guest came. The shops were nearby, the children's school was quite close, and his wife had friends all around.

It was on the whole a peaceful, happy life—till the October of 1947, when he found that the people around had begun to speak and act like savages. Someone or a body of men killed a body of men a thousand miles away and the result was that they repeated the evil here and wreaked their vengeance on those around. It was an absurd state of affairs. But there it was: a good action in a far-off place did not find an echo, but an evil one did possess that power. Our friend saw the tempers of his neighbours rising as they read the newspaper each day. They spoke rashly. "We must smash them who are here—" he heard people say. "They have not spared even women and children!" he heard them cry. "All right, we will teach those fellows a lesson. We will do the same here—the only language they will understand." But he tried to say, "Look here—" He visualized his office colleague sitting on his right, his postman, the fellow at the betel-leaves shop, and his friend at the bank—all these belonged to another community. He had not bothered about their category all these days: they were just friends—people who smiled, obliged, and spoke agreeably. But now he saw them in a new light: they were of another community. Now when he heard his men talk menacingly, he visualized his post office friend being hacked in the street, or the little girl belonging to that colleague of his, who so charmingly brought him lemon squash whenever he visited them, and displayed the few bits of dance and songs she knew—he visualized her being chased by the hooligans of his own community while she was on her way to school carrying a soap carton full of pencils and rubber! This picture was too much for him and he whispered under his breath constantly, "God forbid!" He tried to smooth out matters by telling his fellow men: "You see . . . but such things will not happen here." But he knew that was wishful thinking. He knew his men were collecting knives and sticks. He knew how much they were organizing themselves, with a complete code of operations—all of which sounded perfectly ghastly to his sensitive temperament. Fire, sword, and loot, and all the ruffians that gathered for instructions and payment at his uncle's house, who often declared: "We will do nothing by ourselves yet. But if they so much as wag a tail they will be finished. We will speak to them in the only language they will understand." Life seemed to have become intolerable. People were becoming sneaky and secretive. Everyone seemed to him a potential assassin. People looked at each other with suspicion and hatred. It seemed to him a shame that one should be throwing watchful, cautious looks over one's shoulder as one walked down a street. The air was surcharged with fear. He avoided meeting others. Someone or other constantly reported: "You know what happened? A cyclist was stabbed in —— street last evening. Of course the police are hushing up the whole business." Or he heard: "A woman was assaulted today," or, "Do you know they rushed into the girls' school and four girls are missing. The police are useless; we must deal with these matters ourselves." Such talk made his heart throb and brought a sickening feeling at his throat: he felt his food tasting bitter on his tongue. He could never look at his wife and children without being racked by the feeling, Oh, innocent ones, what perils await you in the hands of what bully! God knows.

At night he could hardly sleep: he lay straining his ears for any mob cries that might burst out all of a sudden. Suppose they stole upon him and broke his door? He could almost hear the terrified screams of his little ones. And all night he kept brooding and falling off into half sleep and struggled to keep awake, awaiting the howl of riotous mobs. The cries of a distant dog sounded so sinister that he got up to see if any flames appeared over the skies far off. His wife asked sleepily, "What is it?" He answered, "Nothing. You sleep," and returned to his bed. He was satisfied that nothing was happening. He secretly resolved that he'd fetch the wood-chopper from the fuel room and keep it handy in case he had to defend his home. Sometimes the passage of a lorry or a cart pulled him out of his scant sleep and set him on his feet at the window: he stood there in the dark to make sure it was not a police lorry racing along to open fire on a murderous crowd. He spent almost every night in this anxious, agitated manner and felt relieved when day came.

Everyone mentioned that the coming Wednesday, the 29th of the month, was a critical day. There was to be a complete showdown that day. It was not clear why they selected that date, but everybody mentioned it. In his office people spoke of nothing but the 29th. The activity in his uncle's house had risen to a feverish pitch. His uncle told him, "I'm glad we shall be done with this bother on the 29th. It is going to end this tension once for all. We shall clean up this town. After all, they form only a lakh and a half of the town population, while we . . ." He went into dizzying statistics.

Zero hour was approaching. He often wondered amidst the general misery of all this speculation how they would set off the spark: will one community member slap the cheek of another at a given moment in a formal manner? "Suppose nothing happens?"

he asked, and his uncle told him, "How can nothing happen? We know what they are doing. They hold secret assemblies almost every night. Why should they meet at midnight?"

"They may not be able to gather everyone except at that hour," he replied.

"We don't want people to meet at that hour. We do not ask for trouble, but if anything happens, we will finish them off. It will be only a matter of a few hours; it will work like a push-button arrangement. But we will avoid the initiative as far as possible."

On the 29th most of the shops were closed as a precaution. Children stayed away from school, and said cheerfully, "No school today, Father—you know why? It seems there is going to be a fight today." The coolness and detachment with which his children referred to the fight made our friend envy them. His wife did not like the idea of his going to the office. "It seems they are not going to office today," she said, referring to some neighbours. "Why should you go?" He tried to laugh off the question and, while setting out, said half humorously, "Well, keep yourselves indoors, if you choose, that is if you are afraid." His wife replied, "No one is afraid. As long as your uncle is near at hand, we have no fear."

At the office, his boss was there, of course, but most of his colleagues were absent. There seemed to be a sudden outbreak of "urgent private business" among them. The few that came wasted their time discussing the frightful possibilities of the day. Our friend's head had become one whirling mass of rumours and fears. He hated to hear their talk. He plunged himself in work with such intensity that he found himself constantly exhausting its sources. So much so that, just to keep himself engaged, he excavated old files and accounts for some minute checking. The result was that it was past seven-thirty when he was able to put away the papers and leave the office.

The old files had had a sort of deadening effect on his mind. But now he felt a sudden anxiety to reach home in the shortest time possible. God knows what is happening to my family, he wondered. The usual route seemed to him laborious and impossible. It seemed to his fevered mind that it might take hours and hours. He felt the best course would be to dash through the alley in front of his office and go home by a short cut. It was a route he favoured whenever he was in a hurry although, under normal circumstances, avoided it for its narrowness, gutters, and mongrels. He snatched a look at his watch and hurried along the dark alley. He had proceeded a few yards when a cyclist coming up halted his progress. The cyclist and the pedestrian had difficulty in judging each other's moves, and they both went off to the left or to the right together, and seemed to be making awkward passes at each other, till the cyclist finally slipped off the saddle, and both found themselves in the road dust.

Our friend's nerves snapped and he yelled out, "Why can't you ride carefully?"

The other scrambled to his feet and cried, "Are you blind? Can't you see a cycle coming?"

"Where is your light?"

"Who are you to question me?" said the other, and shot out his arm and hit the face of our friend, who lost his head and kicked the other in the belly. A crowd assembled. Somebody shouted, "He dares to attack us in our own place! Must teach these fellows a lesson. Do you think we are afraid?" Shouts and screams increased. It was deafening. Somebody hit our friend with a staff, someone else with his fist; he saw a knife flashing out. Our friend felt his end had come. He suddenly had an access of recklessness. He was able to view the moment with a lot of detachment. He essayed to lecture to the crowd on the idiocy of the whole relationship, to tell them that they should stop it at once. But no sound issued from his voice box—he found himself hemmed in on all sides. The congestion was intolerable: everyone in that rabble seemed to put his weight on him and claw at some portion of his body. His eyes dimmed; he felt very light. He mumbled to someone near, "But I will never, never tell my uncle what has happened. I won't be responsible for starting the trouble. This city must be saved. I won't utter the word that will start the trouble, that will press the button, so to say. That'll finish up everybody, you and me together. What is it all worth? There is no such thing as your community or mine. We are all of this country. I and my wife and children: you and your wife and children. Let us not cut each other's throats. It doesn't matter who cuts whose: it's all the same to me. But we must not, we must not. We must not. I'll tell my uncle that I fell down the office staircase and hurt myself. He'll never know. He must not press the button."

But the button did get pressed. The incident of that alley became known within a couple of hours all over the city. And his uncle and other uncles did press the button, with results that need not be described here. Had he been able to speak again, our friend would have spoken a lie and saved the city; but unfortunately that saving lie was not uttered. His body was found by the police late next afternoon in a ditch in that wretched alley, and identified through the kerosene ration coupon in his breast pocket.

Like the Sun

Truth, Sekhar reflected, is like the sun. I suppose no human being can ever look it straight in the face without blinking or being dazed. He realized that, morning till night, the essence of human relationships consisted in tempering truth so that it might not shock. This day he set apart as a unique day—at least one day in the year we must give and take absolute Truth whatever may happen. Otherwise life is not worth living. The day ahead seemed to him full of possibilities. He told no one of his experiment. It was a quiet resolve, a secret pact between him and eternity.

The very first test came while his wife served him his morning meal. He showed hesitation over a titbit, which she had thought was her culinary masterpiece. She asked, "Why, isn't it good?" At other times he would have said, considering her feelings in the matter, "I feel full-up, that's all." But today he said, "It isn't good. I'm unable to swallow it." He saw her wince and said to himself, Can't be helped. Truth is like the sun.

His next trial was in the common room when one of his colleagues came up and said, "Did you hear of the death of so and so? Don't you think it a pity?" "No," Sekhar answered. "He was such a fine man—" the other began. But Sekhar cut him short with: "Far from it. He always struck me as a mean and selfish brute."

During the last period when he was teaching geography for Third Form A, Sekhar received a note from the headmaster: "Please see me before you go home." Sekhar said to himself: It must be about these horrible test papers. A hundred papers in the boys' scrawls; he had shirked this work for weeks, feeling all the time as if a sword were hanging over his head.

The bell rang and the boys burst out of the class.

Sekhar paused for a moment outside the headmaster's room to button up his coat; that was another subject the headmaster always sermonized about.

He stepped in with a very polite "Good evening, sir."

The headmaster looked up at him in a very friendly manner and asked, "Are you free this evening?"

Sekhar replied, "Just some outing which I have promised the children at home—"

"Well, you can take them out another day. Come home with me now."

"Oh . . . yes, sir, certainly . . ." And then he added timidly, "Anything special, sir?"

"Yes," replied the headmaster, smiling to himself . . . "You didn't know my weakness for music?"

"Oh, yes, sir . . ."

"I've been learning and practising secretly, and now I want you to hear me this evening. I've engaged a drummer and a violinist to accompany me—this is the first time I'm doing it full-dress and I want your opinion. I know it will be valuable."

Sekhar's taste in music was well known. He was one of the most dreaded music critics in the town. But he never anticipated his musical inclinations would lead him to this trial. . . . "Rather a surprise for you, isn't it?" asked the headmaster. "I've spent a fortune on it behind closed doors. . . ." They started for the headmaster's house. "God hasn't given me a child, but at least let him not deny me the consolation of music," the headmaster said, pathetically, as they walked. He incessantly chattered about music: how he began one day out of sheer boredom; how his teacher at first laughed at him, and then gave him hope; how his ambition in life was to forget himself in music.

At home the headmaster proved very ingratiating. He sat Sekhar on a red silk carpet, set before him several dishes of delicacies, and fussed over him as if he were a son-in-law of the house. He even said, "Well, you must listen with a free mind. Don't worry about these test papers." He added half humorously, "I will give you a week's time."

"Make it ten days, sir," Sekhar pleaded.

"All right, granted," the headmaster said generously. Sekhar felt really relieved now—he would attack them at the rate of ten a day and get rid of the nuisance.

The headmaster lighted incense sticks. "Just to create the right atmosphere," he explained. A drummer and a violinist, already seated on a Rangoon mat, were waiting for him. The headmaster sat down between them like a professional at a concert, cleared his throat, and began an alapana, and paused to ask, "Isn't it good Kalyani?" Sekhar pretended not to have heard the question. The headmaster went on to sing a full song composed by Thyagaraja and followed it with two more. All the time the headmaster was singing, Sekhar went on commenting within himself, He croaks like a dozen frogs. He is bellowing like a buffalo. Now he sounds like loose window shutters in a storm.

The incense sticks burnt low. Sekhar's head throbbed with the medley of sounds that had assailed his ear-drums for a couple of hours now. He felt half stupefied. The headmaster had gone nearly hoarse, when he paused to ask, "Shall I go on?" Sekhar replied, "Please don't, sir, I think this will do. . . ." The headmaster looked stunned. His face was beaded with perspiration. Sekhar felt the greatest pity for him. But he felt he could not help it. No judge delivering a sentence felt more pained and helpless. Sekhar noticed that the headmaster's wife peeped in from the kitchen, with eager curiosity. The drummer and the violinist put away their burdens with an air of relief. The headmaster removed his spectacles, mopped his brow, and asked, "Now, come out with your opinion."

"Can't I give it tomorrow, sir?" Sekhar asked tentatively.

"No. I want it immediately—your frank opinion. Was it good?"

"No, sir . . ." Sekhar replied.

"Oh! . . . Is there any use continuing my lessons?"

"Absolutely none, sir . . ." Sekhar said with his voice trembling. He felt very unhappy that he could not speak more soothingly. Truth, he reflected, required as much strength to give as to receive.

All the way home he felt worried. He felt that his official life was not going to be smooth sailing hereafter. There were questions of increment and confirmation and so on, all depending upon the headmaster's goodwill. All kinds of worries seemed to be in store for him. . . . Did not Harischandra lose his throne, wife, child, because he would speak nothing less than the absolute Truth whatever happened?

At home his wife served him with a sullen face. He knew she was still angry with him for his remark of the morning. Two casualties for today, Sekhar said to himself. If I practise it for a week, I don't think I shall have a single friend left.

He received a call from the headmaster in his classroom next day. He went up apprehensively.

"Your suggestion was useful. I have paid off the music master. No one would tell me the truth about my music all these days. Why such antics at my age! Thank you. By the way, what about those test papers?"

"You gave me ten days, sir, for correcting them."

"Oh, I've reconsidered it. I must positively have them here tomorrow. . . ." A hundred papers in a day! That meant all night's sitting up! "Give me a couple of days, sir . . ."

"No. I must have them tomorrow morning. And remember, every paper must be thoroughly scrutinized."

"Yes, sir," Sekhar said, feeling that sitting up all night with a hundred test papers was a small price to pay for the luxury of practising Truth.

Chippy

I cannot give a very clear account of Chippy's early life. All that I am in a position to say is that he was born in London, spent several months of his puppyhood in Scotland, and then came out to India with a Major and spent a very happy summer in a hill station. He might well have stayed with the Major, seen something of Peshawar, Quetta, and Delhi, and returned home with that good man, but for a silly little Pekingese. It was the pet of the Major's wife, and Chippy did not like him. One day when no one was about, Chippy forced the puny fellow to realize what he thought of him for living on a lady's lap and eating special biscuits; but the little fellow lost his life in the process. Honestly, Chippy did not intend to kill him; he only wanted to give him a good shake—a thing that could not have killed a mouse. No one was more surprised than Chippy when the little fellow fell down and did not move. The Major's wife became hysterical, and the Major, a devoted husband, easily concluded that Chippy had rabies. He decided to shoot him through the brain next morning. At this stage an Indian friend of the Major, who did not believe in rabies, offered to take away Chippy. Chippy stayed with this gentleman for some time and then drifted on to Mysore, with the Major's friend's brother, Swami. And no dog could have wished for a better master.

Swami and Chippy shared the same room in the house. Swami and Chippy always went out together. Chippy was almost a member of the Champion Tennis Club. Every evening he went there with his master, waited till his master settled down to a good set, and then quietly slipped out and explored all the lanes nearby.

There were gangs of brown dogs and black dogs of uncertain colours, lounging in every square and crossing, challenging all newcomers. Chippy bit and was bitten, tore and was torn, before he could establish his right to wander where he liked. There was nothing very special to attract him to that part of the town; all that he wanted was a place to wander about while his master was playing. The game was, perhaps, dull to watch. One was not allowed even to chase the ball and retrieve it. And why should these street-loafers question a decent dog's movements? Chippy had to shed several mouthfuls of blood and fur before he could gain citizenship in those lanes.

After tennis Swami usually attended some lecture or debate in the College. Chippy never missed a single meeting. He climbed the gallery in the lecture hall, took a seat beside Swami, and never stirred till the vote of thanks was proposed. After the meeting, Chippy went home, had his plateful of bone and rice, and then went out for an hour or two to meet his old friends and sweethearts. He returned at night, slept under his master's cot, and woke him up early in the morning by applying his cold nose to the sleeper's cheek.

On the whole Chippy led a very happy and contented life till one day Swami brought into the house another dog. Chippy would not have objected to another dog as such, but what he objected to was that this dog was short.

It could not be said that Chippy was of an ungenerous disposition, but he hated short dogs. One might notice a hint of this prejudice very early in him in the Pekingese affair. It was Chippy's habit, whenever he was out, to knock down and scratch and bite all the short dogs that he met on the way. And now he was to have a fellow standing on the height of a two-month-old puppy, pitch dark in colour, and with a long loose tail, as a companion at home! Entering the hall one afternoon, Chippy saw the newcomer standing between his master's legs, and dashed forward with a growl. The newcomer would have gone the way of the Pekingese but for a timely kick from Swami, which sent Chippy rolling in the opposite direction. Chippy picked himself up and went out. He lapped a little water from under the garden tap, dug up his bone from the jasmine bed, went to the shady spot behind the garage, and lay down. Rolling the bone between his jaws, he reflected on the latest developments at home. One was evidently not permitted to scare off the newcomer. At this point, his master's voice reached him, calling, "Chippy! Chippy!" Chippy rose and went bounding towards him. He slackened his pace when he saw the short cur standing beside Master, held by a chain.

"Come on, Chippy, come here," cajoled Swami. Chippy went forward to him, meekly expressing as best he could that he realized that he ought not to have gone at a dog standing between his master's legs, as if it were a street meeting. Master accepted the apology, stroked his coat, and held him close to the newcomer, which was squirming at the end of the chain. What a dreadful position! Master was insistent and went on saying, "Now be friends, come on, you are a good boy," and so on and so forth; and Chippy actually had to wag his tail and give a nod.

In a short time the newcomer made himself quite at home. He invaded every favourite place of Chippy's in the house—he came and lounged under the sofa in the hall, sat at Master's feet in the room, stuck to Chippy's side during the mealtime, and even slept under Master's cot at night. There was no getting away from him. Chippy bore his company for some time and then gradually ceased to go into the house. He spent his time, when he was at home, in the shady spot behind the garage. Let the short cur gambol and strut in the house as much as he liked, but he was not going to have Chippy's company.

The only consoling feature in the whole business was that Chippy still retained the honour of going out with the master, because the other was too puny to trot beside Master's bicycle.

The puny fellow had the impudence one day to sidle up to Chippy, more or less hinting a run round the house. Since no one was about, Chippy frowned and bit him a little. That ought to make the dwarf understand that he was presumptuous. This no doubt taught the little fellow his place, but he had the meanness, when Master was there, to behave as if Chippy and he were the thickest of friends in the world. In such a situation, Chippy could not very well bare his teeth and growl. So that when the short fellow played with his ears or teased his tail, Chippy merely turned away his head and tried to think of other things; or if its attentions became too insistent, Chippy rose and left the place.

Almost a fortnight after the arrival of the newcomer, one afternoon, Chippy lay chewing his bone in the shady spot behind the garage, when he was startled out of his wits to see the newcomer standing before him. The newcomer had not discovered the place till now, and now even this was invaded. Chippy stood up in mingled anger and despair. He would have had a fine excuse for choking the other if only he had tried to sidle up and make friends. But the newcomer, exhibiting a profound sense of time and place, looked at Chippy only for a moment, went past him in a business-like manner, lay down a few yards from him, and closed his eyes. Chippy was baffled! He could not chastise the other for just coming there. His last refuge was now gone.

Chippy rose and trotted away from the house. He stopped just for a moment for a plunge in the stagnant water before the police station.

He wandered about the town, without any aim or plan till nightfall, and then went in search of a place where he could get some food and shelter. He went to the market to try his luck there. But urchins flung stones at him, and there were the old dogs of the place who followed him, growling and grumbling, wherever he went. It was all most annoying. He left the market by the western gate, and strayed into the crazy lane behind it. This lane is a nest of tea and liquor shops, from which gramophones shriek into the night; the clatter of mincing meat on iron frying pans keeps the air lively. The lane has no electric lights, but gets a chequered illumination from the blinding petrol lamps hung inside the shops, with their patrons seated on iron chairs and packing cases. This part of the town is unknown to the average citizen of Mysore, but Chippy was drawn there by the smell of chops sizzling on stoves.

He stopped at the first shop. Somebody threw him a delicious bit of curry puff—and more came. The feast went on all night. People were generous to a fault here. There were of course dozens of other dogs, but there was no trouble since the territory did not belong to any gang in particular.

Chippy found everything so satisfactory that he decided to

spend the rest of his life here—far away from the short cur. In about a week he had become the favourite of the place.

The glamour, however, lasted only for a week. Before the end of another week he had lost his appetite. He never touched the chops thrown at him. He really preferred to go without food. He hungered now for his master's company.

One morning Swami was solving a tough problem in mathematics when he felt a cold touch on his feet. He looked under the table and shrieked. "Rascal, where have you been all these days?" Chippy curved his hind half, tucked in his tail, and stood before him with bowed head. He had lost his white colour; his coat had acquired the colour of road dust, with patches of tea stains here and there. Someone had removed his thick leather collar: he was looking perfectly nude without it.

Swami dragged him out and turned the garden tap on him. Rubbing a piece of soap on his back, Swami informed him: "I am sure you will be miserable to hear this: your little friend is gone. It seems he had been stolen and sold to us. His original owners traced him here and took him away yesterday. . . . Do not worry: I'll get you another companion soon."

Uncle's Letters

Little man, just a line to welcome you into this world, my newest nephew. How do you like it? It is full of glare, isn't it? You will have to get used to it. I was told that you let out a lusty cry the moment you set foot on this earth, which is a good sign, showing that you are responding properly to our conditions. You are yet a very ignorant man. I think your only interest now is the spoonful of sugar syrup that they drop on your tongue from time to time. That is all very well, young man, but there are other things to come.

Well, well, a creditable piece of performance indeed! Your father came over to me thoroughly excited. It seems you smiled at him at 5 a.m. yesterday. He parted the tiny curtain and peeped into your cradle since he noticed a slight stirring. And what happened? You wriggled your little body, blinked at him, and threw off a toothless smile. He nearly jumped with joy and woke up your mother to witness the miracle. But by the time she came over, you had changed your mind and kicked your legs and cried. Your father asserts that you did it because he did not show proper appreciation of your performance by picking you up in his arms. Parents are prone to read a lot of meaning into such things.

Yes, cutting one's first tooth is an awkward job; most of us seem unequal to it at first but we survive it without much damage to ourselves. Don't take a too tragic view of it. Bear it up like a man.

You may think that two solid years entitle you to act as you think best. But you should not have exercised this liberty first on the staircase. That is full of real perils, you know. No wonder your feet would not support you more than half-way up and you had to come tumbling down. At your age, whatever high notions you may have about your abilities, you are still not good enough to battle against the pull of gravity. You had better bear it in mind when you toddle about the house next time. I felt very sorry to see your nose so red and swollen. I could hardly recognize you, my dear fellow! Your mother was sure that the resounding impact of your head on the landing must have cracked your skull.

Your mother is confirmed in her belief about the skull-crack she mentioned some months ago. It was borne out by your behaviour today. Why did you treat that little girl from the next house in the manner you have done? It was perhaps because she would not part with the half orange she had in her hand and you had finished off yours. It is reported that you tried to bite off a slice of her arm as a protest against her selfishness. In human society we do not usually settle our differences in this manner. I must warn you to give up this practice definitely.

School? It is a thing you can't escape. You will have to endure it, say, for the next twelve years, unless you feel disposed to prolong it. It is no use looking for sympathy to anyone in this matter. You are no doubt bewildered by the attitude of your elders at home every morning. I learn that your father tries to put up a show of great violence in order to make you feel that the school is the lesser of the two evils. I sympathize with you, but I can do no more. You will have to survive the menaces of your teachers, the awful tortures of arithmetic (especially if you inherit your uncle's capacity), the ups and downs of classroom relationships, its shifting alliances, treaties, and battles. And then the agony of the examination hall and the results. Don't stand awed before this prospect. You will come through it all right.

You are entitled to preen yourself like a peacock, drawing the red-lined hood about your shoulders, and trailing your gown behind. You will, I suppose, photograph yourself in a studio clutching the scroll in your hand. You must have had your earful of platitudes at the convocation. I hope you have not felt unduly depressed by the speech. It is customary for the celebrity who presides over the occasion to tell you what to do with yourself, what to look for in life, and how to live a life of wisdom and glory. Of course you don't pay much attention to what he says since you are full of thoughts of your own. Let me close this with just one more addition to the platitudes which must be ringing in your ears today: life's troubles start only now.

Your mother is not what she used to be, and you are her sole guide and support now. Her life is full of sad memories, but she can forget much in a new home which you can create with the help of a wife. You are earning quite well. You had better give the proposal every consideration.

Fifty blue envelopes and letter paper to match, of the highest quality, with your address written on each one of them, and properly stamped, are left with your wife, I believe. You hope she will write to you daily of her welfare during her stay at her father's house. I fear I must warn you that not more than a tenth of the stock will be used by the party. You will for ever be on the verge of dispatching a wire to demand why there is no letter. However, it is too much to expect a young wife to perform the feat that only professional journalists can.

It always happens this way. The right bridegroom turns up verily like the Prince Charming all of a sudden when the time comes. When you were in doldrums the other day about the problems of daughters I knew all along that life would have a nice surprise in store for you. I dare say you have read from your daughter's face what she thinks of the boy. I used to know the boy's father and uncles. They were my classmates, as it seems, centuries ago. They are good people, but I am not prepared to swear it before a magistrate. Perhaps I have a suspicion they are rather fond of money, and they may ask for this and that. You are certainly prepared for it. So don't worry about anything. Go ahead.

There is no use sighing over a bank pass-book at this stage. It was bound to look emasculated after you had paid the bills of the wedding ceremonies and the feasts. With all this, you bitterly reflect that your bridegroom's people created scenes during the grand occasion, criticizing the arrangements, presents, and so forth. Such things are a part of our social life and you are not to brood over it any more. What is a bridegroom's party for unless it is to hector the bride's. It is a warfare with its own set laws. In any case here is a tip for consolation. You can have your vengeance in your turn when your three sons (or is it going to be four?) are ready for marriage. Your eldest should be entering the market very soon, if I am not mistaken. He is a promising fellow and a lot of people have their eyes on him.

Fretting will do you no good. Your eldest son seems to you to spend too much and save too little. Your other son insists on escorting his wife to her parents' house every other month. Your last boy insists upon adventuring for himself in Bombay. Your first son-in-law is indifferent about the marriage of his daughters and the education of his sons. You find him too busy to bother about such things. Your second son-in-law has definitely taken his place as a ne'er-do-well. No one seems to come to you for guidance in any matter. In fact your general grouse seems to be that people are minding their business. Why don't you leave them alone? You will find that it makes for so much more peace of mind. I fear that you are working it off on that good lady, your wife. But I am sure she is well seasoned to take in such attacks.

I am delighted to learn that they are going to celebrate the occasion of your seeing the one thousandth moon. It is a very significant and triumphant function, my boy, at eighty. Please give my very best wishes to that wonderful woman, your wife, who can feel a legitimate pride on this day. Let me tell you that on this day you will shed your years and feel like a bridegroom as drums and pipes go off, and holy smoke arises, and the scent of flowers and incense hangs in the air, and the cheerful voices of all your children and their children ring in your ears. It is the finest function one can imagine on this earth.

I think, with this, I will close my letters. For one thing, I feel you are now of an age to observe and understand matters of life yourself. Secondly, you know that I find it difficult to hold a pen and shape out the letters, having had my own thousandth moon celebrated about eighteen years ago.

All Avoidable Talk

He was told to avoid all quarrels that day. The stars were out to trouble him, and even the mildest of his remarks likely to offend and lead to a quarrel. The planets were set against him, and this terrified him beyond description. Many things that were prophesied for him lately were coming true. He sat in a corner of a big jeweller's shop and added up numbers all day. He left it at the end of a day, and on his way home, dropped in for a moment to exchange titbits with a friend near his house, who affected great knowledge of the stars. Occasionally the friend gave out free prophecies. Many things that he said came true. "You will have bother about money matters . . . for a fortnight. Even your legitimate dues will not reach your hand in time. . . ." Too true. The usual rent he received from his village by money order went all over India before coming to him because of a slight error in the address. And then his friend told him: "Saturn will cause minor annoyances in the shape of minor ailments at home. . ." And the following week everyone, from his old mother down to the four-month-old, went down with cold and fever. He himself felt like taking to bed, but his jeweller chief would not let him go. And now his friend had told him on the previous evening, "I see your worst period is coming to an end, but avoid all avoidable talk tomorrow—the whole of Monday. There is always the danger of your irritating others and finding others irritating."

The moment he opened his eyes and lay in bed, he told himself: Must not talk to anyone today—who can see where a word will lead? He pinched the cheek of the youngest, patted the back of another, found the boy of seven unwilling to start for school: was about to shout at him, but decided not to interfere, a happy godsend for the boy. His wife appealed: "Why do you allow him to have his own way?" He merely shook his head and went off to the bathroom. His daughter had locked herself in—that meant she would not come out for an hour; she had once again broken the specific order not to go in to bathe at office time. He tapped the door twice or thrice, glared at it, and went away and put himself under the tap in the front garden. All through his dinner he sat with bowed head, maintaining a determined silence, answering his wife's questions with a curt Yes or No. While starting for his office it was his usual practice to stand in the passage and ask for a little betel-nut and leaves, with a cynical remark that they might have consideration for a man who had to catch an early tram. . . . Today he stood on the threshold waiting to see if anyone would serve him and stepped out into the street, with the reflection: If they have not the sense to do a piece of regular duty without reminder . . . I won't chew betel, that is all. . . .

The tram was crowded as usual. Somebody stood on his toe. He bore it patiently. The tram conductor pushed him aside and uttered rude remarks for standing in the way. He kept quiet. The inspector who hopped into the tram for checking would not budge at the magic word "Pass" but insisted on seeing it, and fretted and swore while Sastri fumbled with his buttons and inner pocket. Sastri never uttered a word, and bore it like a martyr.

At the office he was only two minutes late, but his employer, already seated on his cushion, glared at him and behaved as if he had been two hours late. Sastri stood before him dumb, listening patiently to all the charges. "You stand there like a statue, saying nothing, it must be very convenient, I suppose . . ." said his employer, looking him up. "What has come over you?" nearly escaped Sastri's lips, but he checked himself as he came to "What has . . ."

"Eh?" demanded his employer.

"What is . . . What is the time now, sir?" he said.

"You ask me the time! Go, go to your seat, Sastri, before I am very angry with you. . . ." Sastri slunk back to his place. The routine of office life started. The attendant wiped and rearranged the showcases: customers started coming in to buy and sell gold trinkets and jewellery, the small fan whirred and gyrated, wafting cool air on his chief's face, the other partner came in at about midday and took his seat. The younger son of the master came in demanding cash for some extravagance and went away, and Sastri sat in his corner surrounded by heavy registers. Looking at the figures in the pages, he reflected, Nearly two o'clock; another eight hours of this place, and the day will be over. A customer stopped before him, held up a trinket and asked: "Look here, can this diamond be taken out and reset in platinum?" Sastri looked dully at the trinket and said: "You must ask over there." "It's all right, I know that," replied the customer haughtily. "Answer my question first. . . ." Sastri shook his head. "Evidently you know nothing about these matters."

"I know nothing," Sastri said.

"Then get out of a shop like this," answered the other, and moved on and sat before the proprietor. The proprietor presently called, "Sastri, come here."

"Yes, sir," Sastri said, without lifting up his head. There were three more lines to be added to complete the page. If he was interrupted, he would have to start from the top of the gigantic folio all over again. So there was some delay before he could respond to his master's call. Before that his master lost his temper and shouted: "Drop the pen and come here when I call, will you?" There was still one more line to go in. If this link was missed, there was the ghastly prospect of having to spend the whole evening in the company of figures. The master's call became insistent. Sastri looked up for a moment from his ledger; he caught a glimpse of the other's face—a red patch, flushed with anger. He compressed his lips and resolved more than ever not to rise without completing the totalling. He sat as if deaf, calmly going through the work. By the time he stood before his master, the latter had gripped in his hand a leaden paperweight. Perhaps he wanted to fling it at me, Sastri reflected, and was overwhelmed for a moment with resentment. The troublesome customer sat there comfortably and watched the scene with a self-satisfied grin. Looking at him Sastri felt it was an added indignity. He pays me fifty rupees not for nothing; I slave for him. But what right has he to insult me . . . ? He felt desperate. His brow puckered; he asked, looking at the paperweight in his master's hand: "What's that for?"

"Idiot! What has come over you? Mind your own business," said his boss. "Why can't you come up when you are called?" Sastri had meantime recovered his temper, realizing how near an explosion he had been. "I was totalling up, sir," he said, disciplining himself resolutely. "Learn to come when called. Why were you rude to this gentleman?" "I wasn't," replied Sastri briefly.

"Do you think I'm lying?" shouted the customer, and scowled. Sastri gulped down his reply, just remembering in time the injunction, Avoid all avoidable talk, though he felt like hitting his adversary now. His boss looked up at him and said: "Sastri, I must warn you for the last time. You must be courteous to all my customers: otherwise you may get out of this shop." "I merely said I didn't know about platinum."

"I don't want all that. Everyone in this shop must be able to answer about any department. Otherwise I don't want him in my service. Do you understand?" Sastri turned back to go. The customer added: "I only wanted to know if this could be set in platinum. Can't he answer that simple question?"

"Oh, is that all! Even a child should be able to answer that," echoed his master. "Sastri, come here." Sastri again stood before him: "What do you know of platinum setting?"

"I don't know anything, sir."

"You say that to me! All right, go back to your seat. I will deal with you presently. Get out of my sight now. . . ." Sastri sighed and turned back. While returning to his seat, he overheard the customer saying: "These fellows have become very arrogant nowadays." "All due to their unions, I tell you. I've taken care about that! Still—one has to be watchful."

Sastri, sitting in his corner, tried to drown his thoughts in figures. He partly succeeded, but one part of his mind kept smarting: Some fool comes in, and because of him, I must stand every insult! I've served here for twenty years. The customer had finished his work and was going past him, throwing at him a triumphant and contemptuous look. Sastri quickly turned away and gazed at the folio. Is this man born to torment me? I don't know who he is.

A blue beam of sunlight strayed in through a coloured window pane and moved up to the ceiling: that meant it was nearing dusk. His boss got up and passed out: as the motor car started down below, the others in the office also rose to go, and filed past the door, all but Sastri and the watchman. The interruption from his boss had cut in so badly that numbers jumped at each other's throats, and knotted themselves into hopeless tangles, which meant he would have to go over immense areas of the ledgers; he switched on the light and worked till nine. Stretching his cramped fingers, he descended the staircase and was on the road. I have been called names. I have been insulted by strangers and by my officer, before everyone. Platinum! Platinum! I've served for twenty years for less than fifty rupees a month . . . He wondered why he had become so degenerate as not to be able to earn this anywhere else. Tonight I will not dine without extracting an apology from my boss. Otherwise I shall throw off this work. I don't care what happens . . . He had in a flash a vision of his wife and children starving. It seemed insignificant to him now. I will somehow manage. Open a small shop, with a loan or something, and manage somehow. I don't care. Nothing seemed to him important now except redeeming his dignity as an ordinary human being without any reference to his position as an accountant or the head of a family. He remembered the lead paperweight: that hurt his mind more than anything else. He walked down the tramline, sunk in thought. A tram for Royapetta stopped near him. He checked his impulse to climb into it and go home. He let it go. He sought out the bus for Kilpauk and got into it.

It was nearly ten when he reached the gates of his master's bungalow. AMBER GARDENS. The watchman said: "So late, sir!" "Yes, I've to see the master," he replied. "Is he awake?" "Yes, he has just had his dinner and is sitting in the front room. . . ."

Half-way up, Sastri felt uneasy as he recollected the advice of his friend. "Avoid all avoidable talk . . ." But he could not turn back now. Fate seemed to be holding him by the scruff and propelling him forward. He stood in the hall. His boss had spread himself on a sofa with a sheet of newspaper before him. Sastri stood hesitating: "Avoid all . . . avoidable . . ." his friend's words drumming themselves through his brain. Nothing more avoidable than this, he told himself. He wished he could turn back and go away. Better to tackle him in the office. . . . It is difficult to talk to a boss in his home.

Before he could make up his mind about it, his boss, turning over a page, observed him standing meekly; he stared at him for a while and then said: "Sastri! H'm. I see now that you have e..ough sense to feel sorry for your own conduct. I was thinking of you. If I find you again talking back to me I will dismiss you on the spot, remember. And again, I find you are rude to others too. That man comes asking about a platinum setting."

"Yes, sir, platinum setting," echoed Sastri.

"That was a madman. You saw me with a paperweight in my hand, while he sat before me . . ."

"Yes, sir, I noticed it."

"But it is none of your concern. Whether mad or sane, whoever it may be, it is your business to answer politely whether it be about platinum, silver, clay, or rag. Everyone in my office should know about every other department. I would have dismissed you for your speech and conduct today. But you have saved yourself now. It is my principle to forgive a fellow who sincerely repents. It is late. You may go now."

"I am very grateful to you. Good night, sir," Sastri said, putting extreme politeness in his tone. While going home he did not feel the tediousness of the way or the hour, for he was quietly gloating over the fact that he had triumphed over his stars that day.

A Snake in the Grass

On a sunny afternoon, when the inmates of the bungalow were at their siesta, a cyclist rang his bell at the gate frantically and announced: "A big cobra has got into your compound. It crossed my wheel." He pointed to its track under the gate, and resumed his journey.

The family consisting of the mother and her four sons assembled at the gate in great agitation. The old servant, Dasa, was sleeping in the shed. They shook him out of his sleep and announced to him the arrival of the cobra. "There is no cobra," he replied and tried to dismiss the matter. They swore at him and forced him to take an interest in the cobra. "The thing is somewhere here. If it is not found before the evening, we will dismiss you. Your neglect of the garden and the lawns is responsible for all these dreadful things coming in." Some neighbours dropped in. They looked accusingly at Dasa: "You have the laziest servant on earth," they said. "He ought to keep the surroundings tidy." "I have been asking for a grass-cutter for months," Dasa said. In one voice they ordered him to manage with the available things and learn not to make demands. He persisted. They began to speculate how much it would cost to buy a grass-cutter. A neighbour declared that you could not think of buying any article made of iron till after the war. He chanted banalities of wartime prices. The second son of the house asserted that he could get anything he wanted at controlled prices. The neighbour became eloquent about the black market. A heated debate followed. The rest watched in apathy. At this point the college boy of the house butted in with: "I read in an American paper that 30,000 people die of snake bite every year." Mother threw up her arms in horror and arraigned Dasa. The boy elaborated the statistics. "I have worked it out, 83 a day. That means every twenty minutes someone is dying of cobra bite. As we have been talking here, one person has lost his life somewhere." Mother nearly screamed on hearing it. The compound looked sinister. The boys brought in bamboo sticks and pressed one into the hands of the servant also. He kept desultorily poking it into the foliage with a cynical air. "The fellow is beating about the bush," someone cried aptly. They tucked up their dhoties, seized every available knife and crowbar, and began to hack the garden. Creepers, bushes, and lawns were laid low. What could not be trimmed was cut to the root. The inner walls of the house brightened with the unobstructed glare streaming in. When there was nothing more to be done Dasa asked triumphantly, "Where is the snake?"

An old beggar cried for alms at the gate. They told her not to pester when they were engaged in a snake hunt. On hearing it the old woman became happy. "You are fortunate. It is God Subramanya who has come to visit you. Don't kill the snake." Mother was in hearty agreement: "You are right. I forgot all about the promised Abhishekam. This is a reminder." She gave a coin to the beggar, who promised to send down a snake-charmer as she went. Presently an old man appeared at the gate and announced himself as a snake-charmer. They gathered around him. He spoke to them of his life and activities and his power over snakes. They asked admiringly: "How do you catch them?" "Thus," he said, pouncing upon a hypothetical snake on the ground. They pointed the direction in which the cobra had gone and asked him to go ahead. He looked helplessly about and said: "If you show me the snake, I'll at once catch it. Otherwise what can I do? The moment you see it again, send for me. I live nearby." He gave his name and address and departed.

At five in the afternoon, they threw away their sticks and implements and repaired to the veranda to rest. They had turned up every stone in the garden and cut down every grass blade and shrub, so that the tiniest insect coming into the garden should have no cover. They were loudly discussing the various measures they would take to protect themselves against reptiles in the future, when Dasa appeared before them carrying a water-pot whose mouth was sealed with a slab of stone. He put the pot down and said: "I have caught him in this. I saw him peeping out of it. . . . I saw him before he could see me." He explained at length the strategy he had employed to catch and seal up the snake in the pot. They stood at a safe distance and gazed on the pot. Dasa had the glow of a champion on his face. "Don't call me an idler hereafter," he said. Mother complimented him on his sharpness and wished she had placed some milk in the pot as a sort of religious duty. Dasa picked up the pot cautiously and walked off saying that he would leave the pot with its contents with the snake-charmer living nearby. He became the hero of the day. They watched him in great admiration and decided to reward him adequately.

It was five minutes since Dasa was gone when the youngest son cried: "See there!" Out of a hole in the compound wall a cobra emerged. It glided along towards the gate, paused for a moment to look at the gathering in the veranda with its hood half open. It crawled under the gate and disappeared along a drain. When they recovered from the shock they asked, "Does it mean that there are two snakes here?" The college boy murmured: "I wish I had taken the risk and knocked the water-pot from Dasa's hand; we might have known what it contained."

The Evening Gift

He had a most curious occupation in life. Having failed in every effort, he had to accept it with gratitude and enthusiasm; he received thirty rupees a month for it. He lived on fifteen rupees in a cheap hotel, where he was given a sort of bunk in the loft, with rafters touching his head. He saved fifteen rupees for paying off the family loan in the village incurred over his sister's marriage. He added a rupee or two to his income by filling money order forms and postcards for unlettered villagers, whom he met on the post office veranda. But his main work was very odd. His business consisted in keeping a wealthy drunkard company. This wealthy man wanted someone to check his drink after nine in the evening and take him home. Sankar's physique qualified him for this task. "Don't hesitate to use force on me if necessary," his employer had told him. But that was never done. Sankar did all that he could by persuasion and it was a quite familiar sight at the Oriental Café Bar—the wrangling going on between the employer and his servant. But Sankar with a margin of five minutes always succeeded in wresting the gentleman from his cups and pushing him into his car. On the following morning he was asked: "What time did we reach home last night?"

"Nine-fifteen, sir—"

"Did you have much trouble?"

"No, sir—"

"Nine-fifteen!—very good, very good. I'm glad. On no account should you let me stay on beyond nine, even if I am in company—"

"Yes, sir."

"You may go now, and be sure to be back in the evening in time—"

That finished his morning duty. He went back to his garret, slept part of the day, loitered about post offices, courts, etc., and returned to work at six o'clock.

"Come on," said his employer, who waited for him on the veranda, and Sankar got into the front seat of the car and they drove off to the Oriental Café.

Today he was in a depressed state, he felt sick of his profession, the perpetual cajoling and bullying, the company of a drunkard. He nearly made up his mind to throw up this work and go back to the village. A nostalgia for his home and people seized him. "I don't care what happens, I will get back home and do something else to earn this money." On top of this mood came a letter from home: "Send a hundred rupees immediately. Last date for mortgage instalment. Otherwise we shall lose our house—" He was appalled! Where could he find the money? What was the way out? He cursed his lot more than ever. He sat for a long time thinking of a way out. "Our good old home—! Let it go if it is to go." It was their last possession in this world. If it went, his mother, brothers, and his little sister would have to wander about without a roof over their heads. But could he find a hundred rupees? What did they mean by putting it off till the last moment? He cursed his lot for being the eldest son of a troubled family.

He swung into duty as usual. He held the curtain apart for his master as he entered the cubicle. He pressed a bell. He might be a machine, doing this thing for thirty days in the month for nearly twelve months now. The waiter appeared. No talk was necessary. Sankar nodded. The waiter went away and returned a few minutes later with an unopened flat bottle, a soda, and a glass tumbler; he placed these on the table and withdrew.

"Bring this master a lemon squash," the gentleman said.

"No, sir—" Sankar would reply; this ritual was repeated every day. Now Sankar's business would be to pour out a measure of drink into the tumbler, push it up, and place the soda near at hand, go out on to the veranda, and read a newspaper there (with the flat bottle in his pocket), and stay there till he was called in again to fill the glass. By about ten to nine the last ounce of drink would be poured out, and Sankar would sit down opposite his master instead of going out to the veranda. This was a sort of warning bell.

"Why do you sit here? Go to the veranda."

"I like this place, sir, and I will sit here."

"It is not time for you to come in yet."

"Just ten minutes more, sir."

"Nonsense. It is just seven o'clock."

"About two hours ago—"

"You people seem to turn up the clock just as you like—let me see how much is left in the bottle—"

"Nothing," Sankar said, holding up the bottle. "The last drop was poured out." He held up the bottle and the other became furious at the sight of it. "I think," he said with deep suspicion, "there is some underhand transaction going on—I don't know what you have been doing on the veranda with the bottle—" Sankar learnt not to answer these charges. As the clock struck nine, he tapped the other's shoulder and said, "Please finish your drink and get up, sir—" "What do you mean by it? I'm not getting up. Who are you to order me?" Sankar had to be firm.

"Look here, don't you be a fool and imagine I am talking in drink. I am dead sober—leave me alone—"

Sankar persisted.

"I dismiss you today, you are no longer in my service. I don't want a disobedient fool for a companion, get out—" Usually Sankar sat through it without replying, and when the drink was finished he gently pulled the other up and led the way to the car, and the other followed, scowling at him with red eyes and abusing him wildly. Today when his employer said, "I dismiss you, get out this minute—" Sankar replied, "How can you dismiss me all of a sudden! Must I starve?"

"No. I will give you four months' salary if you get out this moment." Sankar thought it over.

"Don't sit there. Make up your mind quickly—" said his master. One hundred and twenty rupees! Twenty rupees more than the debt. He could leave for his village and give the cash personally to his mother, and leave his future to God. He brushed aside this vision, shook his head, and said: "No, sir. You have got to get up now, sir." "Get out of my service—" shouted his master. He rang the bell and shouted for the waiter: "Get me another—" Sankar protested to the waiter. "Get out of here—" cried his master. "You think I'm speaking in drink. I don't want you. I can look after myself. If you don't leave me, I will tell the waiter to neck you out—" Sankar stood baffled. "Now, young man—" He took out his wallet: "What is your salary?"

"Thirty rupees, sir."

"Here's your four months'. Take it and be off. I have some business meeting here, and I will go home just when I like, there is the car." He held out a hundred-rupee note and two tens. Mortgage instalment. How can I take it? A conflict raged in Sankar's mind, and he finally took the money and said: "Thank you very much, sir."

"Don't mention it."

"You are very kind."

"Just ordinary duty, that is all. My principle is 'Do unto others as you would be done by others' is my principle is 'Do . . .' You need not come in the morning. I've no need for you. I had you only as a temporary arrangement—I'll put in a word for you if any friend wants a clerk or something of the sort—"

"Goodbye, sir."

"Goodbye." He was gone. The gentleman looked after him with satisfaction, muttering: "My principle is . . . unto other. . . ."

Next morning Sankar went out shopping, purchased bits of silk for his younger sister, a pair of spectacles for his mother, and a few painted tin toys for the child at home. He went to the hotel, looked into the accounts, and settled his month's bill. "I'm leaving today," he said. "I am returning to my village. . . ." His heart was all aflame with joy. He paid a rupee to the servant as a tip. He packed up his trunk and bed, took a last look round his garret; he had an unaccountable feeling of sadness at leaving the familiar smoke-stained cell. He was at the bus stand at about eleven in the day. The bus was ready to start. He took his seat. He would be at home at six in the evening. What a surprise for his mother! He would chat all night and tell them about the drunkard. . . .

He was shaken out of this reverie. A police inspector standing at the footboard of the bus touched his shoulder and asked:

"Are you Sankar?"

"Yes."

"Get down and follow me."

"I am going to my village. . . ."

"You can't go now." The inspector placed the trunk and bed on a coolie's head and they marched to the police station. There Sankar was subjected to much questioning, and his pockets were searched and all his money was taken away by the inspector. The inspector scrutinized the hundred-rupee note and remarked: "Same number. How did you get this? Be truthful. . . ."

Presently the inspector got up and said: "Follow me to the gentleman's house. . . ." Sankar found his employer sitting in a chair on the veranda, with a very tired look on his face. He motioned the inspector to a chair and addressed Sankar in a voice full of sorrow. "I never knew you were this sort, Sankar. You robbed me when I was not aware of it. If you'd asked me I'd have given you any amount you wanted. Did you have to tie me up and throw me down?" He showed the bruises on his arm. "In addition to robbing?" Sankar stood aghast. He could hardly speak for trembling. He explained all that had happened in the evening. His master and the police inspector listened in grim silence with obvious scepticism. His master said to the inspector: "Can you believe anything of what he says?"

"No, sir," replied the inspector.

"Nor can I. The poor fellow is driven to a corner and is inventing things. . . ." He thought for a moment. "I don't know . . . I think . . . since you have recovered the amount . . . how much did you find with him?"

"About one hundred and ten rupees and some change . . ." said the inspector.

"What happened to the balance?" He turned to Sankar and asked:

"Did you spend it?"

"Yes, I bought some toys and clothes. . . ."

"Well, well," said the gentleman with a flourish. "Let it go, poor devil: I'm sorry for you. You could have asked me for money instead of robbing me by force. Do you know where they found me?" he asked, showing the bruises on his elbow. "Do you know it was nearly next day they took me home? You'd left me unconscious: I will, however, withdraw the complaint. 'Do unto others as you would be done by' is my motto. You have served me faithfully all these months . . . but don't come before me again, you are a rogue. Get away now. . . ."

"Inspector, after the formalities are over you may send me the seized amount tomorrow, thank you very much. . . ."

Sankar starved for two days, and wandered about the street without a place for his head or trunk. At last, loitering near the post office one day, he had a few money orders and postcards to write, which earned him a rupee. With it he ate a meal, and took the bus for his village and back to all the ancient never-ending troubles of his family life.

A Breath of Lucifer

PROLOGUE

Nature has so designed us that we are compelled to spend at least eight hours out of twenty-four with eyes shut in sleep or in an attempt to sleep. It is a compensatory arrangement, perhaps, for the strain the visual faculty undergoes during our waking hours, owing to the glut of images impinging upon it morning till night. One who seeks serenity should, I suppose, voluntarily restrict one's range of vision. For it is mostly through the eye that the mind is strained or disturbed. Man sees more than what is necessary or good for him. If one does not control one's vision, nature will do it for one sooner or later.

Unnoticed, little by little, my right eye had been growing dimmer in the course of a year or two. I felt annoyed by the presence of a smudge of oil on the lens of my spectacles, which I pulled out and wiped with a handkerchief every other minute. When I tried to read, the smudge appeared on the first line and travelled down line by line, and it also touched up the faces of friends and foes alike whenever I happened to examine a photograph. As I raised my eyes the blot also lifted itself upward. It grew in circumference. I couldn't watch a movie without noticing an unseemly mole on the star's much prized face. No amount of cleaning of my spectacle lens was any use.

My eye doctor, after a dark-room test, pronounced that the spot was not on my spectacle lens but in the God-given lens of the eye itself, which was losing its transparency. He recorded it for my comfort on a piece of paper as "Lentil Opacity," to be remedied by means of a simple operation in due course.

Everyone speaks of the simplicity of the operation. It's simple in the sense that it is painless, accomplished without bloodshed. But to the surgeon it is a delicate and responsible task, demanding the utmost concentration of his powers at his finger tips, which will have to hover with the lightness of a butterfly over the patient's eye while detaching a tiny opalescent piece from its surface.

After the operation, total immobility in a state of total blackout for nearly a week, with both eyes sealed up with a bandage; not even the faintest ray of light may pass this barrier. The visual world is shut off. At first I dreaded the prospect. It seemed an inhuman condition of existence. But actually it turned out to be a novel experience. To observe nothing. To be oblivious of the traffic beneath my window, and of the variety of noise-makers passing up and down. I only hear the sound of the traffic but feel no irritation. Perhaps such irritations are caused as much by the sight of the irritant as by its decibel value. When you have no chance of observing the traffic, you cease to bother about it. A soundproof room may not be the only way to attain tranquillity—a bandage over one's eyes may achieve the same result. I never notice the weather, another source of despair, dismay, disappointment, or ecstasy for everyone at all times. I never know whether it is cloudy or sunny outside my window; when it rains I relish the patter of raindrops and the coolness without being aware of the slush and mess of a rain-sodden landscape. I am blissfully free alike from elation as from fury or despair. The joy stimulated by one experience could be as fatiguing as the despair caused by another. I hear words and accept them without any reservation as I am unaware of the accompanying facial expression or gesture which normally modulates the spoken word. In this state, in which one accepts the word absolutely, human relationships become suddenly simplified. For this same reason, I think, the yogis of yore advocated as a first step (and a final step also) in any technique of self-development the unwavering concentration of one's eyes on the tip of one's nose. Mahatma Gandhi himself advised a youth whose heart was constantly agitated by the sight of women to walk with his eyes fixed on his toe, or on the stars above.

When the outside world is screened off thus, one's vision turns immediately inward. In the depths of one's being (according to the terms of philosophers and mystics) or in the folds of one's brain (according to physiologists and psychologists) there is a memory-spot for every faculty. "Music when soft voices die, vibrates in the memory," said Shelley. One can recollect the fragrance of a bygone flower or a perfume, the softness of a touch. Similarly there is a visual memory too, which revives in all its sharpness under some extraordinary stimulus. The visual memory brings forth something not only seen and cherished but also wished for. My interests, let me confess, broadly speaking, are archaeological and geological. All my life I have been excessively fond of rocks, monuments, and ancient sculptures. I can never pass by a rock formation indifferently, or an old temple or a monument. So I now watch through my bandaged eyes night and day breath-taking friezes, cornices, pillars, and carvings, countless numbers of them, as on a slow-moving platform, as if one were present at the stone-cluttered yard of a superhuman sculptor. Sometimes I see a goddess enthroned on a lotus seat in a corner, and not far from her is a formless slab smoothed out by time, but faint etchings, possibly edicts of some ancient emperor, are still visible on it. A closer scrutiny reveals that this whole setting is not actually a corner—there is no corner, no direction, east, west, south, or north; it is a spot without our familiar spatial relationships.

Strangely, my visual memory does not present to me any white walls or bright ceilings. Every surface is grey and ancient, as if centuries of the burning of lamps have left congealed layers of holy oil on every surface. Sometimes I am enmeshed in a jumble of chariot wheels, crowns without heads, maces, and fragments of a dilapidated throne; suddenly this jumble sorts itself out and forms into a single regal figure standing on its feet, spanning the ground and the sky. Presently all this melts out of view. The floor is strewn with sawn-off timber, and a lot of grim metallic artifacts, perhaps the leftovers of an ancient torture chamber. A fantastic contrast occurs presently—an endless billowing stretch of tarpaulin or canvas envelops the whole landscape, such enormous billows that I wonder how I can take a step forward without getting enmeshed in them. Now I find myself in a corridor of an ageless cave-temple. Although I am supposed to remain in the dark I find a subdued, serene light illuminating every object and corner softly for me, a light that throws no shadow. Nothing looks fearsome or unpleasant. Everything is in harmony with everything else and has a pleasant quality all its own. Even an occasional specimen of fauna, a tiger in shape but with the face of an angel—it is not clear what creature is represented—smoothly glides past me, throwing a friendly smile at me.

Reality is of the moment and where we are. The immediate present possesses a convincing solid quality; all else is mere recollection or anticipation. This room with the bed on which I lie day and night is very real to me, with all the spectacle that passes before me; other things seem remote and dreamlike. The present rhythm of my life is set by a routine from morning at six (as I guess from the hawkers' voices in the street), when I summon my attendant (whose company and conversation have inspired me to write the accompanying story), till the night, when I am put to bed with the announcement by the same attendant, "Light is shut off, sir," punctuated by the arrivals and departures of the doctors' team and visitors who bring me news of the unreal world in which they live. Within the confines of this existence I feel snug and contented. Its routines are of the utmost importance to me. I am so much at home within it that I suspect I shall feel a regret when it ends.

R.K.N.
March 1969

Sam was only a voice to me, a rich, reverberating baritone. His whispers themselves possessed a solid, rumbling quality. I often speculated, judging from his voice, what he might look like: the possessor of such a voice could be statuesque, with curls falling on his nape, Roman nose, long legs able to cover the distance from my bed to the bathroom in three strides although to me it seemed an endless journey. I asked him on the very first day, "What do you look like?"

"How can I say? Several years since I looked at a mirror!"

"Why so?"

"The women at home do not give us a chance, that is all. I have even to shave without a mirror." He added, "Except once when I came up against a large looking glass at a tailor's and cried out absent-mindedly, 'Ah, Errol Flynn in town!' "

"You admired Errol Flynn?"

"Who wouldn't? As Robin Hood, unforgettable; I saw the picture fifty times."

"What do you look like?"

He paused and answered, "Next week this time you will see for yourself; be patient till the bandages are taken off. . . ."

Sam had taken charge of my bodily self the moment I was wheeled out of the operation theatre at the Malgudi Eye Clinic in New Extension with my eyes padded, bandaged, and sealed. I was to remain blindfolded for nearly a week in bed. During this confinement Sam was engaged for eight rupees a day to act as my eyes.

He was supposed to be a trained "male nurse," a term which he abhorred, convinced that nursing was a man's job and that the female in the profession was an impostor. He assumed a defiant and challenging pose whenever the sister at the nursing home came into my room. When she left he always had a remark to make, "Let this lady take charge of a skull-injury case; I will bet the patient will never see his home again."

Sam had not started life as a male nurse, if one might judge from his references. He constantly alluded to military matters, commands, campaigns, fatigue duties, and parades. What he actually did in the army was never clear to me. Perhaps if I could have watched his facial expressions and gestures I might have understood or interpreted his words differently, but in my unseeing state I had to accept literally whatever I heard. He often spoke of a colonel who had discovered his talent and encouraged and trained him in nursing. That happened somewhere on the Burma border, Indo-China, or somewhere, when their company was cut off and the medical units completely destroyed. The colonel had to manage with a small band of survivors, the most active among them being Sam, who repaired and rehabilitated the wounded and helped them return home almost intact when the war ended.

Which war was it? Where was it fought? Against whom? I could never get an answer to those questions. He always spoke of "the enemy," but I never understood who it was since Sam's fluency could not be interrupted for a clarification. I had to accept what I heard without question. Before they parted, the colonel composed a certificate which helped Sam in his career. "I have framed it and hung it in my house beside Jesus," he said.

At various theatres of war (again, which war I could never know) his services were in demand, mainly in surgical cases. Sam was not much interested in the physician's job. He had mostly been a surgeon's man. He only spoke of incidents where he had to hold up the guts of someone until the surgeon arrived, of necks half severed, arms amputated, and all aspects of human disjointedness and pain handled without hesitancy or failure. He asserted, "My two hands and ten fingers are at the disposal of anyone who needs them in war or peace."

"What do you earn out of such service?" I asked.

He replied, "Sometimes ten rupees a day, five, two, or nothing. I have eight children, my wife, and two sisters and a niece depending on me, and all of them have to be fed, clothed, sent to schools, and provided with books and medicines. We somehow carry on. God gives me enough. The greater thing for me is the relief that I am able to give anyone in pain. . . . Oh, no, do not get up so fast. Not good for you. Don't try to swat that mosquito buzzing at your ear. You may jam your eye. I am here to deal with the mosquito. Hands down, don't put up your hand near your eyes." He constantly admonished me, ever anxious lest I should by some careless act suffer a setback.

He slept in my room, on a mat a few feet away from my bed. He said that he woke up at five in the morning, but it could be any time since I had no means of verifying his claim by a watch or by observing the light on the walls. Night and day and all days of the week were the same to me. Sam explained that although he woke up early he lay still, without making the slightest noise, until I stirred in bed and called, "Sam!"

"Good morning, sir," he answered with alacrity and added, "Do not try to get up yet." Presently he came over and tucked up the mosquito net with scrupulous care. "Don't get up yet," he ordered and moved off. I could hear him open the bathroom door. Then I noticed his steps move farther off as he went in to make sure that the window shutters were secure and would not fly open and hit me in the face when I got in and fumbled about. After clearing all possible impediments in my way, he came back and said, "Righto, sir, now that place is yours, you may go in safely. Get up slowly. Where is the hurry? Now edge out of your bed, the floor is only four inches below your feet. Slide down gently, hold my hand, here it is. . . ." Holding both my hands in his, he walked backward and led me triumphantly to the bathroom, remarking along the way, "The ground is level and plain, walk fearlessly . . ."

With all the assurance that he attempted to give me, the covering over my eyes subjected me to strange tricks of vision and made me nervous at every step. I had a feeling of passing through geological formations, chasms, and canyons or billowing mounds of cotton wool, tarpaulin, or heaps of smithy junk or an endless array of baffle walls one beside another. I had to move with caution. When we reached the threshold of the bathroom he gave me precise directions: "Now move up a little to your left. Raise your right foot, and there you are. Now you do anything here. Only don't step back. Turn on your heel, if you must. That will be fine." Presently, when I called, he re-entered the bathroom with a ready compliment on his lips: "Ah, how careful and clean! I wish some people supposed to be endowed with full vision could leave a W.C. as tidy! Often, after they have been in, the place will be fit to be burnt down! However, my business in life is not to complain but to serve." He then propelled me to the washbasin and handed me the toothbrush. "Do not brush so fast. May not be good for your eyes. Now stop. I will wash the brush. Here is the water for rinsing. Ready to go back?"

"Yes, Sam!"

He turned me round and led me back towards my bed. "You want to sit on your bed or in the chair?" he asked at the end of our expedition. While I took time to decide, he suggested, "Why not the chair? You have been in bed all night. Sometimes I had to mind the casualties until the stretcher-bearers arrived, and I always said to the boys, 'Lying in bed makes a man sick, sit up, sit up as long as you can hold yourselves together.' While we had no sofas in the jungle, I made them sit and feel comfortable on anything, even on a snake-hole once, after flattening the top."

"Where did it happen? Did you say Burma?" I asked as he guided me to the cane chair beside the window.

He at once became cautious. "Burma? Did I say Burma? If I mentioned Burma I must have meant it and not the desert—"

"Which campaign was it?"

"Campaign? Oh, so many, I may not remember. Anyway it was a campaign and we were there. Suppose I fetch you my diary tomorrow? You can look through it when your eyes are all right again, and you will find in it all the answers."

"Oh! that will be very nice indeed."

"The colonel gave me such a fat, leather-bound diary, which cost him a hundred rupees in England, before he left, saying, 'Sam, put your thoughts into it and all that you see and do, and some day your children will read the pages and feel proud of you.' How could I tell the colonel that I could not write or read too well? My father stopped my education when I was that high, and he devoted more time to teach me how to know good toddy from bad."

"Oh, you drink?" I asked.

"Not now. The colonel whipped me once when he saw me drunk, and I vowed I'd never touch it again," he added as an afterthought while he poured coffee for me from the Thermos flask (which he filled by dashing out to a coffee-house in the neighbourhood; it was amazing with what speed he executed these exits and entrances, although to reach the coffee-house he had to run down a flight of steps, past a veranda on the ground floor, through a gate beyond a drive, and down the street; I didn't understand how he managed it all as he was always present when I called him, and had my coffee ready when I wanted it). He handed me the cup with great care, guiding my fingers around the handle with precision. While I sipped the coffee I could hear him move around the bed, tidying it up. "When the doctor comes he must find everything neat. Otherwise he will think that a donkey has been in attendance in this ward." He swept and dusted. He took away the coffee cup, washed it at the sink and put it away, and kept the toilet flush hissing and roaring by repeated pulling of the chain. Thus he set the stage for the doctor's arrival. When the sound of the wheels of the bandage-trolley was heard far off, he helped me back to my bed and stationed himself at the door. When footsteps approached, the baritone greeted: "Good morning, Doctor sir."

The doctor asked, "How is he today?"

"Slept well. Relished his food. No temperature. Conditions normal, Doctor sir." I felt the doctor's touch on my brow as he untied the bandage, affording me for a tenth of a second a blurred view of assorted faces over me; he examined my eye, applied drops, bandaged again, and left. Sam followed him out as an act of courtesy and came back to say, "Doctor is satisfied with your progress. I am happy it is so."

Occasionally I thumbed a little transistor radio, hoping for some music, but turned it off the moment a certain shrill voice came on the air rendering "film hits"; but I always found the tune continuing in a sort of hum for a minute or two after the radio was put away. Unable to judge the direction of the voice or its source, I used to feel puzzled at first. When I understood, I asked, "Sam, do you sing?"

The humming ceased. "I lost practice long ago," he said, and added, "When I was at Don Bosco's, the bishop used to encourage me. I sang in the church choir, and also played the harmonium at concerts. We had our dramatic troupe too and I played Lucifer. With my eyebrows painted and turned up, and with a fork at my tail, the bishop often said that never a better Lucifer was seen anywhere; and the public appreciated my performance. In our story the king was a good man, but I had to get inside him and poison his nature. The princess was also pure but I had to spoil her heart and make her commit sins." He chuckled at the memory of those days.

He disliked the nurse who came on alternate days to give me a sponge bath. Sam never approved of the idea. He said, "Why can't I do it? I have bathed typhoid patients running one hundred and seven degrees—"

"Oh, yes, of course." I had to pacify him. "But this is different, a very special training is necessary for handling an eye patient."

When the nurse arrived with hot water and towels he would

linger on until she said unceremoniously, "Out you go, I am in a hurry." He left reluctantly. She bolted the door, seated me in a chair, helped me off with my clothes, and ran a steaming towel over my body, talking all the time of herself, her ambition in life to visit her brother in East Africa, of her three children in school, and so forth.

When she left I asked Sam, "What does she look like?"

"Looks like herself all right. Why do you want to bother about her? Leave her alone. I know her kind very well."

"Is she pretty?" I asked persistently, and added, "At any rate I can swear that her voice is sweet and her touch silken."

"Oh! Oh!" he cried. "Take care!"

"Even the faint garlic flavour in her breath is very pleasant, although normally I hate garlic."

"These are not women you should encourage," he said. "Before you know where you are, things will have happened. When I played Lucifer, Marie, who took the part of the king's daughter, made constant attempts to entice me whenever she got a chance. I resisted her stoutly, of course; but once when our troupe was camping out, I found that she had crept into my bed at night. I tried to push her off, but she whispered a threat that she would yell at the top of her voice that I had abducted her. What could I do with such a one!" There was a pause, and he added, "Even after we returned home from the camp she pursued me, until one day my wife saw what was happening and gashed her face with her fingernails. That taught the slut a lesson."

"Where is Marie these days?" I asked.

He said, "Oh! she is married to a fellow who sells raffle tickets, but I ignore her whenever I see her at the market gate helping her husband."

When the sound of my car was heard outside, he ran to the window to announce, "Yes sir, they have come." This would be the evening visit from my family, who brought me my supper. Sam would cry from the window, "Your brother is there and that good lady his wife also. Your daughter is there and her little son. Oh! What a genius he is going to be! I can see it in him now. Yes,

yes, they will be here in a minute now. Let me keep the door open." He arranged the chairs. Voices outside my door, Sam's voice overwhelming the rest with "Good evening, madame. Good evening sir. Oh! You little man! Come to see your grandfather! Come, come nearer and say hello to him. You must not shy away from him." Addressing me, he would say, "He is terrified of your beard, sir," and, turning back to the boy, "He will be all right when the bandage is taken off. Then he is going to have a shave and a nice bath, not the sponge bath he is now having, and then you will see how grand your grandfather can be!" He then gave the visitors an up-to-the-minute account of the state of my recovery. He would also throw in a faint complaint. "He is not very co-operative. Lifts his hands to his eyes constantly, and will not listen to my advice not to exert." His listeners would comment on this, which would provoke a further comment in the great baritone, the babble maddening to one not able to watch faces and sort out the speakers, until I implored, "Sam, you can retire for a while and leave us. I can call you later"—thus giving me a chance to have a word with my visitors. I had to assume that he took my advice and departed. At least I did not hear him again until they were ready to leave, when he said, "Please do not fail to bring the washed clothes tomorrow. Also, the doctor has asked him to eat fruits. If you could find apples—" He carried to the car the vessels brought by them and saw them off.

After their departure he would come and say, "Your brother, sir, looks a mighty officer. No one can fool him, very strict he must be, and I dare not talk to him. Your daughter is devoted to you, no wonder, if she was motherless and brought up by you. That grandson! Watch my words, some day he is going to be like Nehru. He has that bearing now. Do you know what he said when I took him out for a walk? 'If my grandfather does not get well soon I will shoot you.' " And he laughed at the memory of that pugnacious remark.

We anticipated with the greatest thrill the day on which the bandages would be taken off my eyes. On the eve of the memorable day Sam said, "If you don't mind, I will arrange a small celebration. This is very much like the New Year Eve. You must sanction a small budget for the ceremony, about ten rupees will do. With your permission—" He put his hand in and extracted the purse from under my pillow. He asked for an hour off and left. When he returned I heard him place bottles on the table.

"What have you there?" I asked.

"Soft drinks, orange, Coca-Cola, this also happens to be my birthday. I have bought cake and candles, my humble contribution for this grand evening." He was silent and busy for a while and then began a running commentary: "I'm now cutting the cake, blowing out the candles—"

"How many?"

"I couldn't get more than a dozen, the nearby shop did not have more."

"Are you only twelve years old?"

He laughed, handed me a glass. "Coca-Cola, to your health. May you open your eyes on a happy bright world—"

"And also on your face!" I said. He kept filling my glass and toasting to the health of all humanity. I could hear him gulp down his drink again and again. "What are you drinking?"

"Orange or Coca-Cola, of course."

"What is the smell?"

"Oh, that smell! Someone broke the spirit lamp in the next ward."

"I heard them leave this evening!"

"Yes, yes, but just before they left they broke the lamp. I assured them, 'Don't worry. I'll clean up.' That's the smell on my hands. After all, we must help each other—" Presently he distributed the cake and burst into a song or two: "*He's a jolly good fellow,*" and then, "*The more we are together—*" in a stentorian voice. I could also hear his feet tapping away a dance.

After a while I felt tired and said, "Sam, give me supper. I feel sleepy."

After the first spell of sleep I awoke in the middle of the night and called, "Sam."

"Yes, sir," he said with alacrity.

"Will you lead me to the bathroom?"

"Yes, sir." The next moment he was at my bed, saying, "Sit up, edge forward, two inches down to your feet; now left, right, left, march, left, right, right turn." Normally, whenever I described the fantastic things that floated before my bandaged eyes he would reply, "No, no, no wall, nor a pillar. No junk either, trust me and walk on—" But today when I said, "You know why I have to walk so slowly?—"

"I know, I know," he said. "I won't blame you. The place is cluttered."

"I see an immense pillar in my way," I said.

"With carvings," he added. "Those lovers again. These two figures! I see them. She is pouting her lips, and he is trying to chew them off, with his arm under her thigh. A sinful spectacle, that's why I gave up looking at sculptures!"

I tried to laugh it off and said, "The bathroom."

"The bathroom, the bathroom, that is the problem. . . ." He paused and then said all of a sudden, "The place is on fire."

"What do you mean on fire?"

"I know my fire when I see one. I was Lucifer once. When I came on stage with fire in my nostrils, children screamed in the auditorium and women fainted. Lucifer has been breathing around. Let us go." He took me by my hand and hurried me out in some direction.

At the veranda I felt the cold air of the night in my face and asked, "Are we going out—?"

He would not let me finish my sentence. "This is no place for us. Hurry up. I have a responsibility. I cannot let you perish in the fire."

This was the first time I had taken a step outside the bedroom, and I really felt frightened and cried, "Oh! I feel we are on the edge of a chasm or a cavern, I can't walk." And he said, "Softly, softly. Do not make all that noise. I see the tiger's tail sticking out of the cave."

"Are you joking?"

He didn't answer but gripped my shoulder and led me on. I did not know where we were going. At the stairhead he commanded, "Halt, we are descending, now your right foot down, there, there, good, now bring the left one, only twenty steps to go." When I had managed it without stumbling, he complimented me on my smartness.

Now a cold wind blew in my face, and I shivered. I asked, "Are we inside or outside?" I heard the rustle of tree leaves. I felt the gravel under my bare feet. He did not bother to answer my question. I was taken through a maze of garden paths, and steps. I felt bewildered and exhausted. I suddenly stopped dead in my tracks and demanded, "Where are you taking me?" Again he did not answer. I said, "Had we better not go back to my bed?"

He remained silent for a while to consider my proposal and agreed, "That might be a good idea, but dangerous. They have mined the whole area. Don't touch anything you see, stay here, don't move, I will be back." He moved off. I was seized with panic when I heard his voice recede. I heard him sing "*He's a jolly good fellow, He's a jolly good fellow,*" followed by "*Has she got lovely cheeks? Yes, she has lovely cheeks,*" which was reassuring as it meant that he was still somewhere around.

I called out, "Sam."

He answered from afar, "Coming, but don't get up yet."

"Sam, Sam," I pleaded, "let me get back to my bed. Is it really on fire?"

He answered, "Oh, no, who has been putting ideas into your head? I will take you back to your bed, but please give me time to find the way back. There has been foul play and our retreat is cut off, but please stay still and no one will spot you." His voice still sounded far off.

I pleaded desperately, "Come nearer." I had a feeling of being poised over a void. I heard his approaching steps.

"Yes, sir, what is your command?"

"Why have you brought me here?" I asked.

He whispered, "Marie, she had promised to come, should be here any minute." He suddenly cried out, "Marie, where are you?" and mumbled, "She came into your room last night and the night before, almost every night. Did she disturb you? No. She is such a quiet sort, you would never have known. She came in when I put out the light, and left at sunrise. You are a good officer, have her if you like."

I could not help remarking, "Didn't your wife drive her away?"

Promptly came his reply: "None of her business. How dare she interfere in my affairs? If she tries . . ." He could not complete the sentence, the thought of his wife having infuriated him. He said, "That woman is no good. All my troubles are due to her."

I pleaded, "Sam, take me to my bed."

"Yes, sir," he said with alacrity, took my hand, and led me a few steps and said, "Here is your bed," and gave me a gentle push down until I sank at my knee and sat on the ground. The stones pricked me, but that seemed better than standing on my feet. He said, "Well, blanket at your feet. Call out 'Sam,' I am really not far, not really sleeping. . . . Good night, good night, I generally pray and then sleep, no, I won't really sleep. 'Sam,' one word will do, one word will do . . . will do. . . ." I heard him snore, he was sound asleep somewhere in the enormous void. I resigned myself to my fate. I put out my hand and realized that I was beside a bush, and I only hoped that some poisonous insect would not sting me. I was seized with all sorts of fears.

The night was spent thus. I must have fallen into a drowse, awakened at dawn by the bird-noises around. A woman took my hand and said, "Why are you here?"

"Marie?" I asked.

"No, I sweep and clean your room every morning, before the others come."

I only said, "Lead me to my bed."

She did not waste time on questions. After an endless journey she said, "Here is your bed, sir, lie down."

I suffered a setback, and the unbandaging was postponed. The doctor struggled and helped me out of a variety of ailments produced by shock and exposure. A fortnight later the bandages were taken off, but I never saw Sam again. Only a postcard addressed to the clinic several days later:

"I wish you a speedy recovery. I do not know what happened that night. Some foul play, somewhere. The rogue who brought me the Coca-Cola must have drugged the drink. I will deal with him yet. I pray that you get well. After you go home, if you please, send me a money order for Rs. 48/—. I am charging you for only six days and not for the last day. I wish I could meet you, but my colonel has summoned me to Madras to attend on a leg amputation. . . . Sam."

Annamalai

The mail brought me only a postcard, with the message in Tamil crammed on the back of it in minute calligraphy. I was curious about it only for a minute—the handwriting, style of address, the black ink, and above all the ceremonial flourish of the language were well known to me. I had deciphered and read out to Annamalai on an average one letter every month for a decade and a half when he was gardener, watchman, and general custodian of me and my property at the New Extension. Now the letter began: "At the Divine Presence of my old master, do I place with hesitancy this slight epistle for consideration. It's placed at the lotus feet of the great soul who gave me food and shelter and money in my lifetime, and for whose welfare I pray to the Almighty every hour of my waking life. God bless you, sir. By your grace and the grace of gods in the firmament above, I am in excellent health and spirits, and my kith and kin, namely, my younger brother Amavasai and my daughter, son-in-law, and the two grandchildren and my sister who lives four doors from me, and my maternal uncle and his children, who tend the coconut grove, are all well. This year the gods have been kind and have sent us the rains to nourish our lands and gardens and orchards. Our tanks have been full, and we work hard. . . ." I was indeed happy to have such a good report of fertility and joy from one who had nothing but problems as far as I could remember. But my happiness was short-lived. The rosy picture lasted about ten closely packed lines, followed by an abrupt transition. I realized all this excellence of reporting was just a formality, following a polite code of epistle-writing and not to be taken literally in part or in whole, for the letter started off in an opposite direction and tone. "My purpose in addressing your honoured self just today is to inform you that I am in sore need of money. The crops have failed this year and I am without food or money. My health is poor. I am weak, decrepit, and in bed, and need money for food and medicine. My kith and kin are not able to support me; my brother Amavasai is a godly man but he is very poor and is burdened with a family of nine children and two wives, and so I beg you to treat this letter as if it were a telegram and send me money immediately. . . ." He did not specify the amount but left it to my good sense, and whatever could be spared seemed welcome. The letter bore his name at the bottom, but I knew he could not sign; he always affixed his signature in the form of a thumb impression whenever he had to deal with any legal document. I should certainly have been glad to send a pension, not once but regularly, in return for all his years of service. But how could I be sure that he had written the letter? I knew that he could neither read nor write, and how could I make sure that the author of the letter was not his brother Amavasai, that father of nine and husband of two, who might have hit upon an excellent scheme to draw a pension in the name of a dead brother? How could I make sure that Annamalai was still alive? His last words to me before he retired were a grand description of his own funeral, which he anticipated with considerable thrill.

I looked at the postmark to make sure that at least the card had originated correctly. But the post-office seal was just a dark smudge as usual. Even if it weren't so, even if the name of his village had been clearly set forth it would not have made any difference. I was never sure at any time of the name of his village, although as I have already said I had written the address for him scores of times in a decade and a half. He would stand behind my chair after placing the postcard to be addressed on the desk. Every time I would say, "Now recite the address properly."

"All right, sir," he would say, while I waited with the pen poised over the postcard. "My brother's name is Amavasai, and it must be given to his hand."

"That I know very well, next tell me the address precisely this time." Because I had never got it right at any time.

He said something that sounded like "Mara Konam," which always puzzled me. In Tamil it meant either "wooden angle" or "cross angle," depending on whether you stressed the first word or the second of that phonetic assemblage. With the pen ready, if I said, "Repeat it," he would help me by uttering slowly and deliberately the name—but a new one this time, sounding something like "Peramanallur."

"What is it, where is it?" I asked desperately.

"My village, sir," he replied with a glow of pride—once again leaving me to brood over a likely meaning. Making allowance for wrong utterance you could translate it as "Paerumai Nallur," meaning "town of pride and goodness" or, with a change of the stress of syllables, "town of fatness and goodness." Attempting to grope my way through all this verbal wilderness, if I said, "Repeat it," he generally came out with a brand-new sound. With a touch of homesickness in his tone and with an air of making a concession to someone lacking understanding, he would say, "Write clearly NUMTHOD POST," leaving me again to wrestle with phonetics to derive a meaning. No use, as this seemed to be an example of absolute sound with no sense, with no scope for an interpretation however differently you tried to distribute the syllables and stresses or whether you attempted a translation or speculated on its meaning in Tamil, Telugu, Kannada, or any of the fourteen languages listed in the Indian Constitution. While I sat brooding over all this verbiage flung at me, Annamalai waited silently with an air of supreme tolerance, only suggesting gently, "Write in English . . ."

"Why in English?"

"If it could be in Tamil I would have asked that chap who writes the card to write the address also; because it must be in English I have to trouble you"—a piece of logic that sounded intricate.

I persisted. "Why not in Tamil?"

"Letters will not reach in Tamil; what our schoolmaster has often told us. When my uncle died they wrote a letter and addressed it in Tamil to his son in Conjeevaram and the man never turned up for the funeral. We all joined and buried the uncle after waiting for two days, and the son came one year later and asked,

'Where is my father? I want to ask for money.' " And Annamalai laughed at the recollection of this episode. Realizing that I had better not inquire too much, I solved the problem by writing briskly one under another everything as I heard it. And he would conclusively ask before picking up the card, "Have you written via Katpadi?"

All this business would take its own time. While the space for address on the postcard was getting filled up I secretly fretted lest any line should be crowded out, but I always managed it somehow with the edge of my pen-point. The whole thing took almost an hour each time, but Annamalai never sent a card home more than once a month. He often remarked, "No doubt, sir, that the people at home would enjoy receiving letters, but if I wrote a card to everyone who expected it, I would be a bankrupt. When I become a bankrupt, will there be one soul among all my relatives who will offer a handful of rice even if I starve to death?" And so he kept his communications within practical limits, although they provided a vital link for him with his village home.

"How does one get to your village?" I asked.

"Buy a railway ticket, that's how," he answered, feeling happy that he could talk of home. "If you get into the Passenger at night paying two rupees and ten annas, you will get to Trichy in the morning. Another train leaves Trichy at eleven, and for seven rupees and four annas, it used to be only five fourteen before, you can reach Villipuram. One must be awake all night, otherwise the train will take you on, and once they demanded two rupees extra for going further because I had slept over. I begged and pleaded and they let me go, but I had to buy another ticket next morning to get back to Katpadi. You can sleep on the station platform until midday. The bus arrives at midday and for twelve annas it will carry you further. After the bus you may hire a jutka or a bullock cart for six annas and then on foot you reach home before dark; if it gets late bandits may waylay and beat us. Don't walk too long; if you leave in the afternoon you may reach Marakonam before sunset. But a card reaches there for just nine paise, isn't it wonderful?" he asked.

Once I asked, "Why do you have the address written before the message?"

"So that I may be sure that the fellow who writes for me does not write to his own relations on my card. Otherwise how can I know?" This seemed to be a good way of ensuring that the postcard was not misused. It indicated a rather strange relationship, as he often spoke warmly of that unseen man who always wrote his messages on postcards, but perhaps a few intelligent reservations in accepting a friendship improve human relations. I often questioned him about his friend.

"He has also the same name as myself," he said.

I asked, "What name?"

He bowed his head and mumbled, "My . . . my own name . . ." Name was a matter of delicacy, something not to be bandied about unnecessarily, a point of view which had not occurred to me at all until one day he spoke to me anent a signboard on the gate announcing my name. He told me point-blank when I went down to the garden, "Take away the name-board from that gate, if you will forgive my saying so."

"Why?"

"All sorts of people read your name aloud while passing down the road. It is not good. Often urchins and tots just learning to spell shout your name and run off when I try to catch them. The other day some women also read your name and laughed to themselves. Why should they? I do not like it at all." What a different world was his where a name was to be concealed rather than blazoned forth in print, ether waves, and celluloid!

"Where should I hang that board now that I have it?"

He just said, "Why not inside the house, among the pictures in the hall?"

"People who want to find me should know where I live."

"Everyone ought to know," he said, "otherwise why should they come so far?"

Digging the garden he was at his best. We carried on some of our choicest dialogues when his hands were wielding the pickaxe. He dug and kept digging for its own sake all day. While at work he always tied a red bandanna over his head, knotted above his ear in pirate fashion. Wearing a pair of khaki shorts, his bare back roasted to an ebonite shade by the sun, he attained a spontaneous camouflage in a background of mud and greenery; when he stood ankle-deep in slush at the bed of a banana seedling, he was indistinguishable from his surroundings. On stone, slope, and pit, he moved jauntily, with ease, but indoors he shuffled and scratched the cement floor with his feet, his joints creaked and rumbled as he carried himself upstairs. He never felt easy in the presence of walls and books and papers; he looked frightened and self-conscious, tried to mute his steps and his voice when entering my study. He came in only when he had a postcard for me to address. While I sat at my desk he would stand behind my chair, suppressing even his normal breath lest it should disturb my work, but he could not help the little rumbles and sighs emanating from his throat whenever he attempted to remain still. If I did not notice his presence soon enough, he would look in the direction of the gate and let out a drover's cry, "Hai, hai!" at a shattering pitch and go on to explain, "Again those cows, sir. Some day they are going to shatter the gate and swallow our lawn and flowers so laboriously tended by this old fellow. Many strangers passing our gate stop to exclaim, 'See those red flowers, how well they have come up! All of it that old fellow's work, at his age!' "

Annamalai might have had other misgivings about himself, but he had no doubt whatever of his stature as a horticulturist. A combination of circumstances helped him to cherish his notions. I did nothing to check him. My compound was a quarter acre in extent and offered him unlimited scope for experimentations. I had been living in Vinayak Street until the owner of a lorry service moved into the neighbourhood. He was a relative of the municipal chairman and so enjoyed the freedom of the city. His lorries rattled up and down all day, and at night they were parked on the roadside and hammered and drilled so as to be made ready for loading in the morning. No one else in my street seemed to notice the nuisance. No use in protesting and complaining, as the relative of a municipal chairman would be beyond reproach. I decided to flee since it was impossible to read or write in that street; it dawned on me that the place was not meant for my kind any more. I began to look about. I liked the lot shown by a broker in the New Extension layout who also arranged the sale of my ancient house in Vinayak Street to the same lorry-owner. I moved off with my books and writing within six months of making up my mind. A slight upland stretching away to the mountain road; a swell of ground ahead on my left and the railway line passing through a cutting, punctuated with a red gate, was my new setting. Someone had built a small cottage with a room on top and two rooms downstairs, and it was adequate for my purpose, which was to read and write in peace.

On the day I planned to move I requested my neighbour the lorry-owner to lend me a lorry for transporting myself to my new home. He gladly gave me his lorry; the satisfaction was mutual as he could go on with all the repairs and hammerings all night without a word of protest from anyone, and I for my part should look forward to the sound of only birds and breeze in my new home. So I loaded all my books and trunks onto an open truck, with four loaders perched on them. I took my seat beside the driver and bade goodbye to Vinayak Street. No one to sigh over my departure, since gradually, unnoticed, I had become the sole representative of our clan in that street, especially after the death of my uncle.

When we arrived at New Extension the loaders briskly lifted the articles off the lorry and dumped them in the hall. One of them lagged behind while the rest went back to the lorry and shouted, "Hey, Annamalai, are you coming or not?" He ignored their call, and they made the driver hoot the horn.

I said to the man, "They seem to want you. . . ."

His brief reply was "Let them." He was trying to help me put things in order. "Do you want this to be carried upstairs?" he asked, pointing at my table. The lorry hooted outside belligerently. He was enraged at the display of bad manners, went to the doorway, looked at them, and said, waving his arms, "Be off if you want, don't stand there and make donkey noise."

"How will you come back?"

"Is that your business?" he said. "Go away if you like, don't let that donkey noise trouble this gentleman."

I was touched by his solicitude, and looked up from the books

I was retrieving from the packing cases, and noticed him for the first time. He was a thick-set, heavy-jowled man with a clean-shaven head covered with a turban, a pair of khaki shorts over heavy bow legs, and long arms reaching down to his knees; he had thick fingers, a broad nose, and enormous teeth stained red with betel juice and tobacco permanently pouched in at his cheek. There was something fierce as well as soft about him at the same time.

"They seem to have left," I remarked as the sound of the lorry receded.

"Let them," he said, "I don't care."

"How will you go back?" I asked.

"Why should I?" he said. "Your things are all scattered in a jumble here, and they don't have the sense to stop and help. You may have no idea, sir, what they have become nowadays."

Thus he entered my service and stayed on. He helped me to move my trunks and books and arrange them properly. Later he followed me about faithfully when I went round to inspect the garden. Whoever had owned the house before me had not bothered about the garden. It had a kind of battlement wall to mark off the backyard, and the rest was encircled with hedges of various types. Whenever I paused to examine any plant closely, Annamalai also stood by earnestly. If I asked, "What is this?" "This?" he said, stooping close to it, "this is a *poon chedi* [flowering plant]," and after a second look at it declared what I myself was able to observe, "Yellow flowers." I learnt in course of time that his classifications were extremely simple. If he liked a plant he called it "*poon chedi*" and allowed it to flourish. If it appeared suspicious, thorny, or awry in any manner he just declared, "This is a *poondu* [weed]," and, before I had a chance to observe it, would pull it off and throw it over the wall with a curse.

"Why do you curse that poor thing?"

"It is an evil plant, sir."

"What kind of evil?"

"Oh, of several kinds. Little children who go near it will have stomach ache."

"There are no children for miles around."

"What if? It can send out its poison on the air. . . ."

A sort of basement room was available, and I asked Annamalai, "Can you live in this?"

"I can live even without this," he said, and explained, "I am not afraid of devils, spirits, or anything. I can live anywhere. Did I have a room when I lived in those forests?" He flourished his arm in some vague direction. "That lorry-keeper is a rascal, sir; please forgive my talking like this in the presence of a gentleman. He is a rascal. He carried me one day in his lorry to a forest on the hill and would never let me get away from there. He had signed a contract to collect manure from those forests, and wanted someone to stay there, dig the manure, and heap it in the lorries."

"What kind of manure?"

"Droppings of birds and dung of tigers and other wild animals, and dead leaves, in deep layers everywhere, and he gave me a rupee and a half a day to stay there and dig up and load the lorry when it came. I lit a fire and boiled rice and ate it, and stayed under the trees, heaped the leaves around and lit them up to scare away the tigers roaring at night."

"Why did you choose this life just for one rupee and eight annas a day?" I asked.

He stood brooding for a few moments and replied, "I don't know. I was sitting in a train going somewhere to seek a job. I didn't have a ticket. A fellow got in and demanded, 'Where is your ticket?' I searched for it here and there and said, 'Some son of a bitch has stolen my ticket.' But he understood and said, 'We will find out who that son of a bitch is. Get off the train first.' And they took me out of the train with the bundle of clothes I carried. After the train left we were alone, and he said, 'How much have you?' I had nothing, and he asked, 'Do you want to earn one rupee and eight annas a day?' I begged him to give me work. He led me to a lorry waiting outside the railway station, handed me a spade and pickaxe, and said, 'Go on in that lorry, and the driver will tell you what to do.' The lorry put me down late next day on the mountain. All night I had to keep awake and keep a fire going, otherwise sometimes even elephants came up."

"Weren't you terrified?"

"They would run away when they saw the fire, and sometimes

I chanted aloud wise sayings and philosophies until they withdrew . . . leaving a lot of dung around, just what that man required . . . and he sold it to the coffee estates and made his money. . . . When I wanted to come home they would not let me, and so I stayed on. Last week when they came I was down with the shivering fever, but the lorry driver, a good man, allowed me to climb on the lorry and escape from the forest. I will never go back there, sir; that lorry man holds my wages and asserts that he has given it all as rice and potato all these months. . . . I don't know, some day you must reckon it all up for me and help me. . . ."

He left early on the following morning to fetch his baggage. He asked for an advance of five rupees, but I hesitated. I had not known him for more than twenty-four hours. I told him, "I don't have change just at this moment."

He smiled at me, showing his red-tinted teeth. "You do not trust me, I see. How can you? The world is full of rogues who will do just what you fear. You must be careful with your cash, sir. If you don't protect your cash and wife . . ." I did not hear him fully as he went downstairs muttering his comment. I was busy setting up my desk as I wished to start my work without any more delay. I heard the gate open, producing a single clear note on its hinges (which I later kept purposely on without oiling as that particular sound served as a doorbell). I peeped from my western window and saw him go down the road. I thought he was going away for good, not to return to a man who would not trust him with five rupees! I felt sorry for not giving him money, at least a rupee. I saw him go up the swell of ground and disappear down the slope. He was going by a short cut to the city across the level-crossing gate.

I went back to my desk, cursing my suspiciousness. Here was one who had volunteered to help and I had shown so little grace. That whole day he was away. Next afternoon the gate latch clicked, and the gate hummed its single clear note as it moved on its hinges, and there he was, carrying a big tin trunk on his head, and a gunny sack piled on top of it. I went down to welcome him. By the time I had gone down he had passed round the house and was lowering the trunk at the door of the basement room.

He would stand below my window and announce to the air, "Sir, I am off for a moment. I have to talk to the mali in the other house," and move off without waiting for my reply. Sometimes if I heard him I said, as a matter of principle, "Why do you have to go and bother him about our problems now?"

He would look crestfallen and reply, "If I must not go, I won't go, if you order so."

How could I or anyone order Annamalai? It was unthinkable, and so to evade such a drastic step I said, "You know everything, what does he know more than you?"

He would shake his head at this heresy. "Don't talk so, sir. If you don't want me to go, I won't go, that is all. You think I want to take off the time to gossip and loaf?"

A difficult question to answer, and I said, "No, no, if it is important, of course . . ."

And he moved off, muttering, "They pay him a hundred rupees a month not for nothing . . . and I want to make this compound so good that people passing should say 'Ah' when they peep through the gate . . . that is all, am I asking to be paid also a hundred rupees like that mali?" He moved off, talking all the way; talking was an activity performed for its own sake and needed no listener for Annamalai. An hour later he returned clutching a drooping sapling (looking more like a shot-down bird) in his hand, held it aloft under my window, and said, "Only if we go and ask will people give us plants; otherwise why should they be interested?"

"What is it?" I asked dutifully, and his answer I knew even before he uttered it: "Flower plant."

Sometimes he displayed a handful of seeds tied to the end of his dhoti in a small bundle. Again I asked, "What is it?"

"Very rare seeds, no one has seen such a thing in this extension. If you think I am lying . . ." He would then ask, "Where are these to be planted?"

I would point out to a corner of the compound and say, "Don't you think we need some good covering there? All that portion looks bare. . . ." Even as I spoke I would feel the futility of my suggestion, it was just a constitutional procedure and nothing more. He might follow my instructions or his own inclination, no one could guess what he might do. He would dig up the earth earnestly at some corner and create a new bed of his own pattern, poke his forefinger into the soft earth and push the seed or the seedling in. Every morning he would stoop over it to observe minutely how it progressed. If he found a sprouting seed or any sign of life in the seedling, he watered it twice a day, but if it showed no response to his loving touch, he looked outraged. "This should have come up so well, but it is the Evil Eye that scorches our plants. . . . I know what to do now." He dipped his finger in a solution of white lime and drew grotesque and strange emblems on a broken mud pot and mounted it up prominently on a stick so that those that entered our gate should first see the grotesque painting rather than the plants. He explained, "When people say, 'Ah, how good this garden looks!' they speak with envy and then it burns up the plants, but when they see the picture there, they will be filled with revulsion and our flowers will flourish. That is all."

He made his own additions to the garden each day, planting wherever he fancied, and soon I found that I could have no say in the matter. I realized that he treated me with tolerant respect rather than trust, and so I let him have his own way. Our plants grew anyhow and anywhere and generally prospered, although the only attention that Annamalai gave them was an ungrudging supply of water out of a hundred-foot hose-pipe, which he turned on every leaf of every plant until it was doused and drowned. He also flung at their roots from time to time every kind of garbage and litter and called it manuring. By such assiduous efforts he created a generous, massive vegetation as a setting for my home. We had many rose plants whose nomenclature we never learnt, which had developed into leafy menacing entanglements, clawing passers-by; canna grew to gigantic heights, jasmine into wild undergrowth with the blooms maliciously out of reach, although they threw their scent into the night. Dahlias pushed themselves above ground after every monsoon, presented their blooms, and wilted and disappeared, but regenerated themselves again at the next season. No one could guess who planted them originally, but nature was responsible for their periodic appearance, although

Annamalai took the credit for it unreservedly. Occasionally I protested when Tacoma hedges bordering the compound developed into green ramparts, shutting off the view in every direction. Annamalai, a prince of courtesy at certain moments, would not immediately contradict me but look long and critically at the object of my protest. "Don't think of them now, I will deal with them."

"When?" I asked.

"As soon as we have the rains," he would say.

"Why should it be so late?"

"Because a plant cut in summer will die at the roots."

"You know how it is with rains these days, we never have them."

This would make him gaze skyward and remark, "How can we blame the rains when people are so evil-minded?"

"What evil?"

"Should they sell rice at one rupee a measure? Is it just? How can poor people live?"

When the rains did come eventually it would be no use reminding him of his promise to trim the hedges, for he would definitely declare, "When the rain stops, of course, for if a plant is trimmed in rain, it rots. If you want the hedges to be removed completely, tell me, I will do it in a few minutes, but you must not blame me later if every passer-by in the street stares and watches the inside of the house all the time. . . ."

But suddenly one day, irrespective of his theories, he would arm himself with a scythe and hack blindly whatever came within his reach, not only the hedge I wanted trimmed but also a lot of others I preferred to keep. When I protested against this depredation, he just said, "The more we cut the better they will grow, sir." At the end of this activity, all the plants, having lost their outlines, looked battered and stood up like lean ghosts, with the ground littered green all over. At the next stage he swept up the clippings, bundled them neatly, and carried them off to his friend, namesake, and letter-writer, living in the Bamboo Bazaar, who had his cows to feed; in return for Annamalai's generosity, he kept his penmanship ever at Annamalai's service.

His gardening activities ceased late in the evening. He laid away his implements in a corner of his basement room, laboriously coiled up the hose, and locked it away, muttering, "This is my very life; otherwise how can an old fellow feed his plants and earn a good name? If some devil steals this I am undone, and you will never see me again." So much lay behind his habit of rolling up the rubber hose, and I fancied that he slept in its coils as an added safety. After putting it away he took off his red bandanna, turned on the tap, and splashed enormous quantities of water over himself, blowing his nose, clearing his throat, and grooming himself noisily; he washed his feet, rubbing his heels on a granite slab until they shone red; now his bandanna would be employed as a towel; wiping himself dry, he disappeared into the basement and came out later wearing a shirt and a white dhoti. This was his off hour, when he visited the gate shop at the level crossing in order to replenish his stock of tobacco and gossip with friends seated on a teak log. The railway gatekeeper who owned the shop (although for reasons of policy he gave out that it belonged to his brother-in-law) was a man of information and read out a summary of the day's news to this gathering out of a local news sheet published by the man who owned the Truth Printing Press and who reduced the day's radio broadcasts and the contents of other newspapers into tiny paragraphs on a single sheet of paper, infringing every form of copyright. He brought out his edition in the evening for two paise, perhaps the cheapest newspaper in the world. Annamalai paid close attention to the reading and thus participated in contemporary history. When he returned home I could spot him half a mile away from my window as his red bandanna came into view over the crest of a slope. If he found me near at hand, he passed to me the news of the day. That was how I first heard of John Kennedy's assassination. I had not tuned the radio the whole day, being absorbed in some studies. I was standing at the gate when he returned home, and I asked casually, "What is your news today?" and he answered without stopping, "News? I don't go hunting for it, but I overheard that the chief ruler of America was killed today. They said something like *Kannady* [which means glass in Tamil]; could any man give himself such a name?"

When I realized the import of his casual reference, I said, "Look, was it Kennedy?"

"No, they said Kannady, and someone shot him with a gun and killed him, and probably they have already cremated him." When I tried to get more news, he brushed me off with "Don't think I go after gossip, I only tell you what approaches my ears . . . and they were all talking . . ."

"Who?" I asked.

"I don't know who they are. Why should I ask for names? They all sit and talk, having nothing else to do."

He would come into my study bearing a postcard in hand and announcing, "A letter for you. The postman gave it." Actually it would be a letter for him, which he'd never know until told, when he would suddenly become tense and take a step nearer in order to absorb all the details.

"What does he say?" he would ask irritably. His only correspondent was his brother Amavasai, and he hated to hear from him. Torn between curiosity and revulsion, he would wait for me to finish reading the postcard to myself first. "What does that fellow have to say to me?" he would ask in a tone of disgust and add, "As if I could not survive without such a brother!"

I'd read aloud the postcard, which always began formally with a ceremonial flourish: "To my Godly brother and protector, this insignificant younger brother Amavasai submits as follows. At this moment we are all flourishing and we also pray for our divine elder brother's welfare in one breath." This preamble would occupy half the space on the back of the card, to be abruptly followed by mundane matters. "The boundary stone on the north side of our land was tampered with last night. We know who did it."

Pushing the tobacco on his tongue out of the way in order to speak without impediment, Annamalai would demand, "If you really know who, why don't you crack his skull? Are you bereft of all sense? Tell me that first," and glare angrily at the postcard in my hand.

I'd read the following line by way of an explanation: "But they don't care."

"They don't? Why not?" The next few lines would agitate him most, but I had to read them out. "Unless you come and deal with them personally, they will never be afraid. If you keep away, nothing will improve. You are away and do not care for your kith and kin and are indifferent to our welfare or suffering. You did not care to attend even my daughter's naming ceremony. This is not how the head of a family should behave."

The rest of the letter generally turned out to be a regular charge-sheet, but concluded ceremoniously, mentioning again lotus feet and divinity. If I said, in order to divert his mind, "Your brother writes well," he would suddenly grin, very pleased at the compliment, and remark, "He to write! Oh, oh, he is a lout. That letter is written by our schoolmaster. We generally tell him our thoughts and he will write. A gifted man." He would prepare to go downstairs, remarking, "Those fellows in my village are illiterate louts. Do you think my brother could talk to a telephone?" One of his urban triumphs was that he could handle the telephone. In distinguishing the mouthpiece from the earpiece, he displayed the pride of an astronaut strolling in space. He felt an intimacy with the instrument, and whenever it rang he'd run up to announce, "Telepoon, sami," even if I happened to be near it. When I came home at night he'd always run forward to declare while opening the gate, "There was a telepoon—someone asked if you were in. . . ."

"Who was it?"

"Who? How could I know? He didn't show his face!"

"Didn't you ask his name?"

"No, what should I do with his name?"

One morning he waited at my bedroom door to tell me, "At five o'clock there was a telepoon. You were sleeping, and so I asked, 'Who are you?' He said, 'Trunk, trunk,' and I told him, 'Go away, don't trouble us. No trunk or baggage here. Master is sleeping.' " To this day I have no idea where the trunk call was from. When I tried to explain to him what a "trunk call" was (long-distance call) he kept saying, "When you are sleeping, that fellow asks for a trunk! Why should we care?" I gave up.

The only way to exist in harmony with Annamalai was to take him as he was; to improve or enlighten him would only exhaust the reformer and disrupt nature's design. At first he used to light a fire in the basement itself, his fuel consisting of leaves and all sorts of odds and ends swept up from the garden, which created an enormous pall of smoke and blackened the walls; also there was the danger of his setting fire to himself in that room without a chimney. I admonished him one day and suggested that he use charcoal. He said, "Impossible! Food cooked over charcoal shortens one's life, sir. Hereafter I will not cook inside the house at all." Next day he set up three bricks under the pomegranate tree, placed a mud pot over them, and raised a roaring fire. He boiled water and cooked rice, dhall, onion, tomato, and a variety of greens picked from the garden, and created a stew whose fragrance rose heavenward and in its passage enticed me to peep over the terrace and imbibe it.

When the monsoon set in I felt anxious as to how he was going to manage, but somehow even when the skies darkened and the rains fell, between two bouts he raised and kept up the fire under the pomegranate shade. When it poured incessantly he held a corrugated iron sheet over the fire and managed, never bothering to shield his own head. He ate at night, and preserved the remnant, and on the following day from time to time quietly dipped his fingers into the pot and ate a mouthful, facing the wall and shielding his aluminum plate from any Evil Eye that might happen to peep in at his door.

There was not a stronger person in the neighbourhood. When he stalked about during his hours of watch, tapping the ground with a metal rod and challenging in a stentorian voice, he created an air of utter intimidation, like a mastiff. God knows we might have needed a mastiff definitely in the early days, but not now. Annamalai did not seem to realize that such an aggressive watch was no longer necessary. He did not seem to have noticed the transition of my surroundings from a lonely outpost (where I had often watched thieves break open a trunk and examine their booty by torchlight in a ditch a hundred yards from my bedroom window) into a populous colony, nor did he take note of the coming of the industrial estate beyond my house. If any person passing my gate dallied a minute, particularly at night after he had had his supper and the stars were out, Annamalai would challenge him to explain his presence. People passing my gate quickened their pace as a general policy. Occasionally he softened when someone asked for flowers for worship. If he saw me noticing the transaction, he would shout in rage, "Go away. What do you think you are? Do flowers come up by themselves? Here is the old fellow giving his life to tending them, and you think . . ." and charge threateningly towards the would-be worshipper; but if I remained indoors and watched through the window I could see him give a handful of flowers to the person at the gate, muting his steps and tone and glancing over his shoulder to make sure that I was not watching.

Annamalai was believed to earn money by selling my flowers, according to a lady living next door to me, who had constituted herself his implacable enemy. According to Annamalai, whenever I was away on tour she demanded of him the banana leaves grown in my garden, for her guests to dine on, and his steady refusal had angered her. Whenever I passed their compound wall she would whisper, "You are trusting that fellow too much, he is always talking to the people at the gate and always carrying on some transaction." A crisis of the first order developed once when she charged him with the theft of her fowls. She reared poultry, which often invaded my compound through a gap in the fence, and every afternoon Annamalai would be chasing them out with stones and war cries. When I was away for weeks on end, according to the lady, every other day she missed a bird when she counted them at night. She explained how Annamalai dazed the fowl by throwing a wet towel over its head, and carried it off to the shop at the level crossing, where his accomplices sold or cooked it.

Once feathers were found scattered around Annamalai's habitat when it was raided by a watchman of the municipal sewage farm, who wore a khaki coat and pretended to be a policeman. Annamalai was duly frightened and upset. Returning home from a tour one afternoon, I found him standing on a foot-high block of stone, in order to be heard better next door, and haranguing, "You set the police on me, do you, because you have lost a fowl? So what? What have I to do with it? If it strays into my compound

I'll twist its neck, no doubt, but don't imagine that I will thieve like a cheap rascal. Why go about fowl-thieving? I care two straws for your police. They come to us for baksheesh in our village; foolish people will not know that. I am a respectable farmer with an acre of land in the village. I grow rice. Amavasai looks after it and writes to me. I receive letters by post. If I am a fowl-thief, what are those that call me so? Anyway, what do you think you are? Whom do you dare to talk to?" In this strain he spoke for about half an hour, addressing the air and the sky, but the direction of his remarks could not be mistaken. Every day at the same hour he delivered his harangue, soon after he had eaten his midday food, chewed tobacco, and tied the red bandanna securely over his ears.

Sometimes he added much autobiographical detail. Although it was beamed in the direction of the lady next door, I gathered a great deal of information in bits and pieces which enabled me to understand his earlier life. Mounted on his block of stone, he said, "I was this high when I left home. A man who has the stuff to leave home when he is only ten won't be the sort to steal fowl. My father had said, 'You are a thief. . . .' That night I slipped out of the house and walked. . . . I sat in a train going towards Madras. . . . They threw me out, but I got into the next train, and although they thrashed me and threw me out again and again, I reached Madras without a ticket. I am that kind, madam, not a fowl-thief, worked as a coolie and lived in the verandas of big buildings. I am an independent man, madam, I don't stand nonsense from others, even if it is my father. One day someone called me and put me on the deck of a steamer and sent me to a tea garden in Ceylon, where I was until the fever got me. Do you think your son will have the courage to face such things?"

At the same hour day after day I listened and could piece together his life. "When I came back home I was rid of the shivering fever. I gave my father a hundred rupees and told him that a thief would not bring him a hundred rupees. I hated my village, with all those ignorant folk. My father knew I was planning to run away once again. One day all of them held me down, decorated the house, and married me to a girl. I and Amavasai went to the fields and ploughed and weeded. My wife cooked my food. After my daughter appeared I left home and went away to Penang. I worked in the rubber estates, earned money, and sent money home. That is all they care for at home—as long as you send money they don't care where you are or what you do. All that they want is money, money. I was happy in the rubber plantations. When the Japanese came they cut off everybody's head or broke their skulls with their guns, and they made us dig pits to bury the dead and also ourselves in the end. I escaped and was taken to Madras in a boat with a lot of others. At home I found my daughter grown up, but my wife was dead. It seems she had fever every day and was dead and gone. My son-in-law is in a government job in the town. I am not a fowl-thief. . . . My granddaughter goes to a school every day carrying a bag of books, with her anklets jingling and flowers in her hair. . . . I had brought the jewellery for her from Malaya." Whatever the contents of his narrative, he always concluded, "I am not a rascal. If I were a fowl-thief . . . would a government officer be my son-in-law?"

I told him, "No one is listening. Why do you address the wall?"

"They are crouching behind it, not missing a word anyway," he said. "If she is a great person, let her be, what do I care? How dare she say that I stole her fowl? What do I want their fowl for? Let them keep them under their bed. I don't care. But if any creature ever strays here I'll wring its neck, that is certain."

"And what will you do with it?"

"I don't care what. Why should I watch what happens to a headless fowl?"

The postcard that most upset him was the one which said, after the usual preamble, "The black sheep has delivered a lamb, which is also black, but the shepherd is claiming it: every day he comes and creates a scene. We have locked up the lamb, but he threatens to break open the door and take away the lamb. He stands in the street and abuses us every day, and curses our family; such curses are not good for us." Annamalai interrupted the letter to demand, "Afraid of curses! Haven't you speech enough to outcurse him?" Another postcard three days later said, "They came yesterday and carried off the black sheep, the mother, when we were away in the fields."

"Oh, the . . ." He checked the unholy expression that welled up from the bottom of his heart. "I know how it must have happened.

They must have kept the mother tied up in the backyard while locking up the lamb. What use would that be?" He looked at me questioningly.

I felt I must ask at this point, "Whose sheep was it?"

"The shepherd's, of course, but he borrowed ten rupees and left me the sheep as a pledge. Give me my ten rupees and take away the sheep, that is all. How can you claim the lamb? A lamb that is born under our roof is ours." This was an intricate legal point, I think the only one of its kind in the world, impossible for anyone to give a verdict on or quote precedents, as it concerned a unique kind of mortgage which multiplied in custody. "I have a set of senseless dummies managing my affairs; it is people like my brother who made me want to run away from home."

This proved a lucky break for the lady next door as the following afternoon Annamalai left to seek the company of the level-crossing gateman and other well-wishers in order to evolve a strategy to confound the erring shepherd in their village. As days passed he began to look more and more serene. I sensed that some solution had been found. He explained that someone who had arrived from the village brought the report that one night they had found the black sheep being driven off by the butcher, whereupon they waylaid him and carried it back to the bleating lamb at home. Now both the sheep and the lamb were securely locked up, while his brother and the family slept outside on the pyol of the house. I couldn't imagine how long they could continue this arrangement, but Annamalai said, "Give me back my ten rupees and take away the sheep."

"What happens to the lamb?"

"It is ours, of course. The sheep was barren until it came to our house; that shepherd boy did not pledge a pregnant sheep."

It was the tailor incident that ended our association. The postcard from home said, "The tailor has sold his machine to another tailor and has decamped. Things are bound to happen when you sit so far away from your kith and kin. You are allowing all your affairs to be spoilt." Annamalai held his temples between his hands and shut his eyes, unable to stand the shock of this revelation. I asked no questions, he said nothing more and left me, and I saw him go up the slope towards the level crossing. Later I watched him from my window as he dug at a banana root; he paused and stood frozen in a tableau with his pickaxe stuck in the ground, arms akimbo, staring at the mud at his feet. I knew at that moment that he was brooding over his domestic affairs. I went down, gently approached him, pretended to look at the banana root, but actually was dying of curiosity to know more about the tailor story. I asked some casual horticultural questions and when he started to reply I asked, "Why are tailors becoming troublesome, unpunctual, and always stealing bits of cloth?"

My antitailor sentiment softened him, and he said, "Tailor or carpenter or whoever he may be, what do I care, I am not afraid of them. I don't care for them."

"Who is the tailor your brother mentions in his letter?"

"Oh, that! A fellow called Ranga in our village, worthless fellow, got kicked out everywhere," and there the narrative for the day ended because of some interruption.

I got him to talk about the tailor a couple of days later. "People didn't like him, but he was a good tailor . . . could stitch kerchief, drawers, banyan, and even women's jackets . . . but the fellow had no machine and none of his relations would help him. No one would lend him money. I got a money order from Ceylon one day for a hundred rupees—some money I had left behind. When the postman brought the money order, this tailor also came along with him, at the same moment. How could he have known? After the postman left, he asked, 'Can't you give me a hundred rupees? I can buy a machine.' I asked him, 'How did you know that I was receiving a hundred rupees, who told you?' and I slapped his face, spat at him for prying into my affairs. The fellow wept. I was, after all, his elder, and so I felt sorry and said, 'Stop that. If you howl like that I will thrash you.' Then all our village elders assembled and heard both of us, and ordered that I should lend my hundred rupees to him."

I failed to understand how anyone could order him thus. I asked naïvely, "Why should they have told you and what have they to do with it?"

He thought for a while and answered, "That is how we do it, when the elders assemble and order us . . ."

"But you didn't call the assembly?"

"I didn't, but they came and saw us, when the tailor was crying out that I had hurt him. They then wrote a bond on government paper with stamp and made him sign it; the man who sold the paper was also there, and we gave him two rupees for writing the document."

Later I got a picture of this transaction little by little. The tailor purchased a sewing machine with the loan from Annamalai. Annamalai's brother accommodated the tailor and the machine on the pyol of his house; the tailor renewed the bond from time to time, paid the interest regularly and also a daily rent for occupying the pyol. This was a sort of gilt-edged security, and Annamalai preserved the bond in the safety of a tin box in my cellar. When the time for its renewal came each year, he undertook a trip to the village and came back after a month with a fresh signature on the bond, attested by the village headman. But now the entire basis of their financial relationship was shaken. The original tailor had decamped, and the new tailor did not recognize his indebtedness, although he sat on the pyol of their house and stitched away without speaking to anyone.

"You never asked for your hundred rupees back?" I asked.

"Why should I?" he asked, surprised at my question. "As long as he was paying the interest, and renewing his signature. He might have been up to some mischief if I didn't go in person; that is why I went there every time." After all this narration, Annamalai asked, "What shall I do now? The rascal has decamped."

"But where is the machine?"

"Still there. The new tailor stitches everybody's clothes in our house but won't speak to us, nor does he go away from the machine. He sleeps under it every night."

"Why don't you throw him out?"

Annamalai thought for a while and said, "He will not speak to us and he will not pay us the rent, saying when pressed that he paid all the rent to the first tailor along with the price of the machine. . . . Could it be possible? Is it so in the letter you read?"

Very soon another postcard came. It started with the respected preamble, all right, but ended rather abruptly with the words

"We have nowhere to sleep, the tailor will not move. Inside the house the sheep and the lamb are locked. As the elder of our family, tell us where we should sleep. My wives threaten to go away to their parents' houses. I am sleeping with all the children in the street. Our own house has no place for us. If you keep so far away from your kith and kin, such things are bound to happen. We suffer and you don't care."

At this point Annamalai indulged in loud thinking. "Nothing new, these women are always running off to their parents . . . if you sneeze or cough it is enough to make them threaten that they will go away. Unlucky fellow, that brother of mine. He has no guts to say, 'All right, begone, you moodhevi,' he is afraid of them."

"Why can't they throw out the tailor and lock up the machine along with the sheep? Then they could all sleep on the pyol . . ."

"I think he is the son of our wrestler—that new tailor, and you know my brother is made of straw although he has produced nine children." He considered the situation in silence for a while and said, "It is also good in a way. As long as he is not thrown out, the machine is also there. . . . God is helping us by keeping him there within our hold. If my brother has no place to sleep in, let him remain awake."

For the next three days I sensed that much confabulation was going on, as I saw the red bandanna go up the crest more often than usual. His adviser at the Bamboo Bazaar and the well-wishers at the gate shop must have attacked the core of the problem and discovered a solution. When he returned from the gate shop one evening he announced point-blank, "I must go to my village."

"Yes, why so suddenly?"

"The bond must be changed, renewed in the new tailor's name. You must let me go."

"When?"

"When? . . . Whenever you think I should go."

"I don't think you should go at all. I can't let you go now. I am planning to visit Rameswaram on a pilgrimage."

"Yes, it is a holy place, good to visit," he said patronizingly. "You will acquire a lot of merit. After you come back I will go."

So we parted on the best of terms that day. As if nothing had been spoken on the subject till now, he came up again next day, stood behind my chair, and said without any preamble, "I must go."

"Yes, after I return from my pilgrimage."

He turned round and went down half-way, but came up again to ask, "When are you going?"

His constant questioning put me on edge; anyway I suppressed my annoyance and replied calmly, "I am waiting for some others to join me, perhaps in ten days."

He seemed satisfied with the answer and shuffled down. That night when I returned home he met me at the gate. Hardly had I stepped in when he said, "I will be back in ten days; let me go tomorrow. I will be back in ten days and I will guard the house when you are away on pilgrimage. . . ."

"Should we settle all questions standing in the street? Can't you wait until I am in?"

He didn't answer but shut the gate and went away to his room. I felt bad all that night. While I changed my clothes, ate, and read or wrote, there was an uneasiness at the back of my mind at the memory of my sharp speech. I had sounded too severe. I went down to his backyard first thing in the morning, earlier than usual. He sat under the tap with the water turned full blast on his head, and then went dripping to his basement room. He stuck a flower on a picture of God on his wall, lit an incense stick, stuck a flower over his ear, put holy ash on his forehead, knotted the bandanna over his ear, and, dressed in his shorts, emerged ready for the day, but there was no friendliness in his eyes. I spent the time pretending to examine the mango blooms, made some appreciative remarks about the state of the garden, and suddenly said, "You want to be away for only ten days?"

"Yes, yes," he replied eagerly, his mood softening. "I must renew the bond, or gather people to throw out that interloper and seize his machine . . . even if it means bloodshed. Someone has to lose his life in this business. I will come back in ten days."

It sounded to me a too ambitious programme to be completed in ten days. "Are you sure that you want only ten days off?" I asked kindly.

"It may be a day more or less, but I promise to be back then.

Once I return I won't go for two years, even then I won't go unless . . . I will leave the next renewal in my brother's hands."

I found myself irritated again and said, "I cannot let you go now," in a tone of extreme firmness, at which he came nearer and pleaded with his palms pressed together, "Please, I must renew the bond now; otherwise, if it is delayed, I will lose everything, and the people in my village will laugh at me."

"Get me the bond, I will have a look at it," I said with authority.

I could hear him open his black trunk. He came in bearing a swath of cloth, unwound it with tender care, and took out of its folds a document on parchment paper. I looked through it. The bond was worth a hundred rupees, and whoever had drafted it made no mention of a tailor or his machine. It was just a note promising repayment of a hundred rupees with interest from time to time, stuck with numerous stamps, dates, thumb impressions, and signatures. I really could not see how it was going to help him. I read it out to him and commented, with my fingers drumming effectively on the document, "Where is any mention of your tailor or his machine?"

"Surely there is the name Ranga on it!"

"But there is no mention of a tailor. For all it says, Ranga could be a scavenger."

Annamalai looked panic-stricken. He put his eyes close to the document and, jabbing it with his finger, asked, "What does it say here?"

I read it word by word again. He looked forlorn. I said, "I will give you a hundred rupees and don't bother about the bond. What does it cost you to reach your village?"

He made loud calculations and said, "About ten rupees by Passenger from . . ."

"Coming back, ten rupees. You have been going there for years now and you have already spent more than the principal in railway fare alone to get the bond renewed."

"But he pays interest," he said.

"Give me the bond. I will pay the amount and you stay on." I felt desolate at the thought of his going away. At various times I went out on journeys short and long. Each time I just abandoned the house and returned home weeks and months later to find even a scrap of paper in the wastebasket preserved with care. Now I felt desolate.

He brushed aside my economic arguments. "You don't know these things. I can always go to a court as long as the bond is there . . ."

"And involve yourself in further expenses? It will be cheaper to burn that bond of yours." He gave me up as a dense, impossible man whose economic notions were too elementary.

Next day and next again and again, I heard his steps on the stairs. "I will come back in ten days."

I said, "All right, all right, you have too many transactions and you have no peace of mind to do your duty here, and you don't care what happens to me. I have to change my plans for your sake, I suppose?"

All this was lost on him, it was gibberish as far as he was concerned. I was obsessed with flimsy, impalpable things while the solid, foursquare realities of the earth were really sheep and tailors and bonds. He stared at me pityingly for a moment as at an uncomprehending fool, turned, and went downstairs. The next few days I found him sulking. He answered me sharply whenever I spoke to him. He never watered the plants. He ignored the lady next door. More than all, he did not light the fire, as was his custom, in the shade of the pomegranate shrub. He had taken off the red bandanna and hooded an old blanket over his head as he sat in a corner of the basement room, in a state of mourning. When I went out or came in, he emerged from the basement and opened the gate dutifully. But no word passed between us. Once I tried to draw him into a conversation by asking breezily, "Did you hear that they are opening a new store over there?"

"I go nowhere and seek no company. Why should you think I go about, gossiping about shops and things? None of my business."

Another day I asked, "Did anyone telephone?"

"Wouldn't I mention it if there had been telepoon?" he replied, glaring at me, and withdrew mumbling, "If you have no trust in me, send me away. Why should I lie that there was no telepoon if there was one? I am not a rascal. I am also a respectable farmer;

send me away." He looked like someone else under his grey hood; his angry eyes peered at me with hostility. It seemed as if he had propped himself up with an effort all these years but now was suddenly falling to pieces.

A week later, one morning I heard a sound at the gate, noticed him standing outside, his tin trunk and a gunny sack stuffed with odds and ends on the ground at his feet. He wore a dark coat which he had preserved for occasions, a white dhoti, and a neat turban on his head. He was nearly unrecognizable in this garb. He said, "I am going by the eight-o'clock train today. Here is the key of the basement room." He then threw open the lid of his trunk and said, "See if I have stolen anything of yours, but that lady calls me a fowl-thief. I am not a rascal."

"Why do you have to go away like this? Is this how you should leave after fifteen years of service?" I asked.

He merely said, "I am not well. I don't want to die in this house and bring it a bad name. Let me go home and die. There they will put new clothes and a fresh garland on my corpse and carry it in a procession along all the streets of our village with a band. Whereas if I am dead in that basement room while you are away, I will rot there till the municipal scavengers cart me away with the garbage heap. Let me not bring this house an evil reputation. I will go home and die. All the garden tools are in that room. Count them if you like. I am not a thief." He waited for me to inspect his trunk.

I said, "Shut it, I don't have to search your trunk." He hoisted it on his head and placed over it the gunny bundle and was starting off.

"Wait," I said.

"Why?" he asked without stopping, without turning.

"I want to give you—" I began, and dashed in to fetch some money. When I returned with ten rupees, he was gone.

The Shelter

The rain came down suddenly. The only shelter he could run to was the banyan tree on the roadside, with its huge trunk and the spreading boughs above. He watched, with detachment, the rain patter down with occasional sprays coming in his direction. He watched idly a mongrel trotting off, his coat completely wet, and a couple of buffaloes on the roadside eating cast-off banana leaves. He suddenly became aware of another person standing under the tree, beyond the curve of the tree trunk. A faint scent of flower wafted towards him, and he could not contain his curiosity; he edged along the tree trunk, and suddenly found himself face to face with her. His first reaction was to let out a loud "Oh!" and he looked miserable and confused. The lady saw him and suppressed a scream. When he had recovered his composure, he said, "Don't worry, I will go away." It seemed a silly thing to say to one's wife after a long separation. He moved back to his previous spot away from her. But presently he came back to ask, "What brought you here?"

He feared she might not reply, but she said, "Rain." "Oh!" He tried to treat it as a joke and please her by laughing. "It brought me also here," he said, feeling idiotic. She said nothing in reply. The weather being an ever-obliging topic, he tried to cling to it desperately and said, "Unexpected rain." She gave no response to his remark and looked away. He tried to drag on the subject further. "If I had had the slightest suspicion of its coming, I would have stayed indoors or brought my umbrella." She ignored his statement completely. She might be deaf for all it mattered. He wanted to ask, Are your ears affected? but feared that she might feel irritated. She was capable of doing anything when upset. He had never suspected the strength of her feelings until that night of final crisis.

They had had several crises in their years of married life. Every other hour they expressed differing views on everything under the sun: every question precipitated a crisis, none too trivial to be ignored. It might be anything—whether to listen to Radio Ceylon or All India Radio, whether one should see an English picture or a Tamil one, whether jasmine smell might be termed too strong or otherwise, a rose could be termed gaudy or not, and so forth. Anything led to an argument and created tension, and effected a breach between the partners for a number of days, to be followed by a reconciliation and an excessive friendliness. In one such mood of reconciliation they had even drawn an instrument of friendship with elaborate clauses, and signed it before the gods in the puja room with a feeling that nothing would bother them again and that all their troubles were at an end. But it was short-lived and the very first clause of the contract, "We shall never quarrel hereafter," was the first to be broken within twenty-four hours of signing the deed, and all the other clauses, which covered such possible causes of difference as household expenses, criticism of food, budget discussions, references to in-laws (on all of which elaborate understanding had been evolved), did not mean anything.

Now standing in the rain he felt happy that she was cornered. He had had no news of her after he had shut the door on her that night as it seemed so long ago. They had argued over the food as usual, she threatened to leave the home, and he said, "Go ahead," and held the door open while she had walked out into the night. He left the door unbolted for a long time in the belief that she would return, but she didn't.

"I didn't hope to see you again," he ventured to say now and she answered, "Did you think I would go and drown myself?"

"Yes, that I feared," he said.

"Did you look for me in the nearby wells, or ponds?"

"Or the river?" he added. "I didn't."

"It would have surprised me if you had had so much concern."

He said, "You didn't drown yourself after all, how could you blame me for not looking for you?" He appealed to her pathetically. She nearly stamped her foot as she said, "That only shows you have no heart."

"You are very unreasonable," he said.

"Oh, God, you have started giving a reading of my character. It is my ill fate that the rain should have come down just now and driven me over here."

"On the contrary, I think it is a good rain. It has brought us together. May I now ask what you have been doing with yourself all this time?"

"Should I answer?" He detected in her voice a certain amount of concern and he felt flattered. Could he induce her to come back to him? The sentence almost formed itself on the tip of his tongue but he thrust it back. He merely asked, "Aren't you concerned with my own lot? Don't you care to know what I have been doing with myself all these months?" She didn't reply. She simply watched the rain pouring down more than ever. The wind's direction suddenly changed and a gust flung a spray of water on her face. He treated it as an excuse to dash up to her with his kerchief. She recoiled from his approach. "Don't bother about me," she cried.

"You are getting wet. . . ." A bough above shook a few drops on her hair. He pointed his finger at her anxiously and said, "You are getting drenched unnecessarily. You could move down a little this way. If you like I will stand where you are." He expected her to be touched by this solicitude. She merely replied, "You need not worry about me." She stood grimly looking at the rain as it churned up the road. "Shall I dash up and bring an umbrella or a taxi?" he asked. She merely glared at him and turned away. He said something else on the same lines and she asked, "Am I your toy?"

"Why do you say toy? I said no such thing."

"You think you can pick me up when you like and throw me out when you feel that way. Only toys are treated thus."

"I never told you to go away," he said.

"I am not listening to any of that again," she said.

"I am probably dying to say how sorry I am," he began.

"May be, but go and say that to someone else."

"I have no one else to say such things to," he said.

"That is your trouble, is it?" she asked. "That doesn't interest me."

"Have you no heart?" he pleaded. "When I say I am sorry, believe me. I am changed now."

"So am I," she said. "I am not my old self now. I expect nothing in others and I am never disappointed," she said.

"Won't you tell me what you are doing?" he pleaded. She shook her head. He said, "Someone said that you were doing harijan work or some such thing. See how I am following your activities!" She said nothing in reply. He asked, "Do you live all the time here or. . . ?" It was plain that he was trying to get her address. She threw a glance at the rain, and then looked at him sourly. He said, "Well, I didn't order the rain anyway. We have got to face it together."

"Not necessarily. Nothing can hold me thus," she said, and suddenly dashed into the rain and broke into a run. He cried after her, "Wait, wait. I promise not to talk. Come back, don't get drenched," but she was off, vanishing beyond the curtain of raindrops.

The Mute Companions

Other beggars had this advantage over him: they could ask for alms, while he could only make a sort of gurgling at the throat. And this gurgling had to serve him for expressing all his ideas, emotions, and appeals. His home was a corner of the Town Hall veranda.

One day, opening his eyes from a stupor, he saw a tiny monkey ransacking his bag, to which were sticking one or two grains of rice he had collected on the previous day.

Sami pretended to be asleep for a moment and then shot out his arm and gripped the monkey's waist, thus securing a companion, his only companion in life. He tied a piece of cord around the monkey's waist and taught him a number of tricks.

The monkey solved for him the problem of food. He performed his tricks in front of houses and earned for his master rice, edibles, and coins. The opening turn, usually, was a walk around, saluting the assembly, which invariably consisted of a boy, a girl carrying a baby, two other small children, and a grandmother; occasionally also the mother, and, very very rarely indeed, the master of the house. Sami was particular that the monkey should salute everyone assembled, including the young one in the girl's arms. If he omitted anyone he received a tug at his waist which made his teeth chatter. The next turn was the Dancer at the Temple. Other monkey-trainers usually introduced the trick with the question, How did the woman at the temple dance? But Sami merely tickled the monkey under the arm and winked. At this the monkey stood up with one hand on his waist and the other on his head and swayed his hips in a manner that would have done credit to any dancer in a temple. Sami noticed that his patrons said when they saw this, "Ah, really! It is a wonder how he has taught it all this though he is dumb!"

"I don't think he is really dumb. He must be pretending," the callous boy would say. And then they would all try to find out if he was really deaf and dumb by asking him his name and age or telling him point-blank that he was only pretending. At this stage the master of the house would appear on the scene with a scowl on his face. Sami would pick up his bag, staff, and monkey, and hurry away, contented with a handful of rice flung into the bag. There were occasions when he came across amiable patrons, and he held the performance for nearly one hour, exhibiting certain star turns: The Timid Girl Going Back to Her Mother-in-Law. Sami himself played the role of the irate mother-in-law, who, the moment the girl arrived, sent her out to fetch water from a deep well. And then the great Hanuman setting fire to the capital of the Demon King: the monkey would pick up his tail in his hand and prance about. Sami saw, by the laughter in their faces, that his patrons were pleased, and ventured to ask for a little cooked rice for the monkey, a little buttermilk, and sometimes even an old coat or shirt. The stout khaki coat he wore on his bare body had been given him by someone in that bungalow beyond the big shop as a reward for the mother-in-law turn; and the same turn earned him at another place the dark turban on his head.

In the evening he returned to the Town Hall with the monkey serenely riding on his shoulder, and lay down in the corner of the veranda with the monkey snuggling close to him.

There were certain codes of conduct which he expected the monkey to observe. For instance, he never liked his monkey to carry away anything from a house, not even a pebble. Several times the monkey was made to go back and put the stone in its place; and again Sami was very strict in regard to the monkey's behaviour in a front garden: he was never allowed to touch any leaf or flower or even the flower pots. Sami felt that his very existence depended on the behaviour of the monkey.

Thus they spent three years. Three years is a long time when we remember that every second of those three years they were together they worked, ate, and slept together. Well might this companionship have lasted a lifetime but for a very slight temptation that came the monkey's way.

One day Sami was going up the drive of one of those big bungalows. It was only a sporting mood that made him enter the gate. Usually he avoided those big places where people were haughty, aloof, and inaccessible, and kept formidable dogs and servants. He went up hesitatingly, expecting to be shouted off any moment, when he saw a servant coming towards him. Sami held the monkey tight and turned to flee, but the servant caught up with him and poured out a volley of words. Sami indicated that he could not hear, whereupon the servant explained by signs that the master of the house wanted the monkey to be brought to his presence.

He was invited to come up the front steps and hold the show on the veranda. The show was held for the exclusive pleasure of a little boy who lay on a couch amidst pillows, covered with a green shawl. As he watched the monkey perform, his waxen face lit up with life, and he took his medicine and food without a protest. The master of the house beamed on all those assembled. Sami felt he had discovered a treasure house.

The monkey was performing for the third time the turn of The Sweets-Seller Balancing a Tray on His Head. All eyes were on him. The monkey saw on a side table a dish containing a slice of bread and some fruit. Overpowered by this vision, he suddenly darted forward, grabbed the slice of bread, and knocked down a medicine bottle and a flower vase. Instantly there was confusion. Sami, blind with rage, jumped forward to catch the monkey, and knocked down the furniture and very nearly tumbled over the delicate patient. Strong arms gripped him and dragged him down the veranda steps. He turned and saw his monkey sitting on top of a pillar, enjoying his slice of bread. Everyone scowled at Sami and shook his fists at him. They behaved as though they had just saved the little patient from a serious mishap wilfully designed by Sami. He desperately tried to explain that he had had no designs on the boy but only wanted to get the monkey. "Send him out," cried the master of the house. "He is frightening the child. This excitement won't do for him. It is going to take weeks for him to get over this shock. Take him away, the devil!" The servants pushed Sami out. He resisted. He wanted to ask, Where is my monkey? Where is my monkey? But he could only make wild gestures and gurgle, and they thought he was menacing them. They pushed him down the drive, towards the gate. He turned, and just saw his monkey sitting on the tiled roof. He fell at their feet and cringed and begged them to let him call back his monkey. They relented. He stood below the tile and looked up, and by gesture implored the monkey to come down. The monkey looked at his master patronizingly, munching the slice of bread. He didn't understand what his master was saying. He couldn't make out whether he was going to be forgiven or punished if he returned. In any case, he was not thinking of returning. He liked his freedom. It was exhilarating to be able to run about, having lived at the end of a yard-long cord for three years. He merely turned round, walked up the tiles, and put himself through a ventilator which opened into the house. His waist cord lay outside for a moment and then crawled in like a snake and disappeared.

Day after day Sami waited at his corner in the Town Hall hoping that his monkey would come back to him, just as he had come to him on the very first day. Day after day he stood at the gate of the bungalow intently gazing at the ventilator, the roofs, and the trees. The servants chased him away when they noticed him. One day he fell at their feet and begged them to tell him what had happened to the monkey. They replied that they didn't know. Sami believed that after it had gone through the ventilator it was caught and kept in the house.

After waiting for a few weeks he resigned himself to the loss and returned to his old precarious existence—on alms which he could not demand.

At the Portal

If I missed attending a certain committee meeting that evening it was purely unintentional. No doubt, according to my promise to the convener I set out for the meeting hall. The meeting was at five-thirty in the afternoon, but at five-thirty when I turned the university corner I was held up by a couple of squirrels. One might legitimately ask how an adult could ever allow his plans to be diverted by a couple of squirrels, but I still think if there ever was an occasion for an adult to waive all other engagements it was this.

One was the mother and the other a callow youth, ten days old, probably on his second day's outing; the young squirrel had an excessively long bushy tail out of all proportion to his short tiny body, and moved about jerkily. They were going home, which was on the other side of the university wall, probably a niche in the veranda roof of the Registrar's office. The squirrel-home was to be reached through a decorative porthole in the wall at about a height of two feet. But the trouble was the youngster could not reach it. While the mother could jump right from the road on through the gap and pass through, the young one could not do anything more than run to the foot of the wall and look up.

The mother hopped up and, presuming that she was being followed, jumped down on the other side and disappeared. The young one did no more than stand on his hind legs and paw the wall and speculate on the immensity of the fortress obstructing his passage. He stood poised, hoping for a miracle to happen and carry him on to the other side of the wall. This was a very un-squirrel-like attitude to take in life. Presently the mother returned, appearing on the ledge above him. Her tail fluttered lightly, and there was complete astonishment in her look. She looked down, paused for a moment, bit her lip (a truly Disneyan character, and now one could agree with Oscar Wilde when he said Nature imitates Art), and asked, "Still there?" The young one said, "I can't follow you. You climb so high and go off. I can't reach that place."

"Oh!" said the mother, completely surprised. She came down, delivered a couple of licks, murmuring, "Now, now, follow me. It is really not so high. Just a little effort and we will be home. Come on," and she sprang up on the ledge and went out of sight again. The little one made a futile attempt to imitate his mother, fell back, shook off the mud on his coat, and looked about to see who was watching. A slight annoyance came over him at this stage: Mother seemed to think everyone could run about as she did. The mother reappeared and said, "Not made up your mind to come home yet? It will be dark soon." She did not wish to exhibit the anxiety that was coming over her. The sun was about to set and they had to get home soon. She came down, gave a pat and a stroke, and said cheerfully, "Take a deep breath like this. You need not hop up right from zero as I do, though you will do it soon. Take a dozen paces back as I am doing." The young one followed her instructions closely. "And now take it in a run and heave yourself up as I am doing . . ." and soon the mother got out of view again. The young one followed all her instructions except to the extent of reaching the edge of the porthole; he scraped the lime, dropped back, and crouched beside the wall. He knew that his mother would come up presently with a fresh set of instructions. When his mother appeared above him he was so sick of the whole business that he would not look up. His mother cried, "Do you want to stay out tonight?" The young one replied sullenly, without looking up, "I can't help it, I have got to be here, I suppose." The mother grew alarmed. Dusk was falling, an owl was hooting somewhere, some unknown birds or bats were wheeling about, and the deadly crows were returning to their nests—not a safe hour. The mother stood against the wall stock-still till the enemies got out of range; the young one followed her example and stuck close to her. The mother gently pushed him away, saying, "This can't be a lasting solution. You have got to make an honest attempt. I know you can. See, it is so easy." She took a few steps back, took a run, hopped up, came back to the young one, and said, "See how easy it is! I know you can do it. It is not that you can't, only you lack self-confidence. Come on . . ." And she demonstrated. "It is like this. Not like this. Like this. Not like this . . . See . . ." She went up and down a dozen times and the young one attempted to follow her, but every time fell back. Now both of them lay still, panting. The mother bit him on the ear slightly. Her exertions seemed to have given an edge to her temper. "What has come over you?" she asked. The other said tearfully, "Don't leave me here, Mother."

"I don't want to, but . . . but we must not be here now." The young one made a few more attempts, and the mother repeated her demonstrations. It was very tiring. Finally the mother said, "I can't be proud of you. At your age we were . . ." Mother's presence brought back a little liveliness in the young one, and he scampered around unnecessarily, jumping about to no purpose. His attitude showed he was still not aware of the seriousness of their position. He did not realize that it was really a race with time; darkness would be on them in a few moments, and they would not know their way about. The mother said, with real anxiety in her voice, "We ought not to be here any more. See those school youngsters returning from the playground; they will stone us, and there is a dog barking somewhere. This is a very unsafe world. We must go away immediately." The mother again demonstrated, and the young one executed more or less a caricature of her. The mother's patience was at an end now. She appeared for the last time at the porthole and demanded, "Are you coming home or not?"

The young one was in an irresponsible mood and said, "Not unless you carry me as you did that day."

"That day is not this day," said the mother. "If you were young enough to be rolled up and carried between my jaws, I wouldn't wait for your suggestion."

"Then I can't jump up. I am not coming," said the other one.

"Idiot, you don't know what you are in for. Come along quietly. The whole world has retired, we alone are awake and our enemies are about us. Come up quietly."

"I can't, Mother, don't you see . . ." The mother did not wait to hear the full sentence. She quietly turned round, jumped down on the other side, and vanished, pausing only for a split second to say, "After all, God is above. If you are destined to see the morrow you will see it, that is all. What can I or anyone do for you?"

The young one waited, anxiously listening for the footfalls of his mother. Darkness came on. He felt nervous. He was genuinely frightened. He then made several attempts to reach the hole, practising all the tips his mother had given, but it was no use. He was completely fatigued and lay still. Watching him, I felt here was an occasion for me to address an appeal to the university authorities to reduce the height of portholes on their compound walls. I really wished I could help him through. Presently he did the wisest thing under the circumstances. He suddenly left off all effort, made a dash for the nearest avenue tree, and got on to it. From this height, he emitted a couple of calls for his mother, but that Spartan mother did not respond.

I saw by my watch that this episode had gone for exactly an hour and a quarter.

The convener of the meeting said when he saw me next, "You disappointed us again."

"I couldn't really help it this time," and then I used a very convenient phrase: "I was busy—unexpectedly . . ."

Four Rupees

Ranga was never certain what he was going to do next. He set out of his little home in Kabir Lane, and by the time he turned the corner at Market Road, he always found some odd job coming his way. Today a very peculiar task offered itself as he sat near the Market Fountain. A servant from a bungalow in the extension was going round with a searching look in his eyes. He explained, "Our brass pot has fallen into the well. Do you know anyone who can get into the well and bring it out?"

"What will they pay for it?"

"What will you want for the job?"

"I must see the well first, and I can't think of anything less than two rupees," he said.

"Yes, follow me," the other said, and Ranga was astounded. He never thought that his offer would be accepted. He had never gone down a well before. He tried to excuse himself now. But the other would not let him go. He almost gripped him by the wrist and dragged him along. He went protesting. "I don't know anything about wells," he cried. "Oh, don't say that, see the well first," said the servant, and clung to him. He added, "They have made life a hell for me for four days now. They will dismiss me if I don't do anything about it today."

"But I know nothing about wells."

"Hush! None of it with me," admonished the old servant, and smiled significantly. "If you want an anna or two more, ask for it, don't try these tricks."

"But, but," Ranga faltered, but the other offered him a beedi to smoke and silenced him. Ranga followed him resigned to his fate.

At the extension bungalow they were at the gate: the master, his wife, and two boys. At the sight of the servant they cried, "Have you found anyone?"

"Here he is," the servant said, pointing at Ranga. Ranga shuddered and looked about helplessly. The master said, "A brass vessel has fallen into the well. You must take it out."

"How can I, Master?" replied Ranga. The servant interposed at this stage and added, "You leave it to me, Master. He will do it." At this the master felt that here was a deep diplomatic game being played, and merely said, "All right, all right, first see the well." They took him to the backyard. The master and the rest treated him with such consideration that he slowly began to enjoy the importance given to him. All of them surrounded him and explained how it happened. Ranga listened gravely and declared, "The rope must have been worn out." They received this information with such a whoop of approval that Ranga began to feel he had made some pronouncement of profound significance. They then told him of the history of the vessel: how it was an heirloom, given on the occasion of a great-grandfather's marriage and handed from generation to generation. They looked severely at the old servant. The lady added, "This fool has always been warned not to touch that vessel and yet . . ."

"Only zinc pots must be used for drawing water from a well," said Ranga, like an expert speaking. A murmur of approbation went round. Ranga began to feel that he was an established "well-man."

They lifted the covering at the mouth of the well, and Ranga peeked in. His heart sank. Far beyond a great tunnel of rugged darkness a patch of water gleamed. "Seems to be a very deep well," Ranga said.

"Only sixty feet."

"We don't usually go into wells deeper than forty," Ranga said.

"If you want eight annas or so more we won't grudge it," they said.

"You must pay me four rupees, otherwise I can't risk my life." After some haggling they agreed. Ranga's last hope of backing out now vanished. He had never earned four rupees in a lump, and this was attractive. He needn't seek any work for three days at least, and could silence for once his wife and mother-in-law. This looked like a fortune coming his way. But a peep into that sinister patch of water at the bottom of the well neutralized all the attraction four rupees held, and he felt like running away. He said, turning from the well with the air of a man turning from a satisfactory preliminary inspection, "Yes, it is all right. I will come back in the evening. I have to go home now."

"Why?"

He was unable to explain. He murmured that he hadn't eaten his food yet, at which they dragged him to a passage in the bungalow, put up a leaf before him, and served food. Before he knew where he was he had eaten a heavy meal. They stood around and encouraged him to eat more. They gave him betel leaves and areca nut and he chewed till his lips became blood-red. He felt he was an honoured guest in that house. But the obligations involved in this tormented his mind. Now he felt he was irrevocably committed to this expedition. They allowed him to rest for about half an hour and then summoned him to the well. He felt like a condemned man. He stood for a long time gazing into the bottom of the well. He made one final attempt to extricate himself: "I can't. I don't know . . ." "Don't say so," they protested. Ranga felt puzzled why these people were so bent upon seeing him drowned. He had a momentary impulse to dash away and escape. He glanced at those around him. They stood in a ring as if forming a cordon. He felt that if he attempted an escape, they might pick him up bodily and drop him into the well. There seemed to be no hope of escape. He took off his ragged shirt, tucked up his dhoti. He called for a rope, tied its end to the cross-bar of the well, and let the other end down into the well. He climbed the parapet, slid down the rope, and stretched out his legs to reach the foothold out into the sidewall. Thus he progressed downward. He dared not look below him. The air became warm and dark. He looked up—a blue circle of sky, a pipal seedling growing out of a cleft in the cross-bar, and the hazy faces looking at him from the top. "Be careful," someone cried. "Why are you hesitating?" "Let me come up. I can't go down . . ." They cajoled him again and increased his remuneration by a few annas. "You are half-way down already . . ."

"If I don't come up again, please tell my wife . . ." They burst into a laugh on hearing this. He felt so helpless that he said to himself: There is no way out. Let me die. He briskly went down. It became darker and more eerie at every step. His ears grew dull and he felt a heaviness at his chest. His eyes dimmed and he was only partly conscious when he reached the last foothold. His brain kept drumming, Four rupees, four rupees. I am dying, he kept saying to himself. Or am I dead? Ice-cold water lapped his feet. He bent down precariously and took a handful of water and drank it. He then dived into the water muttering, "Four rupees, four rupees." His fingers combed the sandy bed and finally clutched a piece of rope. He dragged it up, and attached to it was the brass pot.

It was a greater adventure going up. They had to haul him up. He lay prone on the ground for nearly an hour. When he awoke they said, "You are a good fellow. We will call you again if anything drops into the well. Where do you live?" He refused to say where he lived. "Give me my wages, let me go." They gave him four rupees and four annas. He looked at it and pleaded, "You promised four rupees and twelve annas, Master." They grew indignant on hearing this. "Is there no limit to your avarice? After all, the vessel costs much less. We have given you food and everything. Go, go. Learn contentment. . . ."

"You can never satisfy 'well-men.' They are like this everywhere," someone added.

When Ranga went home, his wife and mother-in-law were, as usual, at the door. On seeing him his wife snarled, "It is seven o'clock. When am I to buy the things and cook the food? You think I am born to slave. It will be a fine lesson if you are made to do without a meal tonight. . . ." He flourished his four rupees and four annas. "Four rupees! Are you sure you didn't steal it?" He explained, showing the bruises on his elbows and knees. They just laughed and replied, "Never knew you to go near a well; more likely you have been in a scrape and pulled the money out of somebody's pocket. . . ."

Flavour of Coconut

It was a formidable gathering of accusers. People seemed only too ready to pick up and throw just another pebble at one who was already down. The walls of the prison were hemming him in, the bars seemed to be fixed in molten lead. This was both a dock and a prison. The trial was summary, because the times were dangerous. The distinction between prison and dock was a luxury for other prisoners—not for this dangerous creature. He looked up at the faces around, possibly for a sign of hope. The judge, grey-haired and bespectacled, would not betray anything in his face. His mind seemed to be preoccupied with some unfinished work; he looked as though he had been interrupted while doing some more worthwhile job. He had a pen over his ear; any moment he might snatch it and dash off the death sentence. He looked at the prisoner coldly. It was impossible to guess what he had on his mind. Of course, not to be unfair, he looked quite dignified and authoritative and anxious. But he seemed at the same time unduly eager not to displease the prosecution. Though left to himself he seemed to be the sort of judge who would unlock the fetters and cry to the prisoner: "Get out, and let me not catch you again—" But that was just a wishful fancy in the prisoner's fevered mind. It was impossible to guess how a judge would act. The jury looked too grim and behaved queerly. Sometimes they too joined the prosecution vociferously—a most irregular procedure. It was impossible to say who was the prosecutor and who the jury. It looked as though the whole thing was going to be settled by the prosecution alone without so much as a word of defence. Defence? Perhaps there was nothing to defend. The prisoner himself was incapable of doing anything but roll his eyes, which were large and round—they seemed to be made for it. His face looked woebegone. He tried not to show any emotion; only the ends of his whiskers trembled. Someone among his tormentors remarked derisively, "Whiskers? Oh, whiskers for such a puny fellow! Seems to possess whiskers longer than his body!" The prisoner could not mind this raillery. This was not the occasion to weigh the finer points of conduct. More serious things claimed his attention: they were cataloguing their charges against him. The charges were goodly both in number and kind. The prosecutors were clamant and spoke simultaneously, till the judge said, "Hush! Hush! Not so much noise. One at a time. It's not necessary for everyone to talk at once." This was the only good act that the judge seemed capable of doing if one could read anything in it—but this was no time for conjectures. The prisoner had to know definitely one thing—whether they were going to set him free or put an end to him. The suspense was unbearable. Their talk was not encouraging. They spoke of capital punishment as easily as if they were asking someone to leave the room. The death sentence seemed to be a fair certainty. It could not be otherwise. The charges were serious. The prisoner was an antisocial element. His movements were secretive. He came out only in the dark. He was given to looting and dacoity, sabotage and destruction. On the whole a horrible record. The junior-most member of the assembly suddenly felt that he ought to put in a word for mitigation. He ventured to suggest transportation for life instead of capital punishment. The judge sneered, "Transportation! Why?" The defence blinked. The judge added, "So that he may carry on his depredations elsewhere, I suppose!" People were silenced by the grimness of His Lordship's manner. He demanded further, "Even if he is taken away, how are you to make sure that he won't sneak back?"

The subject of all this discussion, as one ought to have guessed by now, was a little mouse who had walked into a trap a moment ago. They had been looking for him for months. Till this moment he had remained practically invisible. Only his movements disturbed the household at night. He rattled the vessels and made so much noise that people often woke up in a fright thinking that a burglar had entered the house. When a plague broke out in the town they became panic-stricken. Whenever they heard vessels clatter in the store-room, they trembled as if they had a time bomb in the house. They dreaded lest this unseen enemy should bring the plague into their house and wipe out the family. The worst of it was that he seemed to know all about exterminating and kept away whenever men from the health department arrived with their apparatus; and when the poison had evaporated he came back, easily passing through any kind of rat-proof floor. They became desperate when they saw how clever and invincible he was. He was like a chess expert, countering their moves all the time.

They tried to tempt him into a trap, baited with onion coated with ghee. He deftly nibbled the outer layers of the onion without disturbing the trigger. They wrung their hands in despair. A rat that was so nimble and sophisticated might destroy mankind itself. It might nibble away at the family some day while it slept. In fact, the enemy seemed to have attempted it. Their eldest son complained one night that something had bitten into his left sole; they saw tooth marks and the doctor immediately ordered a dozen injections costing one hundred and twenty rupees. This boy never forgot the pain of injections and was determined to rid the house of the pest. The ravages in the kitchen continued unabated. The lady of the house was in tears. She looked reproachfully at the entire family and cried, "Can you do nothing about it? Is everyone so useless?" From this she drifted on to related subjects and vehemently denounced food control, ration shops, milkmen, and vegetable vendors. She ended up with a warning that if they did not have their wits about they would all have to starve presently.

The climax came one day when the schoolgirl discovered the voile sari she had put out to dry punctured in four places. Beside this all his other crimes appeared insignificant. One could understand his voraciousness for food, but why should he bite the voile? Sheer devilry! And bought only four days before. The girl was distraught. She was very fond of that sari and every other day she washed it daintily with soap-flakes and put it out to dry on a frame, with her own hands. Unfortunately the frame was placed in the shade outside the store-room window, and presently they found the sari sliced off in four places. The schoolgirl wept for hours; her father, who was very fond of her, ground his teeth in helpless anger and swore vengeance. Her mother felt depressed. The only one who remained unmoved was the youngest son, Ramu, who had one day found his arithmetic book trimmed at the edges and appreciated it as a favour. He told his sister, "You probably tore your sari over a nail, and now blame everything on that poor rat. People blame that rat for everything that happens in this house nowadays. Who knows, there is perhaps no rat at all!"

They looked sourly at their tom-cat curling in a corner. The mother said, "What is the use of pampering this loutish beast?"

"Why do you abuse the cat?" demanded the boy.

"A cat must do its duty. . . . What's a cat for unless it catches rats? This thing seems to be afraid of rats—never goes near one—eats a seer of rice and ghee and milk! What's come over even cats these days! In the old days, I remember, if there was a cat anywhere . . ."

"Probably it wants to be kind to rats, and has also a better taste than other cats," said the boy indignantly.

Someone with profound rodent knowledge suggested that they hold a slice of coconut over fire, roast it slightly, and then use it as bait: its flavour would prove irresistible. He added: "You will have the rat tumbling in, even if he is away in Delhi." Nobody understood why he mentioned Delhi, but they accepted the statement because it sounded nice. This expert also advised them to camouflage the trap with a gunny sack. They followed his instructions and waited anxiously. Nothing happened for hours and hours. And then at about eight in the morning they heard a noise like the report of a rifle-shot. At the same moment several voices went up in a shout from different parts of the house: "The trap has shut!" And at once Mother, who had been circumambulating the tulasi plant in the backyard, left off her worship and came hurrying to the store-room. The schoolgirl, who had been doing her homework in her room, dropped her pen. The eldest son of the house, whose mind was worrying about the B.A. examination but whose fingers were selecting the bush-coat to go with his copper-coloured corduroy trousers, came running. Father, who was just filling his income-tax form, stuck the pen over his ear and hurried to the spot. They brought the cage out of its folds of gunny and there he was, the tiniest mouse, who could hardly be seen as he shrunk away from all the glare of publicity into a corner; he was the very picture of regret—a most carefully planned and guarded existence coming to an end through the flavour of burnt coconut. "He looks like Mickey Mouse!" admired the youngster, falling on his knees and peering in. "Mickey Mouse!" cried his elder brother, and gave out voluble statistics: one hundred thousand tons of grain were lost each day through depredation of rats; twenty thousand bales of cloth and miscellaneous merchandise per week were cut to ribbons by this creature crouching there; and then every fourth person in the subcontinent was in danger of dying of rat bite or of the plague germs it carried. They were astounded at the amount of knowledge the young man displayed. Father was impressed with it. He remembered the wail of his favourite daughter when her voile was bitten into. He said, "Undoubtedly this is a national menace. There is no question of letting it go. Whatever people may say—" He spoke as if it were a matter of national defence. The youngest boy tried to put in a plea of defence. But they brushed him aside, and told him that he wouldn't be allowed to make any further representations on behalf of the prisoner. They stood gravely around for a moment. Father pushed the pen up and down over his ear, adjusted his spectacles, and cleared his throat before delivering the judgment. He said, "Tell the servant to take it to the backyard and drown it in a bucket of water." He looked very grim when he said this. And he immediately left the court. The others dispersed. The little boy wondered if he ought to open the cage and release the prisoner, but his brother stood over him and watched him with suspicion. The little boy scrambled to his feet when he heard footsteps in the corridor. He knew that the servant was coming to take the trap to the execution yard, and wondered for a second whether he should not run away from this sad spectacle, but he was overcome with a morbid curiosity, and followed the servant mutely as the rat trap was picked up and taken out.

Fruition at Forty

Rama Rao obtained his officer's permission to absent himself on the following day. "Happy returns," exclaimed his officer. "Honestly, I did not think you were forty!"

Walking down the road to the bus stand, Rama Rao paused for a minute to view himself in a large mirror that blocked the entrance to a hair-cutting establishment. I don't look forty, he told himself, and passed on.

When he left home he had not known that it was the eve of his birthday. It was while drafting an office note that he realized that the 14th of April was ahead. As a rule they never fussed over birthdays at home, but this was a special event: crossing the fortieth milestone seemed to be an extremely significant affair, which deserved to be marked down with feasting and holiday.

At Parry's Corner he struggled into a bus and hung on to a strap. Good thing we were monkeys once, he reflected. Otherwise how could we perform our clinging and hanging down; exactly the operations of a monkey, the only difference being that they get on smoothly in a herd while we— The conductor had tried to push him out, somebody squeezed his side and scowled at him, and someone was repeatedly trying to stand on his toes, and the driver was pleased to rattle the passengers to their bones by stopping and starting with fierce jerks. Rama Rao wriggled through and fought his way out when the bus stopped at Central Station. He walked down to Moore Market for a little shopping. Nobody at home knew of his birthday. He would surprise them with gifts: printed silk pieces, coloured ribbons, building blocks, and sweets.

It would be such a novelty, giving gifts instead of receiving. He must also buy vegetables and provisions for a modest feast. It was going to be a quiet family party—and if the children were disinclined to go to school he would not force them.

He went round the Moore Market corridor, for a preliminary survey. Shall buy vegetables last, he told himself. He went into a cloth shop and demanded to be shown printed silk and selected three or four bits. The bill was made up. As he scrutinized the items his hand went into his pocket to bring out the purse. It was not in its place. He returned the package. He walked out of Moore Market, rambled aimlessly, his mind all in a boil. He sought a park bench and sat down, trying to recollect when he had last taken out his purse. Must have brushed against a pickpocket in the bus, he told himself. He felt depressed. He looked about: a mendicant was sleeping on another bench, some children were gleefully destroying a flower bed. Some pickpocket to deprive me of my fortieth birthday! He felt angry with the perverse fates which messed up and destroyed all one's plans.

People said forty was a man's best age. Everyone attained maturity of mind and body. A man's habits were fixed, his prejudices and favours were solidified once for all: all his human relationships were well defined and would be free from shocks and surprises. Rama Rao dwelt on these fruitions of forty and was filled with misgivings. What have I achieved at forty? I have lived sixteen years beyond the point marked by the statistician as the expectation of life for an Indian. I have completed three quarters of the longevity of my elders. What have I achieved? He brooded over it and answered. I have four children, the eldest reads in a college. The wife has all the jewellery she had asked for. I have risen to be the head of my section in the office . . . yet I live only in a rented house. The marriage of my daughter and the career of my son will have to be tackled by me within five years. Am I good for it? He was filled with consternation at being forty, at the duties that were definitely expected of him because he was supposed to have reached maturity. He beat his brow at this thought. He wondered if he had really changed. He cast his mind back. The earliest birthday he could remember was the one when his father had presented him with a glittering lace cap; then there was his twentieth birthday soon after his B.A., when he resolved he would not be this or that; it was a catalogue of "I won't this or that"—among them he could recollect only that he had resolved never to marry and never to take up any employment unless they offered him three hundred rupees for a start, some job which would put him on a swivel chair behind a glass door. And then his thirtieth birthday, when he was seized with panic as he realized that he was a father of three. He then believed that things would somehow be clear-cut and settled at forty. And now here he was. What was it going to be like at fifty or sixty? Things would remain just the same. If one did not worry about oneself one started worrying over children and grandchildren. Things did not change. Rama Rao did not feel that the person who was pleased with the gift of a lace cap was in any way different from the one who felt a thrill when the office communicated an increment. The being who felt the home-tutor's malicious grip now felt the same emotion when the officer called him up in a bad temper. Deep within he felt the same anxiety and timidity, and he wondered how his wife and children could ever look up to him for support at all. He suddenly felt that he had not been growing and changing. It was an illusion of his appearance caused by a change of dark hair into grey hair, and by the wearing of longer clothes. This realization brought to his mind a profound relief, and destroyed all notions of years; at the moment a birthday had no more significance and fixity than lines marked in the air with one's fingers. He decided not to mention to anyone at home that it was his birthday.

As he walked back home his mind was still worried about the purse. After all only twenty rupees and an old purse containing receipts, but his wife would get positively distracted if she heard of the loss. Last time when he could not account for five rupees after a shopping expedition she completely broke down. She must on no account be told of the present loss. He would keep her mind free and happy—that would be the birthday gift for her—keeping away from her the theft of the purse just as the purse itself was a gift to an unknown pickpocket.

He went home late, since he had to walk all the way. "Held up by unexpected business on the way," he explained. Next morning he went to his office as usual. "Your birthday over?" asked his chief. "Yes, sir, over earlier than I expected," he explained.

"Very good," said his officer. "I was hoping you would turn up for at least half a day, a lot of things to do." "I knew that, sir," Rama Rao said, going to his desk.

Crime and Punishment

"What is sixteen and three multiplied?" asked the teacher. The boy blinked. The teacher persisted, and the boy promptly answered: "Twenty-four," with, as it seemed to the teacher, a wicked smile on his lips. The boy evidently was trying to fool him and was being contrary on purpose. He had corrected this error repeatedly, and now the boy persisted in saying twenty-four. How could this fellow be made to obtain fifty in the class test and go up by double-promotion to the first form, as his parents fondly hoped? At the mention of "twenty-four" the teacher felt his blood rushing to his head. He controlled himself, and asked again: "How much?" as a last chance. When the boy obstinately said the same, he felt as if his finger were releasing the trigger: he reached across the table, and delivered a wholesome slap on the youngster's cheek. The boy gazed at him for a moment and then burst into tears. The teacher now regained his normal vision, felt appalled by his own action, and begged frantically: "Don't cry, little fellow, you mustn't. . . ."

"I will tell them," sobbed the boy.

"Oh, no, no, no," appealed the teacher. He looked about cautiously. Fortunately this nursery was at a little distance from the main building.

"I'll tell my mother," said the boy.

According to the parents, the boy was a little angel, all dimples, smiles, and sweetness—only wings lacking. He was their only child, they had abundant affection and ample money. They built a nursery, bought him expensive toys, fitted up miniature furniture sets, gave him a small pedal motor car to go about in all over the garden. They filled up his cupboard with all kinds of sweets and biscuits, and left it to his good sense to devour them moderately. They believed a great deal in leaving things that way.

"You must never set up any sort of contrariness or repression in the child's mind," declared the parents. "You'll damage him for life. It no doubt requires a lot of discipline on our part, but it is worth it," they declared primly. "We shall be bringing up a healthy citizen."

"Yes, yes," the teacher agreed outwardly, feeling more and more convinced every day that what the little fellow needed to make him a normal citizen was not cajoling—but an anna's worth of cane, for which he was prepared to advance the outlay. For the teacher it was a life of utter travail—the only relieving feature in the whole business was the thirty rupees they paid him on every first day. It took him in all three hours every evening—of which the first half an hour he had to listen to the child-psychology theories of the parents. The father had written a thesis on infant psychology for his M.A., and the lady had studied a great deal of it for her B.A. They lectured to him every day on their theories, and he got more and more the feeling that they wanted him to deal with the boy as if he were made of thin glass. He had to pretend that he agreed with them, while his own private view was that he was in charge of a little gorilla.

Now the teacher did not know how to quieten the boy, who kept sobbing. He felt desperate. He told the youngster, "You must not cry for these trifling matters, you must be like a soldier. . . ."

"A soldier will shoot with a gun if he is hit," said the boy in reply. The teacher treated it as a joke and laughed artificially. The boy caught the infection and laughed, too. This eased the situation somewhat. "Go and wash your face," suggested the teacher—a fine blue porcelain closet was attached to the nursery. The boy disobeyed and commanded: "Close the lessons today." The teacher was aghast. "No, no," he cried.

"Then I will go and tell my mother," threatened the boy. He pushed the chair back and got up. The teacher rushed up to him and held him down. "My dear fellow, I'm to be here for another hour." The boy said: "All right, watch me put the engine on its rails."

"If your father comes in . . ." said the teacher.

"Tell him it is an engine lesson," said the boy, and he smiled maliciously. He went over to his cupboard, opened it, took out his train set, and started assembling the track. He wound the engine and put it down, and it went round and round. "You are the station master," proclaimed the boy. "No, no," cried the teacher. "You have your tests the day after tomorrow." The boy merely smiled in a superior way and repeated, "Will you be a station master or not?"

The teacher was annoyed. "I won't be a station master," he said defiantly, whereupon the young fellow said: "Oh, oh, is that what you say?" He gently touched his cheek, and murmured: "It is paining me here awfully, I must see my mother." He made a movement towards the door. The teacher watched him with a dull desperation. The boy's cheek was still red. So he said: "Don't, boy. You want me to be a station master? What shall I have to do?"

The boy directed, "When the train comes to your station, you must blow the whistle and cry, 'Engine Driver, stop the train. There are a lot of people today who have bought tickets.' "

The teacher hunched up in a corner and obeyed. He grew tired of the position and the game in thirty minutes, and got up, much to the displeasure of his pupil. Luckily for him the engine also suddenly refused to move. The boy handed it to him, as he went back to his seat, and said: "Repair it, sir." He turned it about in his hand and said: "I can't. I know nothing about it."

"It must go," said the boy firmly. The teacher felt desperate. He was absolutely non-mechanical. He could not turn the simplest screw if it was to save his life. The boy stamped his foot impatiently and waited like a tyrant. The teacher put it away definitely with: "I can't and I won't." The boy immediately switched on to another demand. "Tell me a story. . . ."

"You haven't done a sum. It is eight-thirty."

"I don't care for sums," said the boy. "Tell me a story."

"No. . . ."

The boy called, "Appa! Appa!"

"Why are you shouting like that for your father?"

"I have something to tell him, something important. . . ."

The teacher was obliged to begin the story of a bison and a tiger, and then he passed on to "Ali Baba and the Forty Thieves" and "Aladdin's Lamp." The boy listened, rapt, and ordered: "I want to hear the story of the bison again. It is good. . . ." The teacher was short of breath. He had done six hours of teaching at school during the day. "Tomorrow. I've lost all my breath. . . ."

"Oh! All right. I'll go and tell . . ." exclaimed the boy; he got up and started running all of a sudden towards the house, and the teacher started after him. The boy was too fast for him, wheeled about madly, and made the teacher run round the garden thrice. The teacher looked beaten. The boy took pity on him and stopped near the rose bush. But the moment he went up and tried to put his hand on him, the boy darted through and ran off. It was a hopeless pursuit; the boy enjoyed it immensely, laughing fiendishly. The teacher's face was flushed and he gasped uncomfortably. He felt a darkness swelling up around him. He sank down on the portico step.

At this moment Father and Mother emerged from the house. "What is the matter?" The teacher struggled up to his feet awkwardly. He was still panting badly and could not talk. He had already made up his mind that he would confess and take the consequence, rather than stand the blackmail by this boy. It seemed less forbidding to throw himself at the mercy of the elders. They looked inquiringly at the boy and asked: "Why have you been running in the garden at this hour?" The boy looked mischievously at the teacher. The teacher cleared his throat and said: "I will explain . . ." He was trying to find the words for his sentence. The father asked: "How's he preparing for his test in arithmetic . . . ?" On hearing the word "test" the boy's face fell; he unobtrusively slunk behind his parents and by look and gestures appealed to the teacher not to betray him. He looked so pathetic and desperate that the teacher replied: "Only please let him mug up the 16th table a little more. . . . He is all right. He will pull through." The boy looked relieved. The teacher saw his grateful face, felt confident that the boy would not give him up now, and said: "Good night, sir; we finished our lessons early, and I was just playing about with the child . . . something to keep up his spirits, you know."

Half a Rupee Worth

Subbiah sold rice at the market gate. In his shop you found, heaped in wicker baskets, all varieties: from pebbly coarse rice to Delhi Samba, white as jasmine and slender as a needle. His shop was stuffy and dark but he loved every inch of it. He loved the smell of gunny sack, of rice and husk, and he loved the warm feel of rice cascading into his baskets freshly arriving from the mill. Through good times and bad he flourished. There were days of drought when paddy didn't come up and the rice mills were silenced, when people looked hollow-eyed and half dead. But even then he never closed his shop. If he didn't find stuff for twenty baskets, he scoured the countryside and filled at least two baskets, and sold them. There were times when the harvest was so rich he could hardly accept a quarter of the grain that was offered, when it seemed a fool's business to be selling rice. If you sold rice all day and night you could not hope for a profit of even fifty rupees. They called it "depression in the trade." The God of Harvest was capricious. His bounty was as unacceptable as his parsimony. But Subbiah survived all ups and downs. Rice was in his blood. He had served as an unpaid apprentice when his father ruled. Those were days when Subbiah loathed the rice bags which hemmed him in at the shop; he longed for the crowded streets, cinemas, football matches, and wrestling tournaments, which he glimpsed through the crowded shop door. But his father more or less kept him chained to the shop and discouraged his outside interests: "Boys should be horsewhipped if they are not to become brigands." He practised this theory of child-training with such steadfastness that in due course the little man had no eyes or head for anything except rice and the market. When his father died he slid in so nicely that nobody noticed the difference. Most people thought that the old man was still there counting cash. Business prospered.

Subbiah kept tethered at the backyard of his home five prize cows and buffaloes whose milk, curd, and butter he and his wife and five children consumed day and night and then became rotund and balloonlike. He owned thirty acres of land in a nearby village, and visited it once a month to survey his possessions and make sure they were intact. He lent money at exorbitant rates of interest to desperate persons, and acquired dozens of houses through their default. He became swollen with money. He sent his children to a school, bought them brocaded caps and velvet coats, and paid a home-tutor to shout the lessons at the top of his voice every evening under a lamp in the hall. He loaded his wife with gold ornaments and draped her in gaudy Benares silk; he added on to his house two more stories and several halls and painted all the walls with a thick blue oil paint, and covered them with hundreds of pictures of the gods in gilt frames. All day he sat by his iron safe and kept shoving money into it, watching closely at the same time his assistants measuring out rice into gunny sacks; it was a completely satisfying and tranquil existence. There seemed no reason why it should not go on through eternity—the same set of activities and interests, going on and on, money piling up and rice coming in and going out, and then one or the other of his sons to acquire his shape and appearance and continue the family business. This seemed, for all practical purposes, a region beyond life, death, and change.

It might have continued thus but for the War. It seemed at first to be the end of civilization, but after the first shock, it proved not so unwelcome after all. His profits piled up as never before—Saigon and Burma ceased to send rice, and that meant the stock he held was worth its weight in gold. People flocked to his shop at all hours, and the door of the iron safe could hardly be pushed in. He bought the big house next door for a godown and then the next one and the next; and then bought a dozen more villages. . . . He loaded more gold on his wife and daughters and increased his own girth. War seemed, on the whole, a very beneficial force—till the introduction of Price and Food Control. For the first time in his life he was baffled and worried. He could not see how anyone had the right to say what he should sell and at what rate. He raved night and day to a set of his admiring friends and assistants: "Sircar, what do they know of this business? Let them content themselves with tax-collection, catching thieves, and putting up drains. What do they know of the rice business?" He felt happy when he heard someone say, "The Food Department is a hoax. The Government are making a mess of things." He agreed heartily and implored, "Can't some educated person like you represent to the Government? It's disgraceful."

He soon found that he could still survive under a new garb. By waiting before officials, and seeing people, and filling up forms, he was soon allowed to continue his business as a Fair Price Grain Depot. Still it seemed a poor substitute for his old trade. He groaned unhappily when he learnt that he had to surrender all the rice his peasants laboriously cultivated in his village fields. The whole thing seemed to him atrocious. "They have to fix the price for my produce! They have to give me permission to take what I myself produce!" The scheme seemed to him tyrannical. But he accepted the position without much outward protest. He slept little and lost the taste for food. All through the dark nights his mind dwelt on the problem. Finally a solution emerged. He cried to himself, I still have my rice in the fields, and I still have the bags in my godown. If I can't use my wits and keep my hands on these I might as well perish. After all, what does the Government want? To have things in nice shape on paper—that they shall have. It involved some intricate work, but it was worth it. He retained all the rice he wanted—for sale and personal use—but out of sight and out of paper. He had to give away a lot of money to people who were entitled to examine his stock and accounts, but he never grudged this investment. If he passed a ten-rupee currency note on such an occasion, it meant he had screened from prying eyes a thousand rupees worth of grain. When he thought it over, he realized that all controls and restrictions were really a boon. He reflected philosophically: "God arranges everything for the best." He distributed a few annas for charity twice a week, and broke a coconut at the temple on Fridays in appreciation of God's interest in his affairs. Gradually, with experience, as his technique developed and improved, he became a master of his situation. At his depot, he measured out rice with a deft hand, so that at the end of a day a considerable quantity accumulated which was nobody's, and then he delayed and opened and closed and reopened his shop in such a manner as to make people come to him several times before they could get any rice out of him: when they had money he had no stock, or when he had rice they had no money. By all this manipulation, he accumulated a vast quantity of rice every week; and then out of his village harvest only a small portion reached the Food Department. Very soon he converted one of his houses in a back street into a godown and there piled up rice bags from floor to ceiling. It was supposed to be a store of waste paper and rags, which he collected for the paper mills. "Something to eke out my meagre livelihood," he explained.

He never sold his rice except in small quantities, and to known customers. He took their cash in advance and told them to call later. He always threw in a doubt: "There was a person who had a little rice. I don't know if he still has it. Anyway, leave the cash with me." Sometimes, he returned the money with "Sorry, not available, the man said he had it, but you know how we can never count on these things nowadays—"

One evening, as he had just closed his shop and started out with the key in his pocket, a person halted before him and said, "Oh! You have closed—just my luck." Subbiah usually ignored people who spoke to him in the streets; he always avoided such encounters because people sought him for only one object—to ask for rice. He felt disgusted with all that clamour for rice. Why couldn't they eat maize or millet instead of asking for rice all day when it was not available? Most people could not afford to possess gold.

"I have other business now, no time to stop and talk," said Subbiah. He passed on unceremoniously. The other trotted behind him. He held him by the arm and cried: "You must open your shop and give me rice. I can't let you go." Subbiah was stopped by the fervour of the other's speech. "My two children are crying for food and my old mother is nearly on the point of collapse. They've been starving. My ration card was exhausted three days ago. I can't see them in that condition any more. . . .

Please somehow give me some rice. I have gone round and round the whole town today. . . . But I couldn't get a grain anywhere. At home they will be thinking I'm returning with something. They will . . . God knows what they'll do when they see me go back empty-handed."

"How much do you want?"

"Give me a seer. There are six mouths to feed at home."

Subbiah looked at him with disgust. "Why couldn't you've come earlier?"

"I had to go round in search of rice."

"How much have you?" The other held up a half-rupee coin. Subbiah looked at the coin with contempt. "You expect to get one seer of rice for this?"

"But it's three seers for a rupee, isn't it?"

"Don't talk of all that now. You will starve if you talk of controlled price and such nonsense." He felt enraged. People clung to silly notions even when they were starving. "If you have another eight annas, perhaps, you may get a seer," said Subbiah.

The other shook his head dolefully: "This is the end of the month, you see, this is all I've."

"You will get only half a seer—that's the price a man I know will demand."

"All right," the other said with resignation. "Better than nothing."

"Give the coin here," said Subbiah. He took the coin. "Don't follow me; that fellow is extraordinarily suspicious. He will say No the moment he sees anyone with me. You wait here, I will be back. But I can't promise. If he says No, it will be just your luck, that is all. Give me the coin."

He was gone with the eight annas and the other stood on the street corner. How long shall I have to be here? he wanted to ask as Subbiah's back was turned, but checked himself for fear of irritating him. The man now wished he had cleared the point, for three hours had gone by and yet there was no sign of Subbiah. The night had deepened, traffic thinned, and people were moving about like shadows. Silence descended on the town. The man began to mutter several times to himself, "Well, what has happened, where is he? Where has he gone? When am I to go home and cook the rice? The children, ah, the children." He turned and walked in the direction the other had gone—but that took him nowhere, because the other had pretended to go that way in order not to show where his secret godown was, but actually had turned and gone off in another direction. The man wandered up and down through the silent streets and went back to the main shop, hoping he might be there. He wasn't there either. The lock was still on the door, just as he had seen it before. He felt so puzzled that he wandered aimlessly a little longer, and then called at Subbiah's house. He knocked on the door. Subbiah's wife opened it, remarking on the other side, "You are so late today . . ." She checked herself when she saw the stranger. He asked, "Is Subbiah at home?"

"No. He hasn't come home at all." She looked very anxious. By six next morning they became nervous, and in that condition she could not help saying, "Have you looked for him at the other godown?"

"Where is it?" She had to tell, being the only person who knew its whereabouts. They started out. After wriggling through some bylanes, they came upon the building. The door was bolted inside. They knocked on it. But the house was constructed for safety from intruders, and even rats could not enter except in the right royal manner. Finally they had to break open the front ventilator, slip a boy through it, and then have the main door opened. A faint morning light came in through the broken ventilator. In a corner they saw an electric torch lying on the floor and then a half-rupee coin, and a little off a hand stuck out of a pile of fallen bags. At the inquest they said, "Death due to accidental toppling off of rice bags and suffocation."

The Antidote

His director was already at work on the set—the interior of an office with a large table in the middle and a revolving chair beyond it. Gopal, dressed as decreed in bush-coat and corduroy trousers and with his face painted, went up and did obeisance to the director. The director said, "Go up and take your position four paces from the chair; let us have a couple of rehearsals while the lights are being fixed."

"Yes, sir," said Gopal, going up to his spot. He had no idea what he was expected to do or why. This director was not in the habit of narrating the story to anyone. He took his actors shot by shot, just indicating to them their portion of work for the moment. If they put questions to him, he said, "Just do what I am telling you now, and don't get too curious." It was unnecessary for a puppet to do its own thinking.

Now this superman gently pushed Gopal towards the chair. "Sit down and . . . rest your right elbow on the table . . . that is right . . . look happy because you have just been through a satisfactory business deal. . . ." He surveyed Gopal's posture critically and said, "When that telephone rings, pick it up with your left hand and say . . . remember that you are not to clutch the telephone so desperately, hold it gently, and don't pay any attention to it until it has given three clear rings. A habitual telephone-user will never be in a hurry to take the receiver."

"Yes, sir, I understand," said Gopal.

"You will say into the telephone, 'Ramnarayan speaking. Oh! . . . Hallo . . . Is that so!' in a tone of great astonishment and shock."

"Then do I put down the telephone?" asked the actor.

"That you will know later. . . . This is all for this shot. Don't rush through your lines, speak naturally."

The telephone rang thrice. Gopal acted his part. It was rehearsed a dozen times before a microphone dangling from a cross-arm and moving up and down like the proverbial carrot before a donkey. Gopal delivered his lines with measured precision, yet something always seemed to go wrong. The sound recordist's assistant peeped in at the doorway and repeatedly implored, "Don't swallow the last syllable. Keep the level. Another monitor, if you don't mind." They didn't believe in recording a voice when it was fresh. They always liked it to go husky and inaudible with repetition.

Gopal went through his action and words again and again till he lost all sense of what he was saying or doing. Amidst cries of "Ready," "Start," "Cut," and "Another monitor, please," in various keys, the shot was at last taken. The director was satisfied and grudgingly admitted, "That is the best one can get out of you, I suppose." He added, "Don't shift your position. We are continuing the scene." He ordered the lights to be moved. He viewed the actor through the camera and said, "Don't let go the telephone receiver but you may relax your right arm a bit. Don't be so wooden. Be natural." He came away from the camera, stood before the table, looked critically at Gopal, and said, "Yes, now you have got it right. Only action, no dialogue for this shot."

The microphone on the cross-arm moved away. Gopal felt relieved. Thank God, no speech. I can go home early, I suppose. The director said, "Listen carefully to this. You remember your last dialogue line was 'Hallo . . . Is that so!' It is to be continued in action. You will pause for a tenth of a second, let the telephone drop from your hand, fall back in your chair, and let your head roll to the side ever so lightly."

"Why? Why, sir?" Gopal asked anxiously. This was the first time he was questioning the director's proposal. The director replied, "Because you have just heard shocking news on the phone."

"What is it, sir?" Gopal asked. "Don't bother about it. Don't waste your energy in putting unnecessary questions."

"This bad news makes me swoon?" Gopal asked, his heart palpitating with faint hope. "No," said the director emphatically. "You die on hearing it." He then went on to elaborate the details: how the telephone should slip down, where Gopal's head should strike, how much his arm should convulse, and so on. He approached Gopal's person and gently tapped his forehead. He treated him as lumber; he pushed his head back and rolled it side to side. "Why! You don't look happy!" the director remarked. Gopal hesitated to reply.

The director paused for a moment. Gopal hoped that he would read his thoughts. The director began, "Or would you rather . . ." Gopal waited on his words hopefully. This man was after all going to relent. The director completed his sentence with: ". . . fall on your face and spread out your arms?"

"In a swoon?" Gopal asked again. "No, completely dead. Your heart fails on hearing the bad news," said the director.

Gopal's hand involuntarily strayed near the region of his heart. It was still beating. He looked up at the director. The man stood over him ruthlessly, waiting for an answer. This fellow looks like Yama, Gopal thought. He will choke me if I don't die at his bidding. What a bother!

He asked pathetically, "Can't you change the story, sir?" There was a big lamp directly in front of him, scorching his face. Beyond that was a region of shadow in which a group of persons was assembled, watching him—executives, technicians, and light-shifters.

The director was aghast at his suggestion. "What do you mean? You just do what you are told."

"Certainly, sir. But this, this . . . I don't like."

"Who are you to say what you like or dislike?" asked the director haughtily. This man was ruthless as fate. Even hostile planets might relent occasionally, but this man with the kerchief around his throat was unbudging. He would throttle a baby for effect. He asked, "What is the matter with you, Gopal? Why are you talking absurd things today?"

"This is my birthday, sir," Gopal explained timidly.

"Wish you many happy returns," said the director promptly, and added, "What if it is your birthday?"

"Rather a peculiar birthday," explained Gopal. "This is my

forty-ninth birthday. Astrologers have often told me that I might not see this birthday, and if I lived to see this day I should have nothing more to worry about. . . . I have lived in secret terror of this day all my life. Whenever I saw my wife and children I used to be racked with the thought that I should probably be leaving them orphans. I came late today because we held some propitiatory rites at home for the planets, and we celebrated my survival this day with a feast. My astrologer has suggested that I do nothing unpleasant today, sir. I wish to treat it as a very auspicious day, sir."

The director was impressed. He turned to his assistant, who always shadowed him, carrying a portfolio under his arm, and commanded, "Fetch the story-writer." Presently the story-writer arrived, his lips red with the chewing of betel leaves. He was a successful story-writer who made a lot of money by dashing off plots for film producers. He laughed aloud on hearing of the problem created by the actor. He was not the angry type to feel upset at contrary suggestions. He declared, "Impossible to change the story. How can he refuse to die? I am busy."

He turned on his heel and started out. At the door he stopped to add, "Anyway, send for our boss and tell him about it."

The boss came running into the scene. He asked anxiously, "What is the trouble? What is it all about?"

Gopal sat in his chair unmoving; he was not allowed to shift his position even slightly; continuity would be spoilt otherwise. He felt stuffy. The big lamp scorched his face. They all stood around and looked at him as if he were a freak. Their faces were blurred beyond the shadows. All of them are my Yamas, Gopal thought. They are bent upon seeing me dead.

The boss came over to his table and asked, "Are you in your senses?" Gopal thought he might appeal to the other's box-office sentiment. He said, "People generally like to see happy things on the screen, sir. I have seen the public turn away from pictures which present scenes of death."

"Oh!" exclaimed the boss. He remained thoughtful and said, "You are wrong." He turned to the director and said, "Formerly no doubt the public liked to see only happy stuff. Today is different. I have statistics. Pictures with tragic incidents have grossed thirty per cent more than happy stories, if you take the figures of the last six months. It shows that the public likes to exercise sentiments of sympathy and pity. . . . No, I will not have the story tampered with on any account."

The director patted Gopal's back affectionately and said, "This is a brief shot. I won't take much time. Do make up your mind to cooperate." He adopted a mollifying tone. He was cajoling. But what did it matter? What was the use of cajoling if it was only to persuade a man to die cooperatively? Gopal felt that he was about to lose his job and see his family in the streets. He was wasting precious studio hours. More crowd had gathered to watch the sensational happening today.

The director asked softly, "Will you be prepared to go through this scene tomorrow at least?"

"Certainly, sir," Gopal said with relief. "I shall do whatever you may order tomorrow—even the funeral."

At this the assistant with a portfolio under his arm dashed forward and cried, "We have to finish this scene today. We are not getting this floor tomorrow. The other unit wants it for the palace set. They are only waiting for you to complete the scene in order to dismantle this set. They are already grumbling that we have delayed too long. They are already behind their schedule."

"This puny fellow with the portfolio holds my life in his hand. He won't even hear of a postponement of execution.'

The director retreated for a while into the outer darkness where the technicians were gathered. He spoke to them in whispers.

He stirred them again into activity. Now he advanced towards Gopal with an air of one who had examined all aspects of the case and come to a decision. As he saw him come up, Gopal felt that the man's picture would be complete if he put on a black cap and carried a halter in his hand. Gopal knew that he was a condemned man. The jury had given its verdict. Even before the director opened his mouth to say anything, Gopal said, "All right, sir. I will die."

Lights were on. The camera was ready to shoot. The director howled, "Action." Gopal dropped the telephone. His head fell back and rolled slightly to the side. Scores of persons were gazing on his dying with satisfaction. But before the director cried,

"Cut," Gopal did something which he hoped would pass unnoticed. Though he was supposed to be dead, he shook his head slightly, opened his right eye, and winked at the camera, which he hoped would act as an antidote to the inauspicious role he was doing.

The director, however, shouted: "No good. Repeat action. Retake . . ."

Under the Banyan Tree

The village Somal, nestling away in the forest tracts of Mempi, had a population of less than three hundred. It was in every way a village to make the heart of a rural reformer sink. Its tank, a small expanse of water, right in the middle of the village, served for drinking, bathing, and washing the cattle, and it bred malaria, typhoid, and heaven knew what else. The cottages sprawled anyhow and the lanes twisted and wriggled up and down and strangled each other. The population used the highway as the refuse ground and in the backyard of every house drain water stagnated in green puddles.

Such was the village. It is likely that the people of the village were insensitive: but it is more than likely that they never noticed their surroundings because they lived in a kind of perpetual enchantment. The enchanter was Nambi the story-teller. He was a man of about sixty or seventy. Or was he eighty or one hundred and eighty? Who could say? In a place so much cut off as Somal (the nearest bus-stop was ten miles away), reckoning could hardly be in the familiar measures of time. If anyone asked Nambi what his age was he referred to an ancient famine or an invasion or the building of a bridge and indicated how high he had stood from the ground at the time.

He was illiterate, in the sense that the written word was a mystery to him; but he could make up a story, in his head, at the rate of one a month; each story took nearly ten days to narrate.

His home was the little temple which was at the very end of the village. No one could say how he had come to regard himself as the owner of the temple. The temple was a very small structure with red-striped walls, with a stone image of the Goddess Shakti in the sanctum. The front portion of the temple was Nambi's home. For aught it mattered any place might be his home; for he was without possessions. All that he possessed was a broom with which he swept the temple; and he had also a couple of dhoties and upper cloth. He spent most of the day in the shade of the banyan which spread out its branches in front of the temple. When he felt hungry he walked into any house that caught his fancy and joined the family at dinner. When he needed new clothes they were brought to him by the villagers. He hardly ever had to go out in search of company; for the banyan shade served as a clubhouse for the village folk. All through the day people came seeking Nambi's company and squatted under the tree. If he was in a mood for it he listened to their talk and entertained them with his own observations and anecdotes. When he was in no mood he looked at the visitors sourly and asked, "What do you think I am? Don't blame me if you get no story at the next moon. Unless I meditate how can the Goddess give me a story? Do you think stories float in the air?" And he moved out to the edge of the forest and squatted there, contemplating the trees.

On Friday evenings the village turned up at the temple for worship, when Nambi lit a score of mud lamps and arranged them around the threshold of the sanctuary. He decorated the image with flowers, which grew wildly in the backyard of the temple. He acted as the priest and offered to the Goddess fruits and flowers brought in by the villagers.

On the nights he had a story to tell he lit a small lamp and placed it in a niche in the trunk of the banyan tree. Villagers as they returned home in the evening saw this, went home, and said to their wives, "Now, now, hurry up with the dinner, the storyteller is calling us." As the moon crept up behind the hillock, men, women, and children gathered under the banyan tree. The storyteller would not appear yet. He would be sitting in the sanctum, before the Goddess, with his eyes shut, in deep meditation. He sat thus as long as he liked and when he came out, with his forehead ablaze with ash and vermilion, he took his seat on a stone platform in front of the temple. He opened the story with a question. Jerking his finger towards a vague, far-away destination, he asked, "A thousand years ago, a stone's throw in that direction, what do you think there was? It was not the weed-covered waste it is now, for donkeys to roll in. It was not the ash-pit it is now. It was the capital of the king. . . ." The king would be Dasaratha, Vikramaditya, Asoka, or anyone that came into the old man's head; the capital was called Kapila, Kridapura, or anything. Opening thus, the old man went on without a pause for three hours. By then brick by brick the palace of the king was raised. The old man described the dazzling durbar hall where sat a hundred vassal kings, ministers, and subjects; in another part of the palace all the musicians in the world assembled and sang; and most of the songs were sung over again by Nambi to his audience; and he described in detail the pictures and trophies that hung on the walls of the palace. . . .

It was story-building on an epic scale. The first day barely conveyed the setting of the tale, and Nambi's audience as yet had no idea who were coming into the story. As the moon slipped behind the trees of Mempi Forest Nambi said, "Now friends, Mother says this will do for the day." He abruptly rose, went in, lay down, and fell asleep long before the babble of the crowd ceased.

The light in the niche would again be seen two or three days later, and again and again throughout the bright half of the month. Kings and heroes, villains and fairy-like women, gods in human form, saints and assassins, jostled each other in that world which was created under the banyan tree. Nambi's voice rose and fell in an exquisite rhythm, and the moonlight and the hour completed the magic. The villagers laughed with Nambi, they wept with him, they adored the heroes, cursed the villains, groaned when the conspirator had his initial success, and they sent up to the gods a heartfelt prayer for a happy ending. . . .

On the day when the story ended, the whole gathering went into the sanctum and prostrated before the Goddess. . .

By the time the next moon peeped over the hillock Nambi was ready with another story. He never repeated the same kind of story or brought in the same set of persons, and the village folk considered Nambi a sort of miracle, quoted his words of wisdom, and lived on the whole in an exalted plane of their own, though their life in all other respects was hard and drab.

And yet it had gone on for years and years. One moon he lit the lamp in the tree. The audience came. The old man took his seat and began the story. "... When King Vikramaditya lived, his minister was ..." He paused. He could not get beyond it. He made a fresh beginning. "There was the king ..." he said, repeated it, and then his words trailed off into a vague mumbling. "What has come over me?" he asked pathetically. "Oh, Mother, great Mother, why do I stumble and falter? I know the story. I had the whole of it a moment ago. What was it about? I can't understand what has happened." He faltered and looked so miserable that his audience said, "Take your own time. You are perhaps tired."

"Shut up!" he cried. "Am I tired? Wait a moment; I will tell you the story presently." Following this there was utter silence. Eager faces looked up at him. "Don't look at me!" he flared up. Somebody gave him a tumbler of milk. The audience waited patiently. This was a new experience. Some persons expressed their sympathy aloud. Some persons began to talk among themselves. Those who sat in the outer edge of the crowd silently slipped away. Gradually, as it neared midnight, others followed this example. Nambi sat staring at the ground, his head bowed in thought. For the first time he realized that he was old. He felt he would never more be able to control his thoughts or express them cogently. He looked up. Everyone had gone except his friend Mari the blacksmith. "Mari, why aren't you also gone?"

Mari apologized for the rest: "They didn't want to tire you; so they have gone away."

Nambi got up. "You are right. Tomorrow I will make it up. Age, age. What is my age? It has come on suddenly." He pointed at his head and said, "This says, 'Old fool, don't think I shall be your servant any more. You will be my servant hereafter.' It is disobedient and treacherous."

He lit the lamp in the niche next day. The crowd assembled under the banyan faithfully. Nambi had spent the whole day in meditation. He had been fervently praying to the Goddess not to desert him. He began the story. He went on for an hour without a stop. He felt greatly relieved, so much so that he interrupted his narration to remark, "Oh, friends. The Mother is always kind. I was seized with a foolish fear ..." and continued the story. In a few minutes he felt dried up. He struggled hard: "And then . . . and then . . . what happened?" He stammered. There followed a pause lasting an hour. The audience rose without a word and went home. The old man sat on the stone brooding till the cock crew. "I can't blame them for it," he muttered to himself. "Can they sit down here and mope all night?" Two days later he gave another instalment of the story, and that, too, lasted only a few minutes. The gathering dwindled. Fewer persons began to take notice of the lamp in the niche. Even these came only out of a sense of duty. Nambi realized that there was no use in prolonging the struggle. He brought the story to a speedy and premature end.

He knew what was happening. He was harrowed by the thoughts of his failure. I should have been happier if I had dropped dead years ago, he said to himself. Mother, why have you struck me dumb . . . ? He shut himself up in the sanctum, hardly ate any food, and spent the greater part of the day sitting motionless in meditation.

The next moon peeped over the hillock, Nambi lit the lamp in the niche. The villagers as they returned home saw the lamp, but only a handful turned up at night. "Where are the others?" the old man asked. "Let us wait." He waited. The moon came up. His handful of audience waited patiently. And then the old man said, "I won't tell the story today, nor tomorrow unless the whole village comes here. I insist upon it. It is a mighty story. Everyone must hear it." Next day he went up and down the village street shouting, "I have a most wonderful tale to tell tonight. Come one and all; don't miss it. . . ." This personal appeal had a great effect. At night a large crowd gathered under the banyan. They were happy that the story-teller had regained his powers. Nambi came out of the temple when everyone had settled and said: "It is the Mother who gives the gifts; and it is she who takes away the gifts. Nambi is a dotard. He speaks when the Mother has anything to say. He is struck dumb when she has nothing to say. But what is the use of the jasmine when it has lost its scent? What is the lamp for when all the oil is gone? Goddess be thanked. . . . These are my last words on this earth; and this is my greatest story." He rose and went into the sanctum. His audience hardly understood what he meant. They sat there till they became weary. And then some of them got up and stepped into the sanctum. There the story-teller sat with eyes shut. "Aren't you going to tell us a story?" they asked. He opened his eyes, looked at them, and shook his head. He indicated by gesture that he had spoken his last words.

When he felt hungry he walked into any cottage and silently sat down for food, and walked away the moment he had eaten. Beyond this he had hardly anything to demand of his fellow beings. The rest of his life (he lived for a few more years) was one great consummate silence.

GLOSSARY

bhang: narcotic made from hemp
chappati: wheat-flour pancake
dak: guest house
Deepavali: Hindu Festival of Light, held in October
durbar: audience hall
dwarapalaka: figures of gods placed at the entrance of a home for protection against evil
harijan: Untouchable
kalyani: performance
mali: gardener
mantap: sacred canopy placed over a statue or shrine
namaskarams: greetings
puja: worship, offering
pyol: platform built along the house wall that faces the street
sanyasi: ascetic who has renounced the world
seer: measure of weight (varying from eight ounces to three pounds) or of capacity
shastra: Hindu sacred writings
tank: pool or cistern, often a tank placed on the roof which supplies a house with water
tank bund: dam, dike, embankment
vakil: attorney, pleader in a law court